PROTECTOR

DIANA PALMER

PROTECTOR

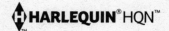

ISBN-13: 978-0-373-77771-6

PROTECTOR

This edition published by arrangement with Harlequin Books S.A.

® and TM are trademarks of Harlequin Enterprises Limited or its corporate affiliates.
Trademarks indicated with ® are registered in the United States Patent and Trademark
Office, the Canadian Trade Marks Office and in other countries.

Printed in U.S.A.

Dear Reader,

As most of you know, Sheriff Hayes Carson has been one of my longest-running characters. He's been in the Long, Tall, Texans series almost from the beginning. He's comforted sad heroines, he's captured bad guys, he's investigated murders, and he's done it all with grace and humor.

Now, finally, his lonely life is coming to a close. I mean that he's finally met the woman of his dreams and she turns out to be his worst enemy, Minette Raynor. I loved the way she stood up to him in *Winter Roses*. I love the way she is with her siblings. She is a woman with grace and guts. Just perfect for a guy like Hayes.

I won't give away the story line, but she proves that women can be heroines as surely as men can, without losing one iota of their femininity. In between her trials and tribulations with Hayes, she has to gain the affection of a very large lizard who hates her.

I have kept iguanas for many years. I think they make wonderful pets, and I love sharing my life with them. I have two new ones now, a large one and a little one, and many thanks to Sam of Backwater Reptiles for helping me keep them alive and healthy while I relearned what I'd forgotten about these sweet and beautiful creatures. My two are captive bred, not wild, and even the dogs and the cats like them.

I hope you enjoy Hayes and Minette as they come face-to-face with danger, and each other, in a wild and tumultuous way. I have enjoyed every minute of the writing of this book.

Barb, you got left out of the last dedication so you're getting in the reader letter here. Ha! And to my guildies on WOW in Knight Owls of Wow and Honor and Duty, and Ice Dragons on Star Wars: TOR, my thanks for letting me be in your guilds and missing events because I was writing.

I also want to say that I am more grateful to all of you who read me than you will ever know, for your loyalty and your kindness and your continued friendship, over all the long years. You are the reason I keep writing. Thank you for being my friends.

Many hugs, much love, from your biggest fan,

Diana Palmer

For my cousin Linda, with much love

1

Sheriff Hayes Carson hated Sundays. It was nothing against religion, or church or anything spiritual. He hated Sundays because he always spent them alone. He didn't have a girlfriend. He'd dated a couple of women around Jacobsville, Texas, but those dates had been few and far between. He hadn't had a serious relationship since he was just out of the military, when he got engaged to a woman who tossed him over for somebody richer. Well, he had dated Ivy Conley before she married his best friend, Stuart York. He'd had feelings for her, too, but it was not returned on her part.

Besides, he thought ruefully, there was Andy. His scaly pet kept him unattached.

That wasn't strictly true, he mused. The reason for the dearth of women in his life was mostly his job. He'd been shot twice since he became sheriff, and he'd been sheriff for seven years. He was good at his job. He was reelected without even a runoff. No criminal had ever escaped him. Well, one had—that man they called El Jefe, the biggest drug lord in northern Sonora, Mexico, who had a network that ran right through Jacobs County. But he was going to land El Jefe one day, he promised himself. He hated drug dealers. His own brother, Bobby, had died of an overdose years ago.

He still blamed Minette Raynor for that. Oh, sure, people said she was innocent and that it was Ivy Conley's sister, Rachel, who'd been killed a year or so ago, who gave Bobby the fatal dose. But Hayes knew that Minette was connected to the tragedy. He really hated her and made no secret of it. He knew something about her that she wasn't even aware of. He'd kept the secret all his adult life. He wanted to tell her. But he'd promised his father not to reveal the truth.

Hell, he thought, sipping Jack Daniel's, he wished he could get rid of that inconvenient conscience that wouldn't let him break his promises. It would save him a lot of grief.

He put the big square whiskey glass down beside his rocking chair, his long legs crossed as he stared out across the bare, rusty-colored meadow to the highway. It was chilly outside most days. Middle November brought frost even to Texas, but it had warmed up a bit today. He'd had supper, so the alcohol wouldn't affect him very much, except to relax him. He was enjoying the late-afternoon sun. He wished he had someone to share that sunset with. He hated being alone all the time.

Part of the reason for his solitude was sitting on the sofa in his living room, in front of the television. He sighed. His scaly best friend terrorized women. He'd tried to keep Andy secret, even putting him in the spare bedroom on the rare occasions when he brought a date home to ride horses. But inevitably, Andy finally got out when he least expected it. On one occasion while he was making coffee in the spotless kitchen, his pet was sneaking over the back of the sofa where the unsuspecting woman was sitting.

The screams were really terrifying. He dropped the coffeepot in his haste to get to the next room. She was standing up on the sofa, brandishing a lamp at the six-foot iguana who was arched on its back, glaring at her.

"It's okay, he's harmless!" he said at once.

That was when his pet decided to drop his dewlap, hiss and strike at her with his long whiplike tail. She actually sprained her ankle jumping off the sofa. The big iguana was ten years old and he didn't like people very much. And he really hated women. Hayes had never figured out why. Andy mostly stayed on top of the refrigerator or under the heat lamp atop his enormous cage, and ate the fresh fruit and salad that Hayes fixed for him every day. He never bothered anybody. He seemed to like Hayes's best friend, Stuart York. He'd even let himself be carried around and petted by total strangers; as long as they were male.

But let a woman walk through the door...

Hayes leaned back with a long indrawn breath. He couldn't give Andy up. It would be like giving away part of his family. And he didn't have any family left. He had a few very distant cousins, like MacCreedy, who had become a local legend in law enforcement for leading funeral processions into bogs before he went to work in San Antonio as a security guard. But Hayes had no close relatives living. His only great-uncle had died three years before.

He glanced through the window at the sofa, where Andy was spread out with the television blaring away. It amused him that his pet liked to watch television. Or at least, it seemed that way. He kept a nice thick waterproof sofa cover on the furniture, in case of accidents. Oddly, Andy never had any. He was house-trained. He went on a small stack of wet papers in a litter box in Hayes's huge bathroom. And he came when Hayes whistled. Odd fellow, Andy.

Hayes smiled to himself. At least he had something living to talk to.

He stared off into the distance. He saw a flash of silver. Probably sunlight reflecting off the wire fence out there, keeping in his small herd of palominos. He had a big cattle dog, Rex, who lived outdoors and kept predators away from the equally small herd of Santa Gertrudis cattle Hayes owned. He didn't have time for a big ranch, but he liked raising animals.

He heard Rex bark in the distance. *Must see a rabbit,* he thought idly. He glanced down at the empty whiskey glass and grimaced. He shouldn't be drinking on a Sunday. His mother wouldn't have approved. He made a face. His mother hadn't approved of anything about him. She'd hated his father and hated Hayes because he looked like his father. She'd been tall and blonde and dark-eyed. Like Minette Raynor.

His face contorted as he processed the thought. Minette was editor-publisher of the weekly *Jacobsville Times.* She lived with her great-aunt and two children, her brother and sister. She never spoke of her biological father. Hayes was sure that she didn't know who her father really was. She knew her late stepfather wasn't her real dad. Hayes knew about her real father because Dallas, his late father and also the former Jacobs County sheriff, knew. Dallas had made Hayes swear he'd never tell Minette. It wasn't her fault, he emphasized. She'd had enough grief for one lifetime, without knowing the truth about her father. Her mother had been a good woman. She'd never been mixed up in anything illegal, either. Let it go.

So Hayes had let it go, but reluctantly. He couldn't disguise his distaste for Minette, however. In his mind, her family had killed his brother, whether or not it was her hand that had delivered the lethal drug that he died from.

He stretched suddenly, yawning, and suddenly bent over to pick up his glass. Something hit his shoulder and spun him around in the chair, throwing him to the bare wood floor of the porch. He lay there, gasping like a fish, numb from a blow he hadn't seen coming.

It took a minute for him to figure out that he'd been shot. He knew the sensation. It wasn't the first time. He tried to move, and realized that he couldn't get up. He was struggling to breathe. There was the copper-scented smell of fresh blood. He was bleeding. It felt as if his lung, or part of it, had collapsed.

He struggled with the case at his belt to retrieve his cell phone. Thank God he kept it charged, in case any emergency required his presence. He punched the code for 911.

"Jacobs County 911, is this an emergency?" the operator asked at once.

"Shot," he gasped.

"Excuse me?" There was a pause. "Sheriff Carson, is that you?"

"Ye...s."

"Where are you?" she asked urgently, knowing that it could take precious time to seek out a cell tower near the call and identify his possible location. "Can you tell me?"

"Home," he bit off. The world was fading in and out. He heard her voice coaxing him to stay on the line, to talk to her.

But he closed his eyes on a sudden wave of pain and nausea and the phone fell from his limp hand.

Hayes came to in the hospital. Dr. Copper Coltrain was bending over him, in a green gown, with a mask pulled down around his chin.

"Hi," he said. "Good to have you back with us."

Hayes blinked. "I was shot."

"Yes, for the third time," Coltrain mused. "I've heard of lead poisoning, but this is getting absurd."

"How am I?" Hayes managed in a raspy tone.

"You'll live," Coltrain replied. "The wound is in your shoulder, but it impacted your left lung, as well. We had to remove a bit of your lung and we're inflating it now." He indicated a tube coming out of Hayes's side under the light sheet. "We removed bone fragments and debrided the tissue, now you're on fluids and antibiotics, anti-inflammatories and pain meds, for the time being."

"When can I go home?" Hayes asked groggily.

"Funny man. Let's talk about that when you're not just out of surgery and in the recovery room."

Hayes made a face. "Somebody's got to feed Andy. He'll be scared to death out there alone."

"We have somebody feeding Andy," Coltrain replied.

"Rex, too, he lives in the barn…"

"Taken care of."

"The key…"

"…was on your key ring. Everything's fine, except for you."

Hayes assumed it was one of his deputies who was helping out, so he didn't argue. He closed his eyes. "I feel awful."

"Well, of course you do," Coltrain sympathized. "You've been shot."

"I noticed."

"We're going to keep you in ICU for a day or so, until you're a bit better, then we'll move you into a room. For now, you just sleep and don't worry about anything. Okay?"

Hayes managed a wan smile, but his eyes didn't open. A few seconds later, he was asleep.

A nurse was bending over him in ICU when he woke again, taking his blood pressure, checking his temperature, pulse and respiration.

"Hi, there," she said with a smile. "You're doing much better this morning," she added, noting her observations on her chart. "How's the chest?"

He moved and winced. "Hurts."

"Does it? We'll ask Dr. Coltrain to up your meds a bit until that passes. Any other problems?"

He wanted to name at least one, but he was unusually shy about mentioning the catheter.

Nevertheless, the nurse noticed. "It's just temporary, and it's coming out tomorrow, Dr. Coltrain said. Try to sleep." She patted him on the shoulder with a maternal smile and left him.

They removed the catheter the next day, which embarrassed Hayes and caused him to mutter under his breath. But he went back to sleep very soon.

Later, when Dr. Coltrain came in, he was barely awake again. "I hurt in an unmentionable place and it's your fault," Hayes muttered at Coltrain.

"Sorry, it was unavoidable. The catheter's out now, and you won't have discomfort for much longer, I promise." He listened to Hayes's chest and frowned. "There's a lot of congestion."

"It's unpleasant."

"I'm going to write up something to clear that out."

"I want to go home."

Coltrain looked very uncomfortable. "There's a problem."

"What?"

He sat down in the chair beside the bed and crossed his legs. "Okay, let's review the mechanics of gunshot injuries. First is the direct tissue injury. Second, temporary cavitation as the projectile makes a path through the tissue and causes necrosis. Third, shock waves if the projectile is ejected at a high rate of speed. You are the luckiest man I know, because the only major damage the bullet did was to your lung. However," he added quietly, "the damage is such that you're going to have a hard time using your left arm for a while."

"Awhile? How long a while?" Hayes asked.

"Micah Steele—remember him?—is our orthopedic surgeon. I called him in on your case. We removed the bone fragments and repaired the muscle damage..."

"What about the bullet?" Hayes interrupted. "Did you get that?"

"No," Coltrain said. "Removing a bullet is up to the discretion of the surgeon, and I considered it too dangerous to take it out..."

"It's evidence," Hayes said as strongly as the weakness would allow. "You have to extract it so that I can use it to prosecute the..." He held his breath. "Guy who shot me!"

"Surgeon's discretion," Coltrain repeated. "I won't risk a patient's life trying to dig out a bullet that's basically disinfected itself on the way into the body. I'd do more damage trying to get it out than I would leaving it in." He held up a hand when Hayes opened his mouth. "I conferred with two other surgeons, one in San Antonio, and they'll back me up. It was too risky."

Hayes wanted to argue some more, but he was too tired. It was an old argument, anyway, trying to make a surgeon remove potential evidence from a victim's body, and it occasionally ended up in a legal battle. Most of the time, the surgeon won. "All right."

"Back to what I was saying," he continued, "there was some collateral damage to your left shoulder. You'll have to have an extended course of physical therapy to keep the muscles from atrophying."

"Extended?" Hayes asked slowly.

"Probably several months. It depends on how quickly you heal and how fast your recovery is," Coltrain said. "It's still going to be a rough ride. You need to know that from the start."

Hayes looked up at the ceiling. "Crackers and milk!" he muttered.

"You'll be all right," Coltrain assured him. "But for the next couple of weeks, you need to keep that arm immobilized and not lift anything heavier than a tissue. I'll have my receptionist get you an appointment with Dr. Steele and also with the physiotherapist here in the hospital."

"When can I go home?"

Coltrain stared at him. "Not for several more days. And even then, you can't go home and stay by yourself. You'll need someone with you for at least a couple of weeks, to make sure you don't overdo and have a relapse."

"A nursemaid? Me?" Hayes frowned. "I was out of the hospital in three or four days the last two times..."

"You had a flesh wound the last time, and the one before that you were only about twenty-seven years old. You're thirty-four now, Hayes. It takes longer to recover, the older you get."

Hayes felt worse than ever. "I can't go home right away."

"That's right. You're going to be extremely limited in what you can do for the next few weeks. You won't be able to lift much while the damage heals and you'll find even ordinary movement will aggravate the wound and cause pain. You're going to need physical therapy three times a week..."

"No!"

"Yes, unless you want to be a one-armed man!" Coltrain said shortly. "Do you want to lose the use of your left arm?"

Hayes glared at him.

Coltrain glared right back.

Hayes backed down. He sank back onto the pillow. His blond-streaked brown hair was disheveled and needed washing. He felt dingy. His dark eyes were bloodshot and had dark circles around them. His lean face was drawn from pain.

"I could get somebody to stay with me," he said after a minute.

"Name somebody."

"Mrs. Mallard. She comes to take care of the house three days a week anyway."

"Mrs. Mallard's sister had a heart attack. She's gone to Dallas. I'll bet she phoned to tell you, but you never check your telephone messages at home," Coltrain said with some amusement.

Hayes was disconcerted. "She's a good woman. I hope her sister does well." He pursed his lips. "Well, there's Miss Bailey," he began, naming a local woman who made her living from staying with recuperating patients. She was a retired practical nurse.

"Miss Bailey is terrified of reptiles," he pointed out.

"Blanche Mallory," he suggested, naming another elderly lady who sat with patients.

"Terrified of reptiles."

"Damn!"

"I even asked old Mrs. Brewer for you," Coltrain said heavily. "She said she wasn't staying in any house with a dinosaur."

"Andy's an iguana. He's a vegetarian. He doesn't eat people!"

"There's a young lady you dated once who might dispute that," Coltrain said with a smile and twinkling eyes.

"It was self-defense. She tried to hit him with a lamp," Hayes muttered.

"I recall treating her for a sprained ankle, at your expense," the other man returned.

Hayes sighed. "Okay. Maybe one of my deputies could be persuaded," he relented.

"Nope. I asked them, too."

He glowered at Coltrain. "They like me."

"Yes, they do," he agreed. "But they're all married with young families. Well, Zack Tallman isn't, but he's not staying with you, either. He says he needs to be able to concentrate while he's working on your case. He doesn't like cartoon movies," he added, tongue-in-cheek.

"Animation bigot," Hayes muttered.

"Of course, there's MacCreedy..."

"No. Never! Don't even speak his name, he might turn up here!" Hayes said with real feeling.

"He's your cousin and he likes you."

"Very distant cousin, and we're not talking about him."

"Okay. Suit yourself."

"So I'm going to be stuck here until I get well?" Hayes asked miserably.

"Afraid we don't have space to keep you," Coltrain replied. "Not to mention the size of the hospital bill you'd be facing, and the county isn't likely to want to pick it up."

Hayes scowled. "I could pick it up myself," Hayes said curtly. "I may not look like it, but I'm fairly well-to-do. I work in law enforcement because I want to, not because I have to." He paused. "What's going on with finding out who shot me?" he asked suddenly. "Have they come up with anything?"

"Your chief deputy is on the case, along with Yancy, your investigator. They found a shell casing."

"Nice work," Hayes commented.

"It was. Yancy used a laser pointer, extrapolated from where you were sitting and the angle of the wound, and traced it to the edge of the pasture, under a mesquite tree. He found footprints, a full metal jacketed shell from an AR-15 semiautomatic rifle and a cigarette butt."

"I'll promote him."

Coltrain chuckled.

"I'll call Cash Grier. Nobody knows more about sniping than the police chief. He used to do it for a living."

"Good idea," Coltrain added.

"Look, I can't stay here and I can't go home, so what am I going to do?" Hayes asked miserably.

"You won't like the only solution I could come up with."

"If it gets me out of the hospital, I'll love it. Tell me," Hayes promised.

Coltrain stood and backed up a step. "Minette Raynor says you can stay with them until you're healed."

"Never!" Hayes burst out. "I'd live in a hollow log with a rattler, sooner than do that! Why would she even volunteer in the first place? She knows I hate her guts!"

"She felt sorry for you when Lou mentioned we couldn't find anybody who was willing to stay in your house," Coltrain replied. Lou was short for Louise, his wife, who was also a doctor.

"Sorry for me. Huh!" he scoffed.

"Her little brother and sister like you."

He shifted. "I like them, too. They're nice kids. We have candy to give away at the sheriff's office on Halloween. She always brings them by."

"It's up to you, of course," Coltrain continued. "But you're going to have a lot of trouble getting me to sign a release form if you try to go home. You'll end up back here in two days, from overdoing, I guarantee it."

Hayes hated the idea. He hated Minette. But he hated the hospital more. Minette's great-aunt Sarah lived with her. He figured Sarah would be looking after him, especially since Minette was at the newspaper office all day every day. And at night he could go to bed early. Very early. It wasn't a great solution, but he could live with it if he had to.

"I guess I could stand it for a little while," he said finally.

Coltrain beamed. "Good man. I'm proud of you for putting aside your prejudices."

"They aren't put away. They're just suppressed."

The other man shrugged.

"When can I leave?" Hayes asked.

"If you're good, and you continue to improve, maybe Friday."

"Friday." Hayes brightened a little. "Okay. I'll be good."

He was. Sort of. He complained for the rest of the week about being awakened to have a bath, because it wasn't a real bath. He complained because the television set in his room didn't work properly and he couldn't get the History Channel and the International History Channel, which appealed to the military historian in him. He didn't like the cartoon channel because it didn't carry the cartoon movies he was partial to. He complained about having gelatin with every meal and the tiniest cup of ice cream he'd ever seen in his life for dessert.

"I hate hospital food," he complained to Coltrain.

"We're getting in a French chef next week," the doctor said wryly.

"Right, and I'm going to be named King of England the following one."

Coltrain sighed. He looked at the chart. "Well, the way you're improving, I plan to release you in the morning. Minette's coming to get you, bring you back to her place and then go on her way to the office."

His heart soared. "I can get out?"

Coltrain nodded. "You can get out. And Minette and her great-aunt are wonderful cooks. You won't have cause for complaint over there."

Hayes hesitated and avoided the doctor's eyes. "I guess it was a kindness on Minette's part to have me stay with her. Especially knowing how I feel about her."

Coltrain moved a little closer to the bed. "Hayes, she never had anything to do with Bobby, except that an older girl at her school was friendly with her and dated Bobby. But she wasn't in their circle of friends, you see? Besides that, she's one of the few people I know who never even tried marijuana. She has nothing to do with drugs."

"Her family..." Hayes began hotly.

Coltrain held up a hand. "We've never spoken of that, and we shouldn't, even now. Minette doesn't know. You promised your father that you'd never tell her. You have to keep that promise."

Hayes took a steadying breath. "It's hard."

"Life is hard. Get used to it," Coltrain told him.

"I'm doing that. This is my third gunshot wound," Hayes pointed out.

Coltrain cocked his head and narrowed his eyes. "You know, that's either damned bad luck or a death wish on your part."

"I don't have a death wish!"

"You walk headfirst into dangerous situations, without any thought of letting your men help."

"They all have families. Young families."

"Zack doesn't. But if it worries you, hire some more single deputies," Coltrain said curtly. "Some men with guts and independent thinking who know the ropes and can calculate the risk."

"Chance would be a fine thing," he huffed. "The last deputy I hired was from up in San Antonio. He commutes. We don't have a big employment pool here. Most of the young men move to the city to find work, and law enforcement is notoriously low-paying, considering where we are. If it was my only source of income, I'd be hard-pressed to pay the bills, even on my salary."

"I know all that."

"The family men needed jobs desperately," he added quietly. "This economy is the worst I've ever experienced in my life."

"Tell me about it. Even physicians are feeling the bite. And it's bad for our patients, many of whom won't come in for early treatment because they don't have insurance to pay for it. So they wait until conditions are life-threatening. It breaks my heart."

"Too true." Hayes leaned back on the pillows. "Thanks for letting me out."

Coltrain shrugged. "What are friends for?" He looked at the chart. "I'm giving you prescriptions to carry with you, and I've made an appointment with the physical therapist who's in a group that practices here. You'll need to go three times a week. Don't argue," he said when Hayes started to protest. "If you want to ever be able to use that arm again, you'll do what I say."

Hayes glared at him. After a minute he sighed. "All right."

"It's not so bad. You'll learn how to exercise the arm, and they'll do heat treatments. Those feel good."

Hayes shrugged, wincing at the brief pain.

"Isn't that drip working?" Coltrain put down the clipboard and fiddled with the drip. "It's clogged." He called a nurse and indicated the drip. She grimaced and quickly fixed it.

"Sorry, Doctor," she said quietly. "I should have checked it earlier. It's just, we're so busy and there are so few of us..."

"Budget cuts," Coltrain nodded, sighing. "Just be more careful," he said gently.

She smiled faintly. "Yes, sir."

She left and Coltrain shook his head. "We have our own staffing problems, as you can see. I'll have that drip removed later and we'll give you a patch for the pain meds."

"Modern technology," Carson chuckled.

"Yes. Some of the new stuff is amazing. I spend an hour on the internet every once in a while researching the new techniques they're experimenting with. I wish I was twenty years younger, so that I could be learning this stuff at medical school. What a future physicians can look forward to now!"

"I've read about some of it. You're right. It is amazing." He was feeling suddenly sleepy.

"Get some rest," Coltrain said. "We'll talk again tomorrow."

Hayes nodded. "Thanks, Copper," he said, using Coltrain's nickname.

"My pleasure."

Seconds later, he was asleep.

The next morning, everything was suddenly bustling. The nurses got him bathed, if you could call a tub bath bathed, and ready to check out by eleven o'clock.

Coltrain came by with the prescriptions and releases. "Now if you have any trouble, any trouble at all, you call me. I don't care what time it is. Any redness, inflammation, that sort of thing."

Hayes nodded. "Red streaks running up my arm..." he teased.

Coltrain made a face. "Gangrene isn't likely."

"Well, you never know," Hayes chuckled.

"I'm glad to see you feeling better."

"Thanks for helping to get me that way."

"That's my job," Coltrain replied with a smile. He glanced toward the door. "Come on in," he said.

Minette Raynor came into the room. She was tall and willowy, with a curtain of pale gold hair that fell almost to her waist in back, neatly combed and clean. Her eyes were almost black and she had freckles just across the bridge of her nose. Hayes recalled that her mother had been redheaded. Perhaps the freckles were inherited. She had pert little breasts and long, elegant fingers. Didn't she play piano at church? He couldn't remember. He hadn't been in a church in a very long time.

"I'm here to drive you home," Minette told Hayes quietly. She didn't smile.

Hayes nodded and looked uncomfortable.

"We'll get him dressed and a nurse will bring him down to the front door in a wheelchair."

"I can walk," Hayes snapped.

"It's hospital policy," Coltrain shot back. "You'll do it."

Hayes glowered at him, but he didn't speak.

Minette didn't speak, either, but she was thinking about the next couple of weeks with pure anguish. She'd felt sorry for Hayes. He had nobody, really, not even cousins who would have taken care of him. There was MacCreedy, but that would be a total disaster. His sweet Mrs. Mallard, who did his housework three days a week, was out of town because her sister was ill. So Minette had offered him room and board until he was healed up.

She was having second thoughts. He looked at her with angry dark eyes that wished her anywhere but here.

"I'll just wait outside," Minette said after a minute, one hand on her purse.

"He won't be long," Coltrain promised.

She left and went down to the waiting room.

"This is a bad idea," Hayes gritted as he started to get out of bed and had to hesitate because his head was swimming.

"Don't fall." Coltrain helped him up. "You can stay another day or two…"

"I'm fine," Hayes muttered. "Just fine."

Coltrain sighed. "All right. If you're sure."

Hayes wasn't sure, but he wanted out of the hospital. Even

Minette Raynor's company was preferable to another day of gelatin and forced baths.

He got into the clothes he'd been wearing when he was shot, grimacing at the blood on the shoulder of his shirt.

"I should have had somebody get fresh clothing for you. Zack Tallman would have brought it over if we'd asked," Coltrain said apologetically.

"It's no big deal. I'll ask Zack to get them for me," Hayes said, hesitating. "I guess Minette's afraid of reptiles, too?"

"I've never asked," Coltrain replied.

Hayes sighed. "He's like a lizardly cow," he said irritably. "Everybody's scared of him because of the way he looks, but he's a vegetarian. He wouldn't eat meat."

"He looks scary," Coltrain reminded him.

"I suppose so. Me and my dinosaur." That tickled Hayes, and he laughed. "Right. Me and my dinosaur."

Once he was dressed, a nurse came in with a wheelchair. Hayes got into it with rare docility and she put his few possessions in his lap, explaining the prescriptions and the care instruction sheets she handed him on the way out the door.

"Don't forget, physical therapy on Monday, Wednesday and Friday," she added. "It's very important."

"Important." Hayes nodded. He was already plotting ways to get out of it. But he didn't tell her that.

Minette was waiting at the door with her big SUV. It was black with lots of chrome and the wood on the dash was a bright yellow. The seats were tan. It had a CD player and an iPod attachment and automatic everything. There was an entertainment system built in so that the kids could watch DVDs in the back-seat. In fact, it was very much like Hayes's personal car, a new Lincoln. He drove a big pickup truck to work. The Lincoln was for his rare nights out in San Antonio at the opera or the ballet. He'd been missing those because of work pressure. Maybe he'd get to see *The Nutcracker* next month, at least. It was almost Thanksgiving already.

He noticed the signature trademark on the steering wheel and chuckled. The SUV was a Lincoln. No wonder the dash instruments looked so familiar.

He was strapped in, grimacing because the seat belt hurt.

"Sorry," Minette said gently, fumbling with the belt to make it less confining.

"It's all right," Hayes said through his teeth.

She closed the door, got in under the wheel and pulled out of the hospital parking lot. Hayes was tense at first. He didn't like being a passenger. But Minette was a good driver. She got him home quickly to the big beautiful white Victorian house that had belonged to her family for three generations. It was surrounded by fenced pastures and a horse grazed, a palomino, all by itself.

"You've got a palomino," he mused. "I have several of my own."

"Yes, I know." She flushed a little. She'd seen his and loved the breed. "But, actually, I have six of them. That's Archibald."

His pale, thick eyebrows rose. "Archibald?"

She flushed a little. "It's a long story."

"I can't wait to hear it."

2

In another pasture, Hayes noted milling cattle, some of which were black-baldies, a cross between Black Angus and Herefords. Most mixed-breed cattle were popular in beef herds. The Raynor place was a ranch.

Along with the ranch, when her stepmother and stepfather died just a few months apart, she inherited two siblings, Julie and Shane. They weren't actually related to her, but they were hers as surely as if they'd been blood siblings. She loved them dearly.

The children were school-age now. Julie was in kindergarten and Shane was in grammar school. Minette seemed to take that responsibility very seriously. No one ever heard her complain about the kids being a burden. Of course, they also kept her single, Hayes mused. Most men didn't want a ready-made family to support.

Minette's great-aunt, Sarah, a tiny little woman with white hair whom Minette always addressed as "Aunt" instead of "Great-

Aunt," was waiting on the front porch. She rushed down the steps as Hayes climbed laboriously out of the SUV.

"Here, Hayes, you lean on me," she said.

Hayes chuckled. "Sarah, you're too little to support a man my size. But thanks."

Minette smiled and hugged her aunt. "He's right. He needs a little more help than you can give." She got under Hayes's arm and put her arm around his back. Her hand twitched when she felt a cavity under his shirt.

"It's another wound," he said quietly, feeling her consternation. "I'm pockmarked with them. That one was from a shotgun blast a few years back. I didn't duck fast enough."

"You're a walking advertisement for the perils of law enforcement," she muttered.

He was trying not to notice how nice it felt to have her close to him. They'd been adversaries for years. He'd blamed her for Bobby's death. He still blamed her family for that, but she didn't know who she really was. She had illusions, and he was hesitant to shatter them. After all, she'd given him a home when nobody else offered.

"Thanks," he said stiffly as they went up the steps and into the roomy, high-ceilinged house.

She paused and looked up at him. She was trying not to let him see the effect his nearness had on her. She'd always adored Hayes Carson, who hated her for reasons that were incomprehensible to her.

"For what?" she stammered.

He searched her black eyes far longer than he meant to. He wondered if she ever questioned the color of those eyes. Her mother had had blue eyes. But he wasn't going to ask.

"For letting me stay here," he said.

"You're welcome." She hesitated. "I'm afraid all the bedrooms are upstairs..."

"I don't mind."

She sighed. "Okay."

Sarah came bustling in behind them and closed the front door. "I changed the bed in the guest room and turned on the heat," she told Carson. "It's not the warmest room in the house, I'm afraid," she added apologetically.

"Not to worry. I like a cool bedroom."

"We need to get some fresh clothing for you," Minette said, appalled by the gunshot wound in the fabric of the shirt he was wearing, and the blood on it.

"I'll call Zack and have him bring some over," he said, naming his chief deputy. "He's been feeding Andy and Rex for me."

"Okay."

She helped him into the guest bedroom. It was decorated in shades of blue, brown and beige. The walls were an eggshell-blue, the coverlet was quilted and included browns and blues. The carpet was a soft beige. The curtains matched the coverlet. The windows, two of them, overlooked the pasture where the palomino was grazing.

"This is very nice," Hayes remarked.

"I'm glad you like it," Minette said gently. "You should call Zack."

He nodded. "I'll do that right now." He eased onto the coverlet and laid back on the pillow, shivering a little from the exertion and the pain and the weakness that was still making him uncomfortable. "That feels so good."

Minette hovered. He was pale and he looked terrible. "Can we get you anything?"

He looked at her hopefully. "Coffee?"

She laughed. "They wouldn't give it to you in the hospital, I gather."

"They did give me a little hot brown water this morning. They called it coffee," he scoffed.

"I make very good coffee," she said. "I have a machine that uses pods, and I get the latte pods from Germany. It's almost sinfully good."

He laughed. "Sounds great."

"I'll make you a cup before I leave." She checked her watch and grimaced. "I need to call and let Bill know I'm going to be later than I expected. It's okay," she added when Hayes looked guilty, "he can handle the office. We go to press on Tuesdays, but today is hectic, because the weekend is coming up."

"I see."

"I won't be a minute."

She went back downstairs, with Sarah trailing her. Hayes dug his cell phone out of his pocket and called Zack.

"Hey," he said. "I escaped."

Zack chuckled. "Way to go, boss. Are you at home?"

"I wish. Coltrain won't let me live by myself. I'm staying with...Minette and her family," he said, almost choking the words out.

"Well!"

Hayes shifted uncomfortably. The stress of riding in the confinement of the seat belt was giving him some problems with his injured chest and shoulder. "I need some fresh clothes. I had to come here in the shirt with the bullet hole."

"Just tell me what you need. I'll bring it over."

Hayes gave him quite a list, including pajamas and robe and slippers. He noticed that his room had not only a television, but a Blu-ray player. "And bring my new movies over," he added. "I'll watch them while I'm bedridden."

"Where are they?"

"On the shelf next to the DVD player."

"Okay."

"Who shot me?" he added curtly.

"We're working on that," Zack assured him. "We have a shell casing and a cigarette butt. We think it may be tied to those recent arrests we made."

"The new Mexican drug cartel mules. Their bosses are fighting a turf war across the border in Cotillo. Its mayor owes his soul to Pedro Mendez, who took over the operation that used to belong to the Fuentes brothers bunch," Hayes added quietly.

"Yes, Mendez is the one his enemies call El Ladrón, the thief," Zack agreed.

"Mendez has a bitter enemy in El Jefe, Diego Sanchez, who has an even bigger drug cartel. Sanchez wants the Cotillo stronghold for himself. It's the easiest path to Texas, through mountains where a sidewinder could get lost." Hayes sighed. "Two of the most evil men on the planet. God knows how many lives they've snuffed out." He didn't add that his own brother was one of those. He'd never shared what he knew with another living soul. Only Coltrain knew, but he had the information from Hayes's late father, not Hayes.

"Hey, at least El Jefe takes care of his people, and he draws the line at killing women and children," Zack reminded him.

"Drugs kill women and children."

"That's true, I guess," Zack said. "I meant, he didn't carry out vendettas against them. But even Manuel Lopez who used to own the drug trade in these parts never hurt children. God knows, he killed enough grown-ups to make up for it before Micah Steele took him out. Not that I know anything about that. Honest. Cross my heart."

Hayes just smiled. "It's an open secret locally, no worries. Maybe El Jefe does have a saving grace or two, but I'd gun him down in a heartbeat if I wasn't sworn to uphold the law."

Zack felt the undercurrents in Hayes's voice, so he didn't ask questions. His boss was closemouthed about some things.

"I imagine one of our drug-distribution czars ordered the hit on me. They don't like local law enforcement interfering with the transport of their product, and they make a public statement with assassinations. But can we prove they tried to kill me?"

Zack chuckled. "The mule who threatened you is in custody in our county detention center. So isn't it a good thing that we keep surveillance devices there?" he mused. "He made a phone call from the facility. We got it on tape, and traced the number. Sadly, it was a throwaway phone. Or that's what we think. The number is no longer in service."

"Damn."

"Not to worry, I've got Yancy on it. He'll go through every scrap of paper, every cigarette butt, every blade of grass on your property to dig the shooter out. Never saw a guy with such an eye for detail."

"Me, neither," Hayes agreed. "He's good." Hayes sighed. "I wish we had the bullet. It might give us an even better lead. But Coltrain wouldn't take it out."

"I've seen lawmen get court orders for bullets to be removed for evidence," Zack replied.

"So have I, but I don't know anybody who's ever forced Coltrain to do anything he didn't want to do. Besides that, he said it was a greater risk to take it out than leave it in." He frowned. "Pity they can't do an invasive scan on me and check out the bullet."

"There's a thought."

Hayes moved and winced, because it hurt. He drew in a long breath. The new antibiotic seemed to be working already. Maybe it was wishful thinking. It still hurt to breathe, but he had to get up and move around, to prevent the development of a bad bronchitis, or even pneumonia.

"Anyway, we're working on your case, along with the other thirty that are current," Zack added drily. "Of course, you're the only shooting victim so far."

"Good enough. If I could get the county commission to listen to me, I'd give you all raises."

"We know that, boss. None of us got into law enforcement because of the money."

Hayes chuckled. "Thanks, Zack."

"I'll be over with the clothes in about an hour. That okay?"

"That's fine."

When he hung up, Minette brought him a big mug of freshly brewed coffee. She handed it to him gently.

"Taste that," she said with a grin.

He did. He rolled his eyes and sighed. "Oh, my gosh," he groaned. "I've never tasted anything so sweet!"

"Told you so." She checked her watch. "I have to go. Is there anything special you'd like for supper?"

He hesitated.

"Come on. We don't live on a budget here. Not yet, anyway," she chuckled.

"Cube steak with onions, mashed potatoes, green beans."

She raised her eyebrows.

"I'm a meat and potatoes man," he confided. "Any variation is a happy one."

"I can handle that. Dessert?"

He swallowed. "Anything but gelatin."

She burst out laughing. "Okay. I'll get Aunt Sarah to make one of her chocolate pound cakes."

"My favorite kind."

She smiled. "Mine, too. Well, gotta go."

"Minette."

She stopped at the door and turned. Hearing her name in Hayes's deep, smooth voice made her toes tingle and she had to hide it. "Yes?"

"Thanks."

He looked very somber. She just nodded and left as quickly as she could. Maybe, she thought hopefully, maybe she could change Hayes's mind about her after all. She was going to work on that, hard.

Zack Tallman was lean, tall, olive-skinned and black-eyed. He had Spanish blood, but he never spoke about his ancestry. He was thirty years old, and one of the best deputies Hayes had ever hired.

He came into the bedroom carrying a huge suitcase. He put it down on a straight chair by Hayes's bed. "I think that's everything you asked for." He opened it.

With some difficulty, Hayes got out of bed and looked into the suitcase. "Yep," he said, smiling as he pulled out the videos. "That's everything."

"You and your cartoon movies," Zack sighed.

"Hey, there's nothing wrong with cartoons," Hayes said defensively. He pulled out pajamas and underwear and a robe and slippers. "I want a shower, but I have trouble standing. You feel like helping me?"

"No problem, boss," Zack chuckled. "You'd do the same for me."

"In a heartbeat," he replied. He managed a smile. "Thanks. I feel dingy."

"No doubt."

Zack helped him into the shower and stood outside the cubicle while Hayes managed to bathe himself and even shampoo his hair, one-handed of course. Minette had even thought of toiletries to put in the bathroom, because the brands were masculine. There was a razor on the sink, and when he was dried and dressed, with a little help from Zack, he even managed to shave.

"I think I'll live," he told the other man as he sank onto the bed under the covers. "Thanks a million, Zack."

"You're welcome. Need anything else?"

"Yes. Get out there with Yancy and find the guy who shot me," Hayes replied.

Zack saluted. "On my way."

"Keep me posted," Hayes reminded him.

"You know I will."

"And can you keep feeding Andy and Rex for me?" he asked hesitantly.

"You bet."

"If you run out of fruit and veggies for Andy…"

"You had more than enough money in the cookie jar to take care of that," Zack assured him. It was where Hayes kept his spare change, and over months of use, it added up to a tidy little sum.

Hayes laughed. "And people say spare change is useless."

"Useless, my left foot," Zack replied. "I'm saving up mine for a trip to Tahiti." He frowned. "I figure by the time I'm seventy-two, I'll have just enough."

"Good grief."

Zack grinned. "Just kidding. I don't even like islands. You get better, boss. I'll take care of Andy, no worries."

"When the cookie jar gets empty…"

"You'll be home by then. I guarantee it. Nice of Minette to let you stay here," he added.

"Yes. Very nice."

"She's such an odd bird," Zack mused. "Never dates anybody. Her whole life is those two little kids and her job. I guess they'd make it hard to have a serious relationship," he said. "Most men don't want somebody else's kids."

"I guess not." Hayes had already thought about that.

"Still, she's a dish," Zack added wistfully. "Pretty and smart and brave. Imagine, taking on a drug cartel after those guys killed a whole newspaper staff over the border a year or so ago for writing bad things about them."

"She takes chances," Hayes agreed.

"Unwise. But brave."

"Very."

Hayes spent the day watching movies. Sarah came in with a light lunch, homemade roast beef sandwiches and hot coffee. Afterward, she brought him a slice of chocolate pound cake.

"You'll never get rid of me if you keep feeding me like this," Hayes said as he bit into the perfect cake. "You're a wonderful cook."

"It's our pleasure to help out," Sarah said.

He finished the cake and coffee and she started to remove the dishes.

"Why did Minette offer to let me stay here?" he asked suddenly.

Sarah hesitated.

"Tell me."

She bit her lower lip. "Well, it bothered her that nobody would stay with you at home," she began. "And she knew you hated being in the hospital. She said..."

"She said what?" Hayes persisted.

She grinned suddenly. "Do you know the passage in the Bible about heaping coals of fire on an enemy's head by being kind to him?"

He burst out laughing.

"Well, it's sort of like that," she added.

He shook his head. "At least I understand it now."

"She never gave drugs to anybody, Hayes," Sarah said softly. "She never even smoked marijuana when she was in high school. Her mother was a fanatic about drugs. She wouldn't even take an aspirin tablet for a headache and she put that attitude into Minette. Never understood why," she said on a sigh. "She was a curious woman. But I loved her dearly."

"Did Minette's father use drugs?" he wondered, averting his eyes.

"Well, I don't know. I never actually met her father." She

flushed. "I mean, the man my niece, Faye, married—Minette's stepfather—didn't use them, ever."

He was shocked. He hadn't been aware that Sarah knew Minette's stepfather wasn't her biological father. He frowned. "Then you don't know what her real father looked like?"

"Not really. My niece didn't speak of him," she said. "I wonder if he had brown eyes, though. It amazed me that my niece produced a girl with Minette's coloring. Nobody in our whole family for generations ever had black eyes. They were always blue."

Hayes didn't look at her. "Genetics are odd."

"I'll say!" She lowered her voice. "You know, Minette's mother married her stepfather when she was about six months pregnant. It was such a scandal!"

Hayes bit his lip. "Was it?"

"Yes! She said her new husband didn't mind about the pregnancy, though, he loved children. They even told Minette, when she was ten, that Stan loved her very much but that he was her stepfather. I wondered if she ever really understood that. She never speaks of it, even to me." She picked up the cup and saucer and fork, looking thoughtful. "Still, as you say, genetics are very odd. If you need anything, you use that," she indicated the speakerphone beside the bed on the table. "And I'll be right up."

"Thanks, Sarah."

She smiled. "You're very welcome." She hesitated at the door. "You won't mention to Minette, that I said anything about her mother?" she worried.

"Of course I won't," he assured her. "Not a word."

She nodded. "Thanks. She's sensitive on the subject."

He watched her go out the door with mingled emotions. So

Sarah didn't speak to Minette about her real father. Curious. They seemed close. But, then, you never knew really went on in families.

Minette showed up just after lunch with Shane and Julie, her little brother and sister, in tow. They ran into the room where Hayes was and jumped into bed with him, shoes and all. Shane was bigger than Julie, a rough and tumble eleven-year-old who loved wrestling and never missed a match that featured his favorites.

"No, kids, calm down! He's been injured!" Minette said frantically. "And we don't climb on beds with shoes on!"

"Sorry, Minette," Julie said, pulling off her shoes and tossing them over the side.

"Me, too," Shane agreed, doing the same.

They moved closer to Hayes, who was fascinated with their lack of fear. He was a stranger, mostly, whom they hardly knew.

"You're gonna live with us," Shane said. "You got shot, yeah?"

He chuckled. "I got shot."

"What a mean thing to do," Julie said solemnly. She moved right up to Hayes's good arm and curled up next to him. "We'll protect you, Hayes," she said softly. "We won't let anybody hurt you ever again."

Hayes felt tears sting his eyes. He hid them, of course, but the child's comment touched him as nothing had in years. His profession kept him bereft of visible emotion. He had to keep it in check, because he had to be strong. He'd seen things most people never had to look at. It affected him. Of course it did. So he buried his feelings deeper and deeper over the years, until he hardly felt anything. But he'd been shot and he was still fragile. Julie's innocent offer to protect him made him melt inside.

"What a sweetheart you are," Hayes said softly, and brushed back the child's pretty blond hair.

She grinned at him and cuddled closer.

"Can we look at where you got shot?" Shane asked. "Is it awful?"

Hayes laughed. "Not a good idea. Yes, it is awful."

"Who shot you?" Shane persisted.

"Someone very mean, and we'll get him," Hayes promised.

"You two come on with me. Aunt Sarah has cookies and milk!"

"Cookies and milk! Woohoo!" Shane cheered, bouncing on the bed.

"Stop that and come down here," Minette said firmly, lifting him off the bed and onto the floor. "Oof, you're getting heavy!" she exclaimed. "Go get cookies. And I think SpongeBob is on television."

"Aw, Minette, that's for little kids like Julie…" Something by the television had caught the boy's attention. He picked up a DVD case and looked at it. "It's *How to Train Your Dragon!*" he exclaimed. "He's got *How to Train Your Dragon!*" He looked excitedly through the other cases. "There's *WALL-E* and *Up* and…!"

"Yes, I love cartoons," Hayes confessed with a faint flush.

"Me, too," Minette said, smiling. "Those are great movies."

"Can we come watch them with you after supper?" Shane pleaded. "Please?"

Hayes laughed at Minette's consternation. "Sure," he said. "Why not?"

"That's very nice of you, Hayes," Julie said in her soft, formal tone. "Thank you."

"You're very welcome." He started to help her off the bed, but Minette was there first. "No lifting," she told Hayes. "Copper Coltrain would let surgical interns practice on me if I dared let you pick up something as heavy as Julie."

"But I'm not heavy, Minette," Julie protested as she was placed gently on the floor.

"Not to me, precious," Minette said, hugging her. "But Hayes has been shot. He can't use his other arm yet."

"That's right. I'm sorry. I forgot."

"Downstairs now, both of you," Minette told the children.

"Yes, Minette," Julie said.

They waved at Hayes and ran clamoring down the steps to the kitchen.

"Sorry," Minette apologized. "They get a little wild."

"It's okay," Hayes said with a genuine smile. "They're great kids."

She was impressed. "Thanks."

"You've done very well with them," he continued. "It must have been difficult." He spoke as if the words were dragged out of him.

Minette smiled faintly. "It wasn't as if I had a choice. I couldn't give them up for adoption or let them be placed in an orphanage. I promised my stepmother I'd take care of them."

"Your stepmother was a good woman," Hayes remarked.

She nodded. "She was one of the sweetest people I've ever known. Always doing good works, taking care of people who needed her. I admired her." She hesitated. "I loved her."

"Your...father was kind, too."

She was hesitant. "He was. He was my stepfather, you know, not my real father. I don't know who my real father is. Mama never told me." She moved closer. "But Stan kept secrets." She frowned. "He said that he knew something that he had to tell me, but he put it off until it was too late. When he was dying, and he lost his voice after the stroke, he even tried to write it down." She drew in a long breath. "But what he wrote was just gibberish. I've wondered about what it could be." She laughed after a minute. "We don't have any dark family secrets. It was probably something about the kids that he wanted me to know."

"Yes." But Hayes was oddly quiet when he said that.

She stared at him. "Hayes, do you know something about me that you're not telling?"

His heart jumped. He stared at her intently. He wanted to say something. He really did. But at the last, he recalled his father's words and the promise he'd been forced to make. When he gave his word, he kept it. Always.

"No," he lied with a straight face. "No, I do not know anything. Anything at all. Honest."

She cocked her head. "I read true crime books. I learn a lot from them. Usually when people don't want to tell the truth, their speech pattern is an indication of that. They speak very formally, without contractions, and they repeat the protest over and above what's called for."

Hayes's high cheekbones actually flushed.

"You do know something," she guessed. "Is it something terrible? I can't believe you wouldn't want to tell me. I'm the enemy, after all, isn't that right?"

His sensuous lips compressed into a straight line. "If I'm the enemy why are you taking care of me?"

Her heart jumped at the way he said it.

He saw her reaction, and his antagonism took a nosedive. She was very pretty when she was upset. Her face became pink and radiant, her freckles stood out. Her black eyes glittered with true beauty.

"People who keep dinosaurs arouse sympathy?" she asked after a minute.

He burst out laughing. "Andy isn't a dinosaur."

"See? When you denied that, you used a contraction."

"Minette, you can't learn everything from books," he pointed out.

"Oh, it's not just books, I'm all over the internet reading case files," she replied.

He frowned. "Why aren't you out dating men?"

"Oh, sure, that's a great idea," she mused. She glanced toward the door and hesitated, listening, to make sure the children couldn't overhear. "So many men want to get serious about a woman with two small dependents. They line up at my door every day."

"I see."

"There was one guy, who was visiting his grandmother here. He asked me out in the newspaper office. I was at a loose end and he seemed very nice. He came to pick me up for the date. Julie and Shane were waiting with me at the door." Her face was sad. "I couldn't believe he was the same man when we went to dinner. He was stiff, polite, formal, and he rushed through the meal and took me straight home. Before he left, he blurted out that I was a nice woman and he liked me, but he wasn't going to saddle himself with someone else's kids. I pointed out that they were my stepfather and stepmother's kids and he said it didn't matter. He wasn't going to start out with a ready-made family. He made it quite clear."

Hayes stared at her intently. "You love those kids."

"Of course I do. I've taken care of them since they were born," she reminded him, her voice soft and gentle with reminiscence. "My stepmother's health was precarious at best, and after Shane and Julie were born, it grew quickly worse. I picked up the slack." She felt tears threaten. "Dawn was one of the kindest people I ever knew. She was very much like what I remember of my mother. I nursed her, right up until the end. I promised her that I'd care for her children as if they were my very own, and I keep my promises."

"So do I," Hayes admitted.

"My stepfather had a stroke, and then a heart attack, not too long after Dawn died. He tried so hard to talk to me, to write to me, to make me understand what he wanted to tell me. But I never could. I looked through all their papers, searching for something they'd written down. There was nothing." She smiled. "Probably it was about the kids."

Hayes managed to look innocent. "I imagine it was."

Her eyes narrowed. She was remembering another conversation. "You might tell me one day, huh?" she asked suddenly.

"When pigs fly," he blurted out.

She moved closer to the bed. "Why won't you tell me?"

He drew in a ragged breath. "I keep my promises, too."

"What does that mean?"

Mercifully there was a small riot downstairs, Julie yelling at Shane about a toy.

"You'd better get down there before bloodshed ensues," Hayes told her, relieved at the interruption.

She threw up her hands and raced down the staircase.

3

It was a new experience for Hayes to have children around, especially children who liked him and curled up with him in bed to watch cartoon movies.

Minette was surprised and touched at how quickly the big, taciturn sheriff melted when the kids cuddled with him. Even Shane did it, although he was older and usually standoffish with people he didn't know. Hayes knew most of the wrestlers by name, which made him Shane's best friend almost at once. They were trying to talk about their favorites while the movie was on, and Julie kept shushing them. It was amusing to Minette.

They watched the movies, but they were always asking questions. What was that place, who did that, could that happen in real life? It went on and on. He never seemed to mind trying to answer those questions, and he was incredibly patient. *Patience* was not a word that Minette had ever associated with Hayes Carson. In fact, he was well-known for the opposite.

"Okay, you two, time for bed," Minette said when the movie finished playing.

"Awwwww," Shane grumbled.

"Do we have to go now?" Julie protested, clinging to Hayes. "What if Hayes gets sick in the night? Can't we stay with him?"

Hayes was touched beyond words. He swallowed, hard. "Thanks, Julie," he said softly, and he smiled.

She grinned at him. "Can you tell us a story?" she asked.

"Yes," Shane agreed. "We want a story!"

Hayes glanced at Minette, who looked confused and faintly irritated. "I'm sorry, kids," he said gently, "but most of the stories I know wouldn't quite suit."

"Do you shoot bad guys like in the movies?" Shane asked, all eyes.

"Not so much, no," Hayes replied. "Actually I'm usually the one getting shot," he added with pursed lips.

"I bet it hurts," Shane said. "Can't we see where you got shot?"

"Okay, that's it, off the bed," Minette clapped her hands to get them moving.

"I bet it looks awful," Shane persisted.

"It does," Hayes said. "And it's bandaged, you know," he added, thinking fast. "Dr. Coltrain would be mad at me if I took it off."

"Good point," Minette said, looking grateful for his quick thinking. "So that's that. Bath time."

"Nooo!" Shane wailed. "I just had a bath yesterday, sis!"

"You're dirty," Julie said, wrinkling her nose. "You smell bad, too."

"Julie," Minette said, exasperated. "We don't say things like that, even to family, now do we?"

"No, Minette," Julie said. She went to her sister and held out her arms. "I'm sorry."

Minette swept her up and hugged her close, smiling. "It's okay. But you mustn't hurt Shane's feelings. You wouldn't like it if he said something like that to you. Now would you?"

"No, Minette," she agreed.

"Aw, she's a girl," Shane returned. "Girls are mean."

"We are not!" Julie said, pouting.

"Baths. Aunt Sarah's waiting. Julie first."

"Can I watch wrestling downstairs while Julie bathes?" Shane asked quickly.

"Just for a very few minutes."

"Okay! Hayes, I'll tell you all about it tomorrow!" He ran out of the room like a small tornado.

Sarah appeared in the doorway, laughing. "Did Shane escape?" she teased.

"He did," Minette said. She put Julie down. "Go with Aunt Sarah," she said gently. "Be good."

"Yes, Minette." She peered around Aunt Sarah toward Hayes. "I wish we could stay with you, Hayes," she sighed.

Hayes looked odd as Sarah swept the child out of the room.

Minette let out a breath. "Two of them." She shook her head. "Some days I wish there were two of me and two of Aunt Sarah, just to cope. I'm sorry if they bothered you..."

"No." He said it abruptly, and then smiled sheepishly. "No, they didn't bother me at all. I like kids."

She stared at him curiously. "You do?"

He nodded. "They're great." He smiled. "Shane's a walking wrestling fact encyclopedia, and Julie has a big heart, for such a little girl."

"She really does," Minette agreed. She moved closer to the bed. He looked ragged. "Pain getting worse?"

He glared at her.

She retrieved a medicine bottle from the bookshelf beside the bed, read the label and shook out two pills. She handed them to Hayes, and pushed his soft drink toward him.

He made a face.

"Copper Coltrain said that your body can't heal if it has to fight the pain at the same time. I'm sure he told you that, too."

"He did. I just hate pills." But he swallowed them, and washed them down with the last of his soft drink.

"We'll bring supper up in a few minutes. It's nothing fancy, just leftover roast beef and mashed potatoes."

He looked as if he'd died and gone to paradise. "Homemade mashed potatoes, again?"

"Well, yes," she said hesitantly. "They don't take long to fix and they go good with beef. It's not fancy," she repeated.

"To a man who lives on takeout and burned eggs and lethal biscuits, it's a feast," he replied. "And you have a gift for cooking potatoes," he added self-consciously.

"Thank you." She hadn't considered that he ate much. But she had heard stories of his cooking. None of them were good. "I guess you're like me," she replied, moving a little closer to the bed. "I don't even have time for lunch. I eat it while I'm writing copy or helping make up the paper."

"I eat in the car most of the time," he confessed. "I go out with the guys to the steak place or the Chinese place about one day a month."

She knew, as most people do, that Hayes could afford to eat out every day if he felt like it. But his deputies couldn't. He wasn't going to indulge his own appetite and emphasize the difference in his bank account and theirs by flaunting it. She liked him for that. She liked him for a lot of things. Not only was he the handsomest man she knew, he was the bravest.

"What are you thinking so hard about?" he wondered aloud.

"How brave you are," she blurted out without thinking and then flushed.

His pale eyebrows arched.

"Sorry, thinking aloud," she replied. "I'll get the kids put to bed, then I'll bring up supper."

"Minette," he called as she reached the door.

She turned.

He averted his eyes. "I really meant it, when I thanked you. For letting me stay here."

She wasn't going to say that she knew he had nobody else to look after him. No close family, no good friends except for Stuart York, who was in Europe with his wife, Ivy. It would have been unkind.

"I know," she said simply.

She managed a smile as she went out the door.

Hayes was almost asleep when she came in with a tray. On it was a light supper of beef with gravy and mashed potatoes, with a faintly elaborate fruit salad on the side.

"That's more trouble than you should have gone to," he began, propping up on the pillows.

"No trouble at all. I like to try and make food look good."

"It does."

She settled the tray on his lap and removed the hot coffee to the side table. "Just so you don't knock it over," she explained. "The tray is a little flimsy."

He smiled. "No problem."

"Well, I'll leave you to it," she said after a minute. "There's pecan pie for dessert."

"Wow."

She laughed. "You really don't cook, do you?"

He shook his head, his eyes closed on a wave of pleasure as he tasted the perfectly cooked roast beef. "This is delicious."

She smiled shyly. "I'm glad you like it."

"I've never had better food anywhere."

She laughed again. "Thanks."

He took a bite of mashed potatoes, perfectly seasoned, and savored them.

"Your investigator wants to come and see you in the morning, to keep you up-to-date on the case," she said suddenly. "Yancy thinks he may have a lead. I wanted to make sure you were feeling up to it first, though."

His face became somber. "I'll be up to it. I want to find out who tried to kill me."

She nodded. "I don't blame you for that. Copper said if you hadn't moved when you did, it would have hit you square in the center of your forehead."

He was grim. "Yes. That means a professional hitman."

"That's what Yancy thinks, too. The shot cartridge was from a sniper rifle, according to Cash Grier."

"It will be a short list of suspects," he added quietly. "That sort of talent doesn't come cheap."

"I know."

He had a sudden thought, and he frowned. "Don't stick your nose in this," he cautioned. "I don't want you in the line of fire."

Her eyes widened.

He glowered at her. "You have two little dependents who need nurturing," he explained. "They don't have anybody else."

"Bull. They have Aunt Sarah. She'd take care of them."

"Not like you do," he replied.

She smiled. "It's one of the biggest stories of the year," she pointed out. "And I've got an exclusive. You can't leave."

"Excuse me?"

She lifted an eyebrow. "We've got all your clothes in the wash, except the pajamas you're wearing. Try walking home like that."

"Walking?"

"Well, I'm not driving you or loaning you a vehicle," she said matter-of-factly. Her eyes were twinkling. "You'd have to have help to break out of here, and I've already threatened everybody who knows you." She leaned forward. "I know things about all of them and I own a newspaper."

He burst out laughing. "That's not fair."

"Hey, this incredible scoop just landed in my lap and you think I'm going to give it up without a fight?"

"Uh-huh," he mused. "So that's why you were so eager to give me a home while I mend."

"Caught me," she laughed.

He cocked his blond head and studied her with open curiosity. It sounded good. But he knew better. Minette didn't have a poker face. At least, not a good one.

She didn't like that intent stare. It made her uncomfortable. "Stop that," she muttered.

He smiled at the color in her cheeks. She was pretty when she blushed. "Sorry."

"I was kidding," she added after a minute. "You're the best sheriff we've ever had. None of us want to lose you. There were lots of people who offered to take you in, you know. I was just quicker than the rest of them."

His dark eyes smiled into hers. "Okay. Thanks. And I'll tell you what I can, when I figure out what's going on."

"I know that."

"But you're not printing a word until I give you a green light."

She crossed her heart.

"I mean it."

She crossed her heart again.

He laughed. "Well, we can argue later. Right now, my excellent mashed potatoes are getting cold."

"You go right ahead and eat. I'll go check on the kids. Sarah or I will be back for the tray in a few minutes. Is the pain easing a bit?"

He nodded. "Thanks," he said stiffly.

"I know you don't like taking medicine," she replied. "I know why."

The truce was over, just that quickly. He saw Bobby's white, dead face, the track marks down his arms from drug abuse. Bobby had died of an overdose. Minette didn't know that she was involved in that death. He wanted to tell her. He wanted her to know. But in the end, he heard his father's voice, and his own promise, and he couldn't do it.

Minette grimaced. "I'm sorry," she said. "I'm really, really sorry."

He averted his eyes. He started eating again and didn't say another word.

Minette went out and closed the door behind her, gritting her teeth. Of all the stupid, stupid things to say! She could have pinched herself. Just when they were getting along, she had to drag up a bitter memory and hit him in the face with it.

"That's the way, Minette," she muttered to herself, "ruin everything, why don't you?"

Aunt Sarah glanced at her as she came into the kitchen. "Talking to yourself again," she observed. "Men with nets are lurking."

She waved her hand. "They'd never catch me. I'd throw down a couple of homemade, buttered rolls and they'd kill themselves fighting over them."

Sarah laughed with delight. "That's true enough, sweet," she agreed. "You really can cook. How's Hayes?" she added.

"Mad," Minette sighed, perching against the counter. "I mentioned why he hated drugs and the truce went over the hill."

Sarah grimaced.

"Me and my big mouth," Minette said heavily. "I just never know when to keep it shut, do I?"

"He won't believe the truth, after all this time, will he?" she asked.

Minette shook her head. "I don't know why he hates me so much."

Neither did Sarah. But she was older than Minette and she'd heard enough gossip to have a faint idea of what might be the problem. She didn't have the heart to share that information with Minette, however. Some secrets should never be told.

Minette frowned at the guilty expression on her great-aunt's face. "What do you know, Aunt Sarah?"

"Me?" Sarah acted for all she was worth. "What do you mean, child?"

The innocent act worked. Minette couldn't see through it. "Sorry," she replied. "I'm just edgy."

"I know." She was somber. "Somebody wants Hayes dead. I hope they can find out who, before they try again."

"Yancy Dean is one of the best investigators we've ever had," Minette reminded her. "He came out here from Dade County, Florida, and a Miami cop is no slouch."

"I agree."

"Besides, Zack Tallman could dig information out of a dry turnip. The pair of them are almost invincible."

"I heard something today."

Minette moved closer. "What?"

"Yancy went to see Cash Grier."

Minette sat down at the table with the older woman. "I know. He's trying to find out who the shooter was."

Sarah leaned forward, as if the walls themselves had ears. "Cash still has contacts in covert ops. He knows where to find out things. If it's local talent, he'll ferret it out, Yancy says."

"Yancy's sharp."

"Yes. So is Zack," Sarah agreed. "You mark my words, it's this drug cartel that's responsible. Somehow, Hayes is in the middle of a turf war."

"He catches crooks. It's an unpopular profession."

Sarah nodded. "And he takes chances, honey."

Minette's black eyes were sad. "I noticed. This is his third gunshot wound. Sooner or later, he's going to get one they can't fix."

"It's so odd, too, isn't it?" Sarah asked, thinking aloud. "I mean, Dallas Carson never got shot even once, and he was sheriff here for twenty years. We've never had a police chief take a bullet, either. But Hayes gets hit three times."

Minette frowned. "Maybe it's just bad luck."

"It's indifference," Sarah said quietly. "He doesn't care if he dies."

Minette's face went pale. She tried to hide it, but the older woman knew her too well.

Sarah laid a hand over Minette's. "He's alone. Well, except for this time, when he needed family around him, and he had nobody. He hasn't had a family since his father died. He lost his mother when Bobby was in high school, then he lost Bobby. Dallas had a heart attack. So now there's just Hayes. He has no girlfriend, no close relatives, nobody. It's almost Thanksgiving, too, which reminds him that he's all by himself in the world."

"He's independently wealthy," Minette inserted.

"What good is money in the middle of the night when you're totally alone and nobody cares what happens to you?" Sarah asked gently.

Minette frowned.

"Hayes doesn't have a reason to care if he lives or dies," the other woman said in a lowered voice. "He loves his job. Of course he does. But he's fearless because he has nothing to lose, don't you see?"

Minette had never understood Hayes's penchant for walking into the jaws of death. She thought it was just cold courage. But what Sarah said made sense.

"You've got me and Shane and Julie," Sarah persisted. "We're your family and we love you. Who loves Hayes?"

Minette bit her tongue. She wasn't going to start making confessions. Not now.

But Sarah knew. She'd always known. She'd seen Minette crying her eyes out when Hayes had carved up her heart with vicious accusations after Bobby's death. She'd watched Minette go from a bright and bubbly teenager to an old woman in the months after Bobby's overdose. Hayes had been relentless in pursuit of his brother's killer, and his trail led straight to Minette.

Sarah had never understood why. Minette wasn't a drug user. She never put a foot out of line, ever. But somehow Hayes convinced himself that she was the guilty party and treated her accordingly. It was odd that Hayes would end up convalescing here, when he'd made a career of hating Minette.

"Sarah?" Minette interrupted her thoughts.

"Sorry. I was just thinking about how long Hayes has blamed you for something you never even did," Sarah replied quietly. "I'm so sorry."

"Yes. So am I. But it won't do any good. Hayes will never change his mind. He knows that Ivy Conley York's sister Rachel supplied the drugs that Bobby overdosed on. She even left a confession of sorts when she died. He knows that Brent and Ella Walsh, Keely York's parents, gave the uncut cocaine to Rachel deliberately for Bobby. But even that hasn't made a dent in his attitude toward me." She rested her chin on her propped hands. "Sometimes I think hating me is a habit he doesn't want to give up. So he finds excuses to justify his dislike."

"It's so wrong."

Minette smiled. "Hayes is stubborn." She toyed with an orange silk flower in the fall arrangement on the dining room table. "I do wish he'd stop walking into bullets, though. For a mortal enemy, he's got class."

Sarah chuckled. "A noble enemy."

"Absolutely." She looked at her watch. "Well, I've got some research to do on the web, so I'd better get to it. You'll be all right here with Hayes?" she added, and couldn't help her worried expression.

"Zack and Yancy will be here in the morning," Sarah reminded her. "They have guns. Big guns."

"Hayes has a big gun. It didn't do him much good on his porch, though, did it?" she asked ruefully.

Sarah had to agree. "Anyway, I keep the doors locked and you will be in the house. We can use the phone to call the sheriff's office." Her eyes twinkled. "I hear the sheriff here is very efficient."

"So are his deputies." Minette sighed. "What a mess." She ran her fingers through her long blond hair and grimaced. "I ought to cut my hair," she muttered. "It takes so much work to keep it clean and brushed!"

"Don't you dare!" Sarah exclaimed. "It's so beautiful. How many years would it take for you to grow it that long again?"

Minette grimaced. "A lot, I suppose." She got up and kissed Sarah's forehead. "I'm going to the den. Call me if the kids act up. Julie's having trouble sleeping, again."

"She's having some problems at kindergarten," Sarah said and then bit her lip. "Oh, dear," she added when she saw her great-niece's expression. "I didn't mean to blurt that out."

Minette sat back down. "What sort of problems?" she asked curtly.

Sarah tried not to tell, but that stare wore her down. "One of the other girls makes fun of her, because she's slow."

"She's slow because she's methodical when she's doing things," Minette said. "I'll have a talk with Miss Banks."

"That might be wise. Miss Banks is a nice woman. She taught

grammar school for a long time, before she started teaching in kindergarten."

"I know." She leaned forward. "She taught me in grammar school!"

Sarah laughed. "Did she? I'd forgotten."

"I hadn't. I'll speak with her tomorrow."

"Good idea."

"Poor Julie," Minette said. "I was picked on in school, too." She made a face. "There should be a special place in the hereafter just for bullies," she said darkly.

"Well, a lot of them just need standing up to," Sarah replied. "Sometimes they have terrible problems of their own and they're making trouble to call attention to themselves. Others are insecure and shy and don't know how to interact with other people. And some…"

"…some are just plain mean," Minette interrupted curtly.

"Well, there's that, too." Sarah laughed suddenly.

"What's funny?"

"I was remembering what you did to your own little problem in middle school," Sarah said with a twinkle in her eyes. "I believe liver and onions and ketchup and rice were involved…?"

"Well, she shouldn't have made me mad in the cafeteria at lunch, should she?" Minette chuckled. "Big mistake."

"Took the wind out of her sails, that did. She was nice to you after you took her down a few inches in front of her girlfriends."

"She had a mother dying of cancer and her brother had just been arrested for stealing a car," Minette replied quietly. "I thought she was the nastiest girl I'd ever met. But her father was a drunk and she didn't have anybody at home who cared about her. She was scared." She smiled. "I didn't know all that at the time, of course."

"How did you find out?"

"She got cancer herself, a few months ago," Minette replied quietly. "She sent me an email and apologized for how she'd treated me when we were kids. She wanted me to forgive her." Minette bit her lower lip. "I spent years hating her for what she did."

"What did you say?"

"Of course I forgave her. She's on her way to recovery, but it will be a long road." She smiled sadly. "The things we learn years after it's too late to do any good."

"I guess we really never know other people."

Minette nodded. "And we judge without knowing."

"Nobody's perfect."

"Least of all, me," Minette said. She got up again. "With that in mind, it might not hurt to find out a little something about Julie's enemy."

Sarah smiled. "Nice thought. And if she's just mean...?"

"Well, then, I'll talk to her parents, won't I?" Minette laughed. Sarah just nodded.

Minette hadn't wanted to revisit those old memories, but they were relentless. It was hard being a child. Without maturity and experience, how could the victim of bullying know how to cope? Schools promised aid, but some people were reluctant to involve themselves in situations of conflict.

Minette sat down at her desk and turned on her computer. So often, children never experienced that happy childhood of which so many novels spoke. Probably, she considered, childhood had more relation to the painful world of Charles Dickens than to a happy cartoon movie that always ended well.

Ironically the first news tidbit she pulled up dealt with a child whose relentless persecution had led to suicide. Minette bit her lip. How horrible, to let things get to that point. But many children were reluctant to tell their parents or caregivers about such situations.

Her own ordeal had lasted for two years. She recalled it with bitterness, even on the heels of the apology that had come so unexpectedly. The experience had ruined school for her, despite the kindness of her few friends. She looked back on those so-called carefree days not with joy, but with sadness.

But, she reminded herself, those days were long gone for her. Now, she had to do for Julie what she couldn't do for herself.

She looked up the contact information for Miss Banks and started composing an email.

Hayes was sitting up in bed, looking very pale and gaunt when Minette went up to check on him before she took the kids to kindergarten and grammar school, respectively.

"Oh, dear," she said worriedly.

He grimaced. "I'm okay," he said. "Just a little dizzy."

She moved to the bed and touched his forehead. "You've got a fever." She pulled out her cell phone and called Copper Coltrain. She filled him in on Hayes's condition and Copper said he'd come out to the house as soon as he got his own kids to school.

"Thanks, Copper," she said.

"All in a day's work," he replied. "Lou can fill in for me until I get to the office. Don't worry about Hayes," he added. "Sometimes we have these little setbacks. He'll be fine. I won't let him die."

Minette laughed softly. "Thanks."

"My pleasure." He hung up.

"No need to look so worried," Hayes told her when she put the phone away. "I'm tougher than I look."

"I know that. But I don't like losing houseguests."

He smiled through the discomfort. "I'm not dying. I'm just sick. Damn, it hurts."

She pulled out the meds and gave him what was prescribed. "Copper's coming by to see you."

"He'll fix me right up."

She glared at the prescription bottle. "This antibiotic always works for me."

"I have an odd constitution and I'm funny about drugs," he said wearily. "Copper will work it out. But thanks for calling him."

"Sure. I'll check back with Aunt Sarah later."

He nodded. "Be careful. It's wet out and the roads get treacherous after a rain."

"I know." She smiled. "I'll see you later. Hope you feel better."

"Thanks. Me, too."

He closed his eyes. She left him there, but not without misgivings and a lot of worry.

4

Minette had her day planned. Interviews in the morning, pick Julie up at kindergarten at one, bring her home, then back to school to talk to Julie's teacher. Then, at three, she would go back to the elementary school to get Shane.

But that wasn't the way it played out...

When she finished the first interview, with a local politician who was thinking about entering the mayor's race, she had a phone call.

"Miss Raynor?" a deep, faintly accented voice inquired.

"Yes?"

"I have a message for your houseguest."

"Who is this?" she asked belligerently.

"My name is not important. Please tell Sheriff Carson that a more accurate marksman is being engaged."

He hung up.

Minette stared at the phone, but she didn't hang it up. She

pulled out her cell phone and called Zack. She explained the phone call she'd just received and asked if he could have the telephone company run a trace. He agreed to try and hung up.

Bill Slater stuck his head in the door. "Trouble?" he asked.

She sighed. Her managing editor looked capable of standing there all day unless she told him. "I think whoever hired the attempt on Sheriff Carson just called me," she confided. "He had a message for Hayes. They're hiring a better shot," she said coldly.

"Well, that's brassy," Bill replied.

She nodded. She felt sick to her stomach. They couldn't watch Hayes night and day. And a good sniper was invisible.

"Zack's good," he reminded her. "So is Yancy."

"I wonder if we know anybody in the mob," she wondered aloud. "Fight fire with fire?" she mused with a laugh.

"Bite your tongue. Hayes will lock you up for just suggesting it."

She sighed. "No doubt." She worried her hair. "It's got to be connected with the turf war," she added. "Hayes interfered. They don't like that."

"Tell me about it. Our recently departed ace reporter almost got you killed and us burned alive with his unmasking of the rougher elements of the drug trade," he added darkly. "I could have punched him. Insolent little toad."

"He wasn't so bad," she replied with a sad smile. "At least he had the guts to dig out the bare facts of the conflict."

"And almost got us killed," Bill repeated. "If it hadn't been for some quick work by the fire department, and then Chief Grier, who found the perp, we'd both be toast."

"That's the truth." She pursed her lips. "You know what, I think I'll wander over to the police department and have a word with Chief Grier." She got up, and pushed her chair toward her desk. "You'll need to have Jerry prompt the florist about that display ad they want—we can't wait too long on the copy."

"I'll tell Jerry to sit on them."

She made a face at him. "Don't sit too hard. We're hurting for advertising."

"So I'll stand on street corners and sell great package deals," he chuckled.

"I don't think it would help. But it's a kind thought. I'll be back when I can. Call if you need me."

He nodded.

Cash Grier was intimidating, even to a woman whose job it was to interview all sorts of personalities. He seemed very businesslike and unapproachable. He was tall and dark, with a handsome face and intelligent black eyes. He'd been married for a couple of years to a former movie star, and they had a little girl. Tippy Grier's young brother also lived with them.

"What can I do for you?" Cash asked when she perched forward on a chair in front of his massive cluttered desk.

She was staring at piles of paper haphazardly stacked on either side of a cleaned-off spot.

He gave her a haughty look. "I'll have you know that those files are logically stacked in priority of need. I myself went through each one with no assistance from my secretary who doesn't know how to file anything!" he added, raising his voice so that the demure, dark-haired young woman in the outer office could hear him through the half-open door.

"Lies," came a lilting voice in answer.

"I can't even find the menu for Barbara's Café!" he shot back.

With a resounding sigh, the young woman walked through the door, dark-haired, slender and neatly dressed in jeans and a blue T-shirt with a knee-length sleeved sweater over it. "There," she said, putting the menu neatly on his desk. She glared at him. "And the files would be in order, sir, if you'd just let me do my job…"

"Those are secret and important files," he pointed out in his deep voice. "Which should not be the subject of local gossip."

"I never gossip," she replied blandly.

"You do so," he retorted. "You told people all over town that I carry a sidearm!"

The secretary looked at Minette, rolled her eyes and went back out again.

Minette was distracted. She stared at Cash Grier curiously. Their very few meetings had been businesslike and brief, mostly when she interviewed him about criminal investigations—and there had only been a handful lately.

"I have trouble getting good help," he said with an angelic smile.

"I'm the best help you've ever had, sir, because I can spell and type and answer the phone!"

"Well, you can't do them all at once, Carlie, now can you?" he shot back.

There was a muttered sound, followed by the muted one of fingers on a computer keyboard.

"What can I do for you?" Cash asked belatedly.

"It's about Sheriff Carson," Minette replied.

"Yes. We're working with his department to find out who shot him, although frankly, it's causing some headaches."

She nodded. "I just had a call from someone who said the next person they send would be a better shot. That's just a summary.

I brought the recording with me." She took out a small cassette and put it on the desk. "We routinely record all our calls. We've had some issues in the past."

"Yes, when someone tried to firebomb your office, I remember. He's doing five to ten up in state prison, one of the few arsonists who ever got convicted." Cash took out a small device from his desk drawer, inserted the tape Minette had brought and played it with his eyes shut. He did that again. He opened his eyes. "Northern Mexico," he murmured, thinking aloud. "But with a hint of Mexico City. A native speaker. Calling from somewhere near a highway."

"You got all that from a few words?" Minette asked, impressed.

He nodded, all business. "I still have a few skills left over from the old days, and I've dealt with telephone threats before. This is gloating, pure and simple. He thinks he's too smart to be caught." His eyes narrowed. "Hayes still at your place?"

"Yes," she said. "He's resisting attempts at rehabilitation and pretending that he doesn't need all that nonsense." She sighed. "He may never leave, at this rate."

He got up from the desk, towering over her. "I'll go out and have a talk with him," he said. "I've been in his situation a few times. It might help. Mind if I hold on to that tape?"

"No. And if we get any more calls, I'll bring them to you." She hesitated. "I have two little kids living in my house, not to mention my elderly great-aunt," she began.

"And you're wondering how safe they are," he replied. He smiled gently. "I'll take care of that. No worries. You just save the world one article at a time."

She laughed. "Okay."

He walked her out. Carlie looked up from her desk with shimmering green eyes.

"The mayor called," she told Cash. "He wants to know if you're coming to the city council meeting."

"No."

"I'll tell him."

"I'll tell you what to tell him..." Cash began heatedly.

She held up a hand. "Please. My father is a minister."

Cash made a face at her and walked Minette to the front door. "I'll see what I can do to motivate Hayes." He hesitated. "Has he still got that huge reptile?"

Minette nodded.

"Is it living with you, too?" he asked with a grin.

She laughed. "No. I'm not going to be lunch for any enormous holdover from the dinosaur age," she promised him.

Later, at Minette's house, Cash was less humorous. Hayes had received a call, also.

"The coward was bragging about his marksman's skill. He said that I moved or I'd be dead now," Hayes muttered.

"Good thing you did move," Cash replied. He drew in a breath. "I gather you've had the number checked out already?"

Hayes gave him a long-suffering look, and Cash laughed.

"Yes. It was a cell phone that's no longer in service. Probably one of those throwaway types. We traced a call one of the cartel mules placed from our jail the day before I was shot. Same story."

Cash nodded. "We've dealt with our share of those," he agreed. He leaned forward in the chair he was occupying beside Hayes's bed. "Lawmen make enemies," he added. "But this is an exceptional one. Do you have any idea who's behind the assassination attempt?"

Hayes nodded. "My investigator dug out a privileged little piece of dark information about a month ago. He was able to tie the death of a border agent with the one they call El Ladrón."

"The thief," Cash translated. He laughed. "How appropriate."

"His men don't call him that," Hayes said. "Only his enemies."

"We can only hope that he has enough of those to help bring him down."

"He has one major enemy who's fighting him for control of Cotillo," Hayes said. "A reclusive, very dangerous leader of a South American cartel making inroads into the Mexican drug trade."

"This reclusive drug trader, do we know who he is?"

Hayes nodded. "The son of an American heiress who ran away with a charming but deadly Mexican gang leader. He used his mother's money to avenge his father, who was killed by agents of El Ladrón."

"Deeper and deeper," Cash mused.

"It gets worse." Hayes's jaw was taut with stress. His dark eyes narrowed. "This reclusive drug lord has ties to our country in a way that could cause some very harsh problems locally."

"Don't tell me. He's related to the mayor of Jacobsville," Cash chuckled.

"Much worse." He drew in a breath. "He has a daughter. She doesn't know it."

Cash frowned. "There's a new wrinkle. Her father is a notorious drug dealer and she doesn't know about him?"

Hayes nodded. He felt a twinge of guilt. "He's the one who supplied Brent and Ella Walsh, who gave Rachel Conley the coke that she injected my brother, Bobby, with…a fatal dose of narcotics."

"Sorry," Cash said gruffly. "That must make it harder."

"It does." He leaned back against the pillows. He felt older than his years. "My father, Dallas, was sheriff here for many years, right up until he died, as you must know. He told me about the connection, in case I ever needed the information, but he made me swear that I'd never tell the woman what I knew about her real father." He made a face. "It's tied my hands in terrible ways."

"I can imagine." He cocked his head. "Which means you can't tell me, either."

"That's the case." Hayes drew in a long breath. "I'm not sure what to do," he confessed. "I don't know how she'd react. I don't know," he added, "if her father even knows about her. But I have to assume that he probably does. If that's the case, and he finds himself in a corner, he might try to use her to help him out of it."

Cash's eyebrows arched. "She has influence?"

"Yes."

"Oh, boy."

"I never thought I'd have to wrestle with a decision like this," he replied. "It's keeping me awake at night."

"Family secrets," he murmured. "Tippy and I have had to deal with those, too. She still doesn't know who her real father was. Her mother couldn't tell her, although her brother's dad is a police chief in Georgia."

"I heard about that," Hayes replied, and frowned.

"What are you going to do?"

Hayes shrugged, wincing when it made his chest uncomfortable. "I'm not sure. It depends on circumstances." He met Cash's eyes. "I'm putting Minette's family in danger by staying here," he added unexpectedly.

"Not really." Cash's dark eyes were amused. "Things are going on that you don't know about." He held up his hand when Hayes tried to speak. "Better you don't know."

"I gather our every move is being watched," Hayes mused.

"Oh, you can count on that." He propped his forearms on his knees. "Now about this physical therapy thing..."

"Stop right there," Hayes muttered.

"Sorry, I promised. I always keep my promises. I know what it's like to be shot, and I have vaster experience than you do," he added. "You don't want to end up losing the use of that arm, do you?"

Hayes's eyes popped. "What do you mean?"

"Surely the doctor explained how muscles atrophy?"

"Well, he said something of the sort. I wasn't really listening. I was trying to get him to sign me out of the hospital at the time. I'd have agreed to paint his house if he'd asked."

Cash chuckled. "I've been there, too." He pursed his lips. "It's just a little sacrifice, having that treatment and doing the exercises. You don't want to have to hire somebody to carry your gun and shoot it for you," he added.

"I have been shot before," Hayes argued.

"Yes, but not this seriously," Cash replied. His dark eyes narrowed. "You know, most people who carry more than two gunshot wounds would be said to have gone looking for trouble."

Hayes glared at him.

"I won't believe you're suicidal, Hayes," Cash continued. "But you do walk in blind. I don't want to have to learn how to work with a new sheriff," he added meaningfully. "It would be time-consuming."

Hayes managed a grin. "I'll buy that. You're not the easiest acquaintance I know."

"I'll get worse with age," Cash promised. "The point is," he sobered, "that you're less cautious than you need to be. Gunshot wounds add up. They cause problems later in life."

"I'm not going to start watching my shadow."

"Not asking you to," Cash replied. "But you need to pay more attention to your surroundings and call for backup. You're not one of those caped heroes. We don't have any radioactive spiders around here."

Hayes chuckled. "You sure about that?"

"Go to rehab," Cash advised. "And take advantage of the last rest you're likely to get in the coming weeks. I think we're going to find that we're in the middle of a drug turf war."

"You've been talking to Cy Parks."

"Yes, I have. You remember that property a former drug trafficker bought that adjoins his?" He waited while Hayes nodded. "Well, it's never been resold and Cy's seen some new activity there. Buildings going up, semitrailers coming in. He checked it out, but the workers don't seem to know much. They say some horse breeder is moving in. Cy thinks it's going to be a front for drug distribution. He's worried."

"He does love his purebred Santa Gerts," Hayes agreed, mentioning the one native breed of cattle, Santa Gertrudis, which hailed from the famous King Ranch in Texas.

"I told him I'd have a few people I know check it out and get back to me. But if you want my opinion, the man behind it is El Ladrón's competition."

Hayes sat straight up. "No. Not him. Not here, for God's sake!"

"Afraid so, if my theory is right."

"Damn. Damn!"

"It might work to our advantage," Cash said. "We'd have him where we could watch him."

Hayes didn't dare say what he was thinking. It would have revealed too much.

"What if he's the gent who sent the shooter after me, instead of the other?" Hayes wondered aloud.

"Not him," Cash replied. "He's got too much class for hired assassins."

Hayes lifted an eyebrow. "Too much class?"

"The man goes to church," Cash replied. "He's devout. He takes care of his workers, buys insurance for all of them, makes sure the kids are educated."

"Is he a drug lord or a saint?" Hayes asked, exasperated.

"Why do you think they call him 'El Jefe'? They speak of him with reverence. He's as far removed from the other one as a saint is from sin." He shook his head. "I don't know how he ever ended up involved in the drug trade in the first place. He's independently wealthy. He doesn't need it."

"Maybe he likes the risk and the rep," Hayes replied.

Cash chuckled. "Maybe he does."

"You're sure he didn't send the shooter?"

"We can't be sure," Cash replied. "But the evidence leans heavily toward the maniac down in Mexico. Minette brought a recording of a call she had at the office, threatening to send another shooter," he added.

"What?"

"Just happened, she'll tell you about it later, I'm sure," Cash told him. "But I listened to the recording. I have a pretty good ear for accents. This was definitely a native Mexican speaker. From what we know of El Jefe, his hires are mostly American. Get this, he feels it exploits native Mexicans to involve them in something so shady, so he uses American criminals to move his product."

"What an interesting guy."

"Interesting. Nuts."

"Probably both."

Cash glanced at his watch. "I have to get home for lunch. You think about what I said. Don't let pride keep you from getting the treatment you need to mend properly."

Hayes sighed. "All right. And thanks for the legwork."

"Your investigator's very good. He'd have turned all this up eventually. I just have deeper sources. Keep getting better."

"I'll do my best. Thanks."

Cash shrugged, smiled and left.

Later, Hayes was eloquent about the fact that Minette didn't phone to tell him about the call she'd received.

"For heaven's sake, it was the middle of the day and I had a teacher conference and other things to do besides worry you about phone calls!" she said finally, exasperated.

"Your family is in as much danger as I am," he gritted. "In fact, I should really go home…"

"No!" she interrupted. "No, no, no! Cash Grier said we're properly watched and nothing is going to happen to us. You can't stay by yourself. You know that."

His sensual lips made a flat line.

"Go ahead, grumble, but if you try to go home I'll have your investigator fetch you right back here," she said, dark eyes flashing.

He glared. She glared back.

"What's the matter, do you think I'll poison you when you aren't paying attention?" she asked with dripping sarcasm.

He drew in a rough breath. "I'm more concerned about a bullet coming through the wall."

She moved closer to the bed. "Listen, Hayes, I love the kids and my great-aunt. I'd never willingly put them in danger. But if you go home, there's a good chance that they'll get you. I can't believe you don't know that."

"I don't want anyone hurt on my account."

She smiled. "I've been taking care of myself and the others for some time now," she pointed out. "Dawn was sickly. She couldn't even take care of Julie when she was born, much less Shane. I did that for her. She was such a sweet person. I still miss her."

"You miss your stepdad, too?"

She nodded. "He was wonderful. After my mother died, I couldn't have asked for a more caring parent."

"How did she meet him?"

"At a fair," she laughed. "She was pregnant and alone, and he was dashing and handsome...." She paused at his expression. "No, I know he wasn't my real father," she said. "My mother was always honest with me, up to a point. She never would tell me who my natural father was. I did try to dig into old records to find out, but I couldn't even get her to tell me where she lived before she met my father—well, the man I always called my father."

"It must have hurt."

She pondered that. She shook her head. "I figured she had good reasons for not wanting me to know," she said. She smiled sadly. "Most likely, he was married and she didn't want to get him into trouble with his family. It doesn't matter. I had a wonderful childhood and loving parents, even if my father was a stepfather. A lot of kids have it worse than that."

Hayes nodded. "My parents fought like tigers, all the time," he confessed after a minute. "I don't know why. They couldn't get along for ten minutes. It made things really hard on Bobby and me." His face hardened. "Bobby couldn't take it. He had a sensitive nature and he took it all to heart. He turned to drugs to escape, and they cost him his life eventually. I hate drug dealers and drug lords more than I hate anything on earth," he added with flashing dark eyes.

"I don't blame you," she said softly. "I know you loved your brother."

He gave her a long, cold glare.

She held up a hand. "We've been here before," she said wearily. "I had nothing to do with it...."

"Like hell you didn't," he said icily.

"How?" She lifted her hands eloquently. "I never used drugs or even associated with people who did!"

He bit his lip. He almost drew blood.

Minette stared at him. She began to piece things together in her mind. The way he hated her. The way he'd treated her for so many years, blamed her for Bobby's death when he had to know that she knew nothing about drug use.

"Hayes," she said softly, "you have to tell me what you know about me. What won't you tell me?"

All at once, his face smoothed out like an ironed cloth. He blinked. "What do you mean?" he asked innocently. "Cash tricked me into promising I'd have the damned therapy," he said suddenly, changing the subject.

"He did?" She let it drop. He was behaving very oddly, but she'd think about it later. "Good for him!"

He grimaced. "I guess I need to be able to use my arm, even if I don't use it for shooting."

"You use it for the shotgun," she pointed out.

He sighed. "Yes."

"Aunt Sarah can drive you to the sessions," she said. "She's already volunteered."

"That's kind of her."

"It's no sacrifice."

He studied her curiously. "I still don't understand why you invited me to come here," he said quietly. "I've treated you very badly, for a long time."

"Coals of fire," she promised.

He chuckled. "Is that it?" he asked, without revealing that her great-aunt had already imparted that tidbit of information.

She nodded enthusiastically.

"Well...it was a kindness."

"Alternatively," she said pertly, "perhaps I'm a closet masochist. I love being persecuted."

"Unlikely."

"Can I get you anything before I start supper?"

"I thought Sarah was cooking."

"She was, but I have a yen for chicken and dumplings. Just between us, I can't cope with her idea of it, so I do it myself."

"That's one of my favorite dishes."

"Mine, too."

"I hope you keep a gun in your desk drawer," he said suddenly.

She arched both eyebrows. "So I can shoot the typesetter?"

"I was thinking of anyone barging in with a gun."

"I remember reading something that President John Kennedy was credited with saying, many years ago," she said suddenly. "He said that if someone was willing to trade his life for yours, there was no way to avoid being killed. It was true then, and it's true now. Besides all that, I believe very strongly that when your time's up, it's up."

"Yes. I believe that way, too."

"Is that why you keep walking into gun battles?" she asked blithely.

He glared at her. "Both times, I didn't realize there was a second shooter."

"Both times, you should have."

"Lady," he said between his teeth, "you don't know hell about gun battles."

"No, it's more than that," she said. Her eyes held his. "You blamed me, you blamed Rachel Conley, you blamed the supplier, you blamed your parents...but you blame yourself more, don't you, Hayes? You think you should have known how badly Bobby was involving himself with drugs, and you should have stopped him."

He didn't say a word. His face was like stone.

"That's it, isn't it?" she asked very quietly. "You're looking for ways to punish yourself because he died."

"That is none of your business."

She moved closer to the bed. "You couldn't have stopped him," she said solemnly. "One of my friends in high school had a father who was an alcoholic. He literally drank himself to death. His mother tried everything, absolutely everything, to stop him, from jail to ministers to psychiatrists—he was even told that if he kept doing it, he was going to die. He hid bottles from them in all sorts of places, and one day when they were at church, he drank too much and mixed the alcohols with pills, and he died. His wife tried to commit suicide, because even though it wasn't her fault, and everyone knew how hard she'd tried to stop him, she blamed herself. It took years of therapy to convince her that he had a choice and he made it." She moved another step closer, because he looked less threatening now. "People make bad decisions. We can try to protect them, but we aren't always successful. You did your best, Hayes. That's all anyone can do. And you're no more to blame for Bobby's death than I am. It was his time. Nothing would have made any difference."

5

Hayes didn't say anything for a minute. He just stared at Minette.

"That's what you've been doing, isn't it?" she prodded gently.

He drew in a breath and averted his eyes. "Not consciously," he said finally.

He was silent after that, but she knew she'd started him thinking.

"I'll just get to work on supper," she said, and pulled the door shut behind her.

A couple of hours later, she presented Hayes with a nice plate of chicken and dumplings and a green salad, with a small portion of apple cobbler for dessert.

He thanked her, but he was subdued. It wasn't until she came back to pick up the supper dishes that he became more communicative.

"I've been thinking about what you said," he began.

She smiled.

"Maybe I did feel guilty," he said after a minute. "Bobby was almost a generation younger than me. I was old enough that I should have noticed when he used drugs."

"You weren't living at home then," she replied quietly.

"I was over there every weekend," he argued.

"It's not the same."

He leaned back against the pillows. His thick blond-streaked brown hair was clean and its disheveled look made it even more attractive. He had a day's growth of beard, which gave him a swashbuckling air. His spotless white T-shirt that he wore with burgundy flannel pajama pants made him look very masculine and showed off his rodeo-rider physique to its best advantage. Minette thought he was the handsomest man alive. She wasn't letting that show, of course.

"My dad was sharp," he continued. "But perhaps he didn't want to look too close. He said Bobby was hanging out with one of the town's bad boys, but Bobby said he was trying to rehabilitate the kid." He laughed humorlessly. "Dad was a churchgoer and he believed that anybody could be turned from a wrong road. Bobby convinced him. Hell, he convinced me, too."

"You and your father looked for the best in people, despite working in a profession that generally teaches you to do the opposite," she pointed out. "I'd know about that. Working in newspaper doesn't exactly point you to the best behavior of the population in general."

"True."

"And to be honest, Hayes, your father was beginning to feel his age."

"He had plenty of health problems at the end, especially his heart," Hayes commented. "He didn't take care of himself, although I did my best for him."

"You did your best for both of them," she said.

"Did I?" The expression in his eyes was wistful. "I was so occupied with my job, even then. And I was only a deputy sheriff at the time."

"You have to be one of the most prosperous lawmen in Texas," she laughed.

He shrugged. "I inherited wealth. It doesn't mean I'm going to sit down and entertain."

"Me, neither," she replied with a smile. Her parents had left her well provided for.

"Workaholics," he mused.

"Count on it," she agreed. "I never liked the idea of fancy clothes and even fancier houseguests. I'd rather make mud pies with the kids."

"You really do that, don't you?" he asked, impressed.

"They're sweet children," she said gently. "I enjoy them more than I can say."

"It's a big responsibility."

"Yes, but I don't mind it," she said, smiling.

He was watching her in an odd way, his dark eyes intent on her face, so intent that she flushed.

He saw her sudden color. That made him arrogant. He smiled slowly, and held her eyes until she became embarrassed. "I'd better get these in the dishwasher," she faltered, picking up the plate and cup and moving to the door. "If you need anything, you can call us."

"Thanks." He was still watching her with that odd half smile as she fumbled her way out the door.

Minette was confused. Hayes had never really talked to her, except to lay blame and make snide comments. Now, he was looking at her in a way he never had before, so that she was uncomfortable being near him.

It didn't help that she'd lost her heart to him years ago when she was at school with Bobby. Hayes had always been the sun in her sky, which was why his antagonism had hurt so much.

But he seemed different now. He was less argumentative than he'd ever been, and he seemed more inclined to be friendly.

It was Minette who had to drive him to therapy the following week when Aunt Sarah had a doctor's appointment.

She used the SUV when she drove the kids around, but she also had a pickup truck. It was funny, because she could have had a fancy sports car or any other sort of second vehicle, but she liked trucks.

"Isn't it cool?" she asked as she drove out of the yard. "It's got all sorts of toots and whistles, but what I like most is how sturdy it is."

"It's sturdy all right," he chuckled. "In fact, I drive one almost identical to it, except for the color. Yours is black and mine's white."

She laughed, trying not to blush when she realized the similarities. She hadn't given it a thought until just now. "What a coincidence."

"You've got this, and an SUV. Don't you like cars?" he asked.

"I do, but I sit higher in trucks. I keep the SUV for the kids, because they're safe. And also," she added with a laugh, "there's that entertainment system so that Julie and Shane can watch movies while I'm driving. It makes for calmer travel."

"What's this interest in safety?"

"I covered a wreck last spring. You remember, the Danes boy who died after he was sideswiped by an old SUV?"

"Yes. It was a tragic case."

"He was in a lightweight little sedan. The SUV was all metal." She grimaced. "I couldn't get the picture out of my mind."

"So you bought an SUV and a truck?"

She nodded, pausing at a red light. "They're not great on gas, because they both have V-8 engines," she explained. "But I like this truck because it's powerful and I don't have to worry about someone hitting me when I'm driving it. It has all sorts of safety features."

"You could probably find a car with the same features."

"Yes, but it would be some flashy, expensive thing."

"And that matters because...?" he prodded.

She grimaced. She pulled back out into traffic. "See, the thing is, I don't want the kids to get ideas about luxury making them better than other kids. I do have top-of-the-line vehicles for them to ride in, but they aren't flashy sports cars. I buy their clothes out of a midrange department store and I don't give them fancy presents even at Christmas. I give them the sort of things any middle-class parent would. Wealth is no measure of worth."

"I approve," he said with a faint smile.

She laughed. "My parents would, too. They brought me up the same way. I was never given expensive presents."

"Come on. There must be one frivolous thing you'd die to have."

She smiled. "No. Not really. Well, there's one..."

"What?"

"I love cameos. Those old-fashioned ones that women used to

wear on dresses or on a necklace. I could wear it on the suits I keep in my closet for special occasions and church. But it always seemed like an unnecessary expense." She laughed. "It's nothing I'd buy myself. Even for Christmas." She glanced at him. "What about you?"

"Oh, I'm easy. I like ties."

She glanced at him with wide eyes until she realized he was holding back laughter.

"I might as well like them, it's all I get," he pointed out.

"Someone should have a word with your deputies," she replied.

"Their wives," he chuckled. "What do you get a guy who has everything? A tie. But the thought is what counts."

"So what would you like?"

"A really good spinning reel," he said with a sigh. "I love to fish."

"Really?" She was surprised. She'd never known him to mention a hobby.

"I like to hunt, too, but I can never spare the time. Fishing's easy. I keep a reel in the truck and stop by the river on my lunch hour when I have a few minutes to spare. I don't catch much, but once in a while I pull out a bass or bream."

She laughed. "I love to fish."

"What? You?"

"Really. My stepfather used to take me with him. I learned how not to talk. He was very serious about that. We sat on a creek bank for two hours once without a single word. Not that we ever caught much. He liked lures. I wanted to fish with worms but he said that was bad bait."

"Worms are good bait."

"I know. But it's hard to argue when you're only ten."

"I guess it is." He grimaced as he saw the hospital coming up fast. "I don't want to have to do this," he muttered.

"You want to use that arm, though, don't you?" she asked pertly.

He glared at her.

"Fine. We'll go home and you can learn to fish one-handed...."

"Crackers and milk!" he burst out.

She gaped at him.

He looked uncomfortable. "I give talks about drugs to little kids," he pointed out. "What if I got used to bad words and they slipped out at school?"

"I think probably the kids would know more of those words than you do, Hayes," she said ruefully.

"Could be, but I'm not using them."

She smiled. "Don't sound apologetic. I like it."

"Do you?" He smiled at her in a new way, one that caused her to go too close to the curb and have to back up.

She pulled up to the entrance and unfastened his seat belt for him. "If you'll call me, I'll be here in five minutes," she promised.

She'd had to lean closer to unfasten the belt. When she started to sit up again, his face was very close, so close that she caught her breath and her heart ran wild.

"You're very nervous around me," he said in a deep, velvety tone. "Why?"

"I'm not...n-nervous," she stammered, flushing. "You'll be late!"

"Will I?" His eyes narrowed. They held hers until she thought her heart would suffocate her.

"Yes," she said.

"Then I'll see you later, Minette." The way he said her name made her even more uncoordinated. It was a mercy when he finally turned away, got out of the truck and closed the door. But before he closed it, he smiled at her again, and in a way that kept her distracted all the way back to work.

She went on her lunch hour to pick Hayes up at the hospital. Despite his objections, they rolled him out to the curb in a wheelchair.

"It's my shoulder, not my legs," he muttered.

"We have rules," the nurse pointed out. "Besides that, I like rolling you around. It makes me feel in control."

He muttered something under his breath.

"What was that?" she queried.

"I said I'm not going to be reclassified as freight," he replied.

She laughed.

Minette jumped out of the truck and opened the passenger door for him.

"I am not an invalid," he said angrily. He started to get in the truck, but as Minette moved to help him, her loafer caught on the curb and she fell.

"Damn the luck!" Hayes said angrily. He reached down to lift her.

"No!" she exclaimed, and the nurse echoed her. "Don't you dare try to lift me with your arm in that condition!"

He was saying something under his breath, and it wasn't "crackers and milk."

"I'm all right," Minette said, catching her breath. She winced as she moved her foot. "I'm so clumsy!"

"We can get you into X-ray," the nurse began worriedly.

"I just turned my ankle," Minette assured her. "I do this all the time. You'd think a grown woman would be able to walk by herself, wouldn't you?" she laughed breathlessly.

"Are you sure you don't want to see a doctor?" the nurse said, looking agitated.

Minette gave her a long look. "I've never sued anybody in my life," she assured her.

The nurse laughed. "I suppose we're all twitchy about accidents these days. I'm glad you're all right. But if that starts to act up later, you come back," she added firmly.

"Yes, Nurse." Minette waited until Hayes was strapped in before she closed his door and went around, slowly, to get in under the steering wheel. The nurse was standing on the curb when they left.

"You'll see a doctor if that isn't better by tonight," Hayes told her.

She made a face. "Not you, too."

"Yes, me, too. Little accidents can have big repercussions."

"I suppose. But it's really okay. Just sore."

"We'll see."

She glanced at him as she drove. "No complaints about that therapy today?"

He shrugged, wincing when it hurt. "Not so many, no. They really know their business in there. And the heat treatments are pretty great."

She laughed. "That's what I've heard."

His cell phone rang suddenly. He dug it out of the holder on his belt. "Carson," he answered professionally. He frowned. "You sure? Okay. Come on over. We're—" he glanced out the window "—about five minutes from Minette's place. Just a sec."

He turned his head. "Is it okay if my investigator comes over to discuss my case?"

She was surprised, and pleased, by his courtesy. "Of course it is."

He nodded. "She says come on over, Yancy. I'll wait for you in the living room. Sure. Thanks."

He hung up, looking pensive. "They think they've got something."

"Quick work," she replied. She glanced at him. "I get an exclusive when you break the case," she pointed out. "Because the shooting is being investigated on my property."

He chuckled. "Always playing the angles, huh, kid?"

"I'm not a kid," she reminded him. "I'll be twenty-six just before Christmas."

"Which isn't that far off, either." He sighed. "I guess you decorate around Thanksgiving?"

She nodded. "The kids are always so excited when the tree goes up. We light it on Thanksgiving night."

"I haven't had a Christmas tree in years. No point, since there's just me at the house."

"There's Mrs. Mallard," she said.

He made a face. "She comes in to clean three times a week. If I put up a Christmas tree she'd think I'd lost my mind and she'd quit." He scowled. "Do you have any idea how long it takes to persuade a woman to clean a house that contains a six-foot-long iguana?"

"Probably weeks," she mused, and laughed.

"Months," he replied. "And I'm not going through that again."

"I'll bet she has a Christmas tree at her house," she said.

He didn't say a word.

"She's got six grandchildren. At least two of them go to her house every year with their families for dinner on Christmas Eve. Of course she would have a tree up."

"Well, I'm not putting one up." He stared at her pointedly.

"You do what you like at your own house," she said. "But at my house, we put up a tree."

He made a rough sound in his throat.

"My goodness, I just realized, Thanksgiving is next Thursday," she exclaimed as they pulled up in front of the big Victorian house. "I've got to start getting things together." She glanced at him with a twinkle in her dark eyes. "I'll have to buy the tree and get it situated before then."

He glared at her. "I am not helping you put up a tree."

"I never asked you to," she said haughtily. "You'd probably drop all the decorations and break them out of spite."

"Wrap a rope around it. That's decorative."

"We have decorations that go back to when I was a kid," she said. "And some that belonged to my great-grandmother. Aunt Sarah keeps them in a cotton-lined box."

"My skin's itching. I think I'm allergic to celebrations."

She laughed. "Well, you can't go home yet," she said. "So I guess you'll just have to cope with a holiday."

"I'll stay in my room. You can slide toast under the door," he said.

She grinned. "Not a chance, Hayes. You'll survive," she added when he looked hunted. "You might even enjoy yourself."

"I don't like turkey."

"We're also having ham."

He hesitated.

"Sweet potato soufflé," she added. "Poached apples. Dressing with homemade giblet gravy. Homemade rolls…"

"Stop," he groaned. "I'm starving."

She grinned. "You still want me to shove a piece of toast under your door?"

"I might sacrifice myself for homemade rolls. I don't remember the last time I had one."

She just laughed.

They got to the house and Minette opened his door for him, but she was limping.

"I knew you should have seen the doctor," Hayes said, concerned.

"It's just wrenched," she argued.

"Here. Lean on me. You won't hurt my arm," he said with a long-suffering expression, "it's the other one that I got shot in. Come on."

She gave up. He was warm and very strong, and it felt good to have his arm around her waist, all that exciting masculinity so close that her skin tingled even through her clothing. He helped her up the steps.

"What's wrong?" Sarah asked, meeting them at the door with a frown.

"She tripped on the curb at the hospital," Hayes began.

"Wrenched the ankle, did you? Come on. I'll soak that for you right now before it swells any more. Hayes, do you need me to help you upstairs?" she added with a smile.

"No, thanks, Sarah, my investigator's on his way over. They've got a break, they think. I asked if it was okay. I should have asked you, too…"

"You're home," Sarah replied easily. "Family doesn't have to ask if visitors can come over. Now you come with me, young lady," she added, turning back to Minette before she saw the expression that washed over Hayes's face.

He hadn't been part of a family since his father's death. It felt odd, to be considered part of Minette's. He turned slowly and went into the living room. He dropped into the big armchair and leaned back into its cushy softness. He was tired from the unfamiliar exertion and still weak form his ordeal. He didn't like admitting that. He was a big, strong, tough lawman.

Right.

Minette let Sarah put her foot in a tub of warm water with Epsom salts in it. "Takes the swelling right down," she was assured.

"I fell like a sack of sand," Minette sighed. "I'm so clumsy!"

"Runs in the family. Your poor mother, God rest her soul, was exactly the same. Remember the time she caught her sleeve on the doorknob out front and ripped it right off?"

Minette laughed. "I'd forgotten that."

"So you come by the gift honestly."

"Are you going shopping before you pick up the kids?" Minette asked the older woman.

"Yes. Anything you need?"

"Next Thursday's Thanksgiving."

"So it is. I'll stock up on cranberry sauce and flour and yeast today. Probably better to get the turkey and ham next Monday so we can thaw the turkey for a couple of days in the fridge," Sarah said, thinking aloud.

"We'd never manage to cram it in the freezer," Minette said. "Freezers should be designed by women," she added irritably.

"Tell me about it."

Out front, a car drove up.

"I'll bet that's Hayes's investigator," she told Sarah. "Can you go let him in?"

"I can let him in," Hayes said from the hallway. "It's my shoulder, not my leg."

Minette made a face at him. He made one back.

Yancy was blond and dashing, very married, with a six-year-old son. He grinned at Hayes. "Looking better there, boss," he commented.

"I wish I was back at my office," Hayes said heavily. "Come on in."

"You want coffee, Yancy?" Sarah called.

"I wouldn't turn down a cup, Sarah, thanks," Yancy replied.

"Be just a minute. Hayes, she still got you hooked on that fancy European coffee?"

Hayes burst out laughing. "Yes. Sorry."

"No problem, I'll fix you a cup of it. Does Yancy want to try a latte?"

"Just plain black coffee, thanks." Yancy held up a hand. "I'm not into those fancy ones."

"You don't know what you're missing, does he, Hayes?" Minette called out.

"No, he doesn't."

"Hi, Minette," Yancy said, frowning as he saw her sitting in the kitchen with her foot in a pan of water. "What happened to you?"

"I was doing my superheroine imitation and I fell down," Minette said with utter disgust. "I guess I'll have to give back the cape, now."

Yancy burst out laughing.

"Just a turned ankle," Minette added. "Feels better already. Aunt Sarah's a magician."

"I practiced on your mother, darling," she told the younger woman with a grin.

"Well, get better," Yancy said.

"Thanks."

Yancy followed Hayes into the living room. He was more somber when they were alone.

"Company's coming," he told Hayes, lowering his voice. "Cy Parks said they're moving in on that property that adjoins his."

"Not another fake honey distributor," Hayes groaned, alluding to a former owner who'd pretended to sell honey while he stocked his barn full of bales of marijuana.

"Actually," Yancy said quietly, "it seems to be a legitimate operation. Horses. Purebred horses. Very expensive. He races them in the Kentucky Derby. He's putting up a barn that uses green power and the horses will live better than a lot of people do."

Hayes frowned. "A legitimate operation."

Yancy held up a hand. "Legitimate horses," he agreed, nodding. "But the owner has been charged twice with drug trafficking and walked out of court a free man both times."

"Damn! It's El Jefe, isn't it?" Hayes asked through his teeth.

"The very same."

"Maybe I'd better get better life insurance and invest in a suit of body armor."

"We're almost positive that he's not the one who had you shot,"

Yancy corrected. "It was the other, Mendez. El Ladrón. The guy's got an attitude problem. Anybody crosses him or causes him trouble, he puts them down. He's worse than Lopez ever dreamed of being," he added grimly.

"Cy Parks could write you a book on that guy."

"Him and half the mercs in town, not to mention a couple of DEA agents," Yancy agreed. "Lopez died in a mysterious yacht explosion very near Dr. Micah Steele's old house in the Bahamas, as I recall."

"Micah was never officially involved."

Yancy's eyes twinkled. "So they say. Convenient location, however, wouldn't you say?"

"Actually——" Hayes began.

"Actually the word on the street was that Micah was up to his ears in it," Minette said, pausing in the doorway. "And sanctioned." She smiled angelically. "Nothing gets past a good reporter."

"You mention that in public, and you could be wearing concrete overshoes," Yancy mentioned wryly.

She put her hand on her heart. "I never tell what I know. Empires would fall."

Hayes was studying her with real interest. That hair invaded his dreams at night. It was the most beautiful curtain of pale gold he'd ever seen. With her black eyes and peaches and cream complexion, she was lovely. Her face wasn't conventionally pretty, but when she smiled, she glowed. He smiled idly at the picture she made, in her nicely fit blue jeans and that long pullover sweater with its turtleneck.

"Is my nose on crooked?" she asked him.

He chuckled. "I was just thinking that pale yellow suits you," he mused, indicating her sweater. He shook his head. "Your hair is amazing."

She flushed. "Thanks. I think."

"Oh, it's a compliment, in case you weren't sure," Hayes added. He glanced at Yancy. "She can cook," he said. "And I mean, cook! She even makes her own bread. I swear, I'll dream of the food here every night long after I'm back home." He winced. "Eating my own bouncy biscuits and burned eggs."

"Why don't you hire a cook?" Yancy asked him. "Your stomach would love you for it."

"Andy," Minette said, venturing a guess.

Hayes sighed. "She's right. I'd try to hire a cook, the cook would walk into the living room and see Andy perched on the sofa watching television, and walk right back out again." He shook his head. "I had this electrician come to replace my ceiling fan. Andy was sprawled on the marble coffee table—it was summer, and he was hot. Well, the electrician thought he was a ceramic piece. You know how still Andy can be," he added, and Yancy nodded. "So, the electrician's up on his ladder, twisting wires together, when Andy notices that the ladder's higher than the coffee table."

"I can see where this is going," Minette chuckled.

Hayes nodded. "Andy started climbing up the ladder. I swear, the electrician actually jumped off the top rung and landed on the sofa. He was screaming like a kid in a sprinkler in midsummer."

"Did he finish fixing the fan?"

"Nope. It took me ten telephone calls, but I did finally find a man who wasn't afraid of reptiles to come and finish the job. He came down from San Antonio." Hayes threw up his hands.

"The electrician told everybody he knew, so now I can't even get a plumber to come over if a pipe breaks!"

"Most people would be unnerved by a six-foot lizard," Minette pointed out.

"Yes, but he's like a cow, he eats vegetables," Hayes moaned.

Yancy pursed his lips. "Green scaly cow. Hmm."

"You hush," Hayes said. "We've got bigger issues to deal with than my pet."

"He isn't kidding," Yancy said, grimacing. "A major drug lord is moving in next to Cy Parks."

Minette's black eyes widened. "You mean, that rumor's really true?"

"It is," Yancy said.

"But, what if he's the one who had you shot?" Minette asked Hayes, and her face was rigid with concern.

Hayes stared back at her with an odd tingling in his body. She was really worried about him. He met her eyes and held them, and the world seemed to go away for that space of seconds.

6

Minette felt as if her legs were melting as she met Hayes's dark eyes. She just stared at him.

"It was the other one," Yancy said.

They both looked at him blankly.

"The other drug lord," he pointed out. "The one they call El Ladrón," he emphasized. "We're almost positive that El Jefe had nothing to do with it. He doesn't believe in hired assassins."

"A drug lord with ethics?" Minette laughed nervously. She avoided Hayes's searching eyes because her heart was beating her to death.

"It would seem so," Hayes agreed. "He even goes to church."

"I think I need a drink," Minette teased.

"Oh, no. You start drinking and the food around here goes to pot, I starve and go back to the hospital to beg for that green jell stuff that makes my stomach churn, and law enforcement in the whole county goes to the dogs. No drinking."

She burst out laughing. So did Yancy.

"Okay. But you have to admit, he does seem like one strange drug lord."

"It gets more complicated," Yancy said. "He raises thoroughbred horses."

"How very odd," Minette said, frowning. "My mother used to talk about breeding thoroughbreds. Someone she knew was in the business. Funny, I'd forgotten that."

"You breed horses, too," Hayes said.

"Just palominos," she said. "Archibald was the first. I fell in love with the breed because of him. They were going to put him down." She made a face. "He killed a man."

"And you've got him here?" Hayes burst out.

She held up a hand. "The man was beating him with a stool," she said, wincing at the memory of what she'd been told. "Archibald was bloody and bruised, and he just took it, but the man had a stepchild, a little boy, and when the child protested what was being done to the horse, the man hit the boy with the stool, too. Archibald reared up and kicked the man in the head. It was all over, just that quickly."

"How did you end up with him?" Yancy asked, curious.

"A man I know at the sale barn was telling me about it. Seemed a shame to him to kill a horse for defending a child. So I intervened." She didn't add that she'd intervened with a lawyer, a friend in network TV reporting and several animal rights activists. But in the end, she got custody of Archibald.

"I imagine that's a very long story," Hayes said, reading between the lines.

"It is, and not a pretty one," she replied solemnly. "But I wasn't about to let the horse pay for what a mean human being had done."

"What about the child?" Hayes asked.

She smiled. "He went back to live with his mother. They found that he had a history of emergency room visits since he'd been with his stepfather, and he'd had a couple of broken bones. The stepfather lied about the boy's mother abusing him to get custody, all to spite his ex-wife for leaving him. A tragic story all around."

"So now Archibald leads a charmed life and he has lots of fillies to keep him company," Hayes said with a smile.

"Yes. He's such a gentle horse." She winced. "It never ceases to amaze me, how some people think animals don't even have feelings and that it's all right to abuse them." She shook her head. "What a world we live in."

"It's getting better," Hayes said. "Enlightenment takes time, grasshopper," he teased.

She grinned. Her face flushed at the teasing.

"Well, I have to go," Yancy said. He got to his feet.

"But I'm just bringing coffee," Sarah protested, entering the room with a tray. She glared at Yancy. "So you just sit right back down there and drink your coffee and eat some of this nice lemon pound cake Minette made," she said belligerently.

Yancy chuckled. "First time I was ever forced to eat cake and drink coffee. I'm not complaining. I've even got the boss himself for a witness," he added, jerking his head toward Hayes. Everybody laughed.

After Yancy left, Minette went back to work, even though Hayes protested that she needed to rest her foot. Hayes stayed in the living room, by himself, brooding.

"You should be resting," Sarah said from the doorway.

He sighed. "I should," he agreed. He turned his head toward her. His dark eyes narrowed thoughtfully. "Sarah, how much do you know about Minette's mother?"

She moved into the room, sat down on the edge of the sofa next to Hayes's chair and looked at him somberly. "I know that the man she married wasn't Minette's natural father," she confessed. "Minette knows that, too."

"Yes, but how much more do you know?"

She looked worried. "She never said much about him. She was very reticent. I thought he was probably married, and that was why." She smiled sadly. "My niece was always very naive. Sweet, but innocent. She wanted Minette very much. I don't think she would have wanted her so badly if she hadn't been in love with the father, you know?"

He nodded.

"I asked her one time if he knew about Minette. She never answered me."

Hayes felt his heart jump. That would be a complication, and it was one that disturbed him a lot.

Sarah was sharp. Her own eyes narrowed. "You know a lot more about this than you're saying, Hayes."

"Maybe I do."

"You gave your word to somebody, that you'd never speak of it, didn't you?"

He smiled. "I guess my reputation follows me around."

She nodded. "We know if you make a promise, you keep it." She leaned forward. "But how is it going to affect Minette, if her father turns out to be somebody really bad and he shows up here?"

Hayes felt his face go taut. "You're reaching, Sarah."

"Am I? Wouldn't it be better, even if you break a promise, to tell her the truth before she finds it out in some public and humiliating way?"

He was troubled, and it showed.

"You need to think about that," Sarah continued. She got up. "I won't say another word about it."

"You see too much." He smiled gently.

She wrinkled her nose. "I just read people very well. Even sheriffs with poker faces," she added with a grin.

Hayes was torn. He did feel bound by the promise he'd made. On the other hand, Minette's life could be in danger. Her real father, El Jefe, might use her as a bargaining chip to save himself from being arrested and prosecuted for drug trafficking. His enemy, the other drug lord, Mendez, might feel inclined to kidnap her, or worse, use her as revenge for the other man's invasion of his own drug territories.

Either way, having El Jefe as a resident of Jacobsville did nothing to help Hayes's recovery. He only wished he had some way, any way, to find out what the neighborhood drug lord was really up to.

Hayes's wish came true unexpectedly. Zack stopped by two days later, his face grim. "Well, I think I may have some answers," he told Hayes when they were behind the closed door in Hayes's bedroom. "I can guarantee you won't like them."

"Go ahead," Hayes replied.

"Well, it seems that El Jefe has a contact in Houston. That guy has a friend who works for one of the foremost private investigators in the business, Dane Lassiter."

"I've heard of him," Hayes said. "He was in law enforcement before being badly injured in a shootout."

"That's the one. He's got branches of his business in every major city in the country, and his reputation is sound. A few weeks ago, El Jefe had his contact hire Lassiter's firm for a private matter."

"If Lassiter finds out who he is, he'll be looking elsewhere for help," Hayes predicted.

Zack smiled. "Exactly. Lassiter did his homework. As an upshot, El Jefe had to find another private investigator."

"Do we know what he's looking for?" Hayes asked quietly.

"It's a who, actually," Zack said. "Or, rather, that's the assumption. Get this, they say that El Jefe has a child somewhere, and he's trying to find it." He sighed, missing Hayes's suddenly tense expression. "If you want my opinion, he's already got the information he wanted. I mean, why would a drug lord who's one jump ahead of the U.S. authorities suddenly pick up and move into Texas?"

"You think El Jefe is related to somebody local," Hayes interpreted.

"You bet I do," Zack replied.

"Any idea who?" Hayes asked, trying his best to sound casual.

"No clue," the other man replied. "But the word is that El Ladrón has also engaged private detectives, no doubt for the same reason." His expression was grim. "So we may find ourselves in the middle of a real turf war, protecting someone who's going to be in a great deal of danger pretty soon."

"Yes."

"So I was thinking, if the drug lords could hire a P.I., why can't we?" Zack continued.

"The county commissioners will be thrilled if I go to them for funding," Hayes remarked, trying to keep his fears about Minette hidden.

"You could send Yancy," Zack suggested. "Old Ben Yates is terrified of him. He'd probably agree at once."

Hayes frowned. "Why is he afraid of Yancy?"

"There was this disagreement about a stand of oak trees that the chamber of commerce planted on the main county road several years ago," Zack reminded him. "Ben decided that they were planted without proper permissions, so he tried to pass a motion to have them cut down."

"Now that just makes no sense at all," Hayes mused.

"It does if you realize that Ben lives on that road, that he just installed a huge wood-burning stove in his house, and that fire-wood's expensive. He suggested that he could perform the labor himself for the wood." He pursed his lips. "Oak's a real slow-burning wood."

"And he could be arrested if I catch him cutting down a single tree," Hayes said, irritated.

"Well, that's exactly what Yancy said, and a lot more besides. You know, Yancy's pretty intimidating when he loses his temper, plus he curses in some odd dialect of Spanish that nobody in this county even understands. So Ben didn't understand what he was saying at all, but he actually ran out of the hardware store where the discussion took place, and went home. Ever since then, if you mention Yancy's name, he gets real nervous and mentions that he doesn't even own an ax." He chuckled. "I think it's funny."

"And people think politicians are honest." Hayes shook his head.

"Well, some of them probably are," Zack replied.

He bit his lower lip. "There should be a private detective some-where around here that we could hire, closer than Houston."

"I'll look into it. But whether or not the county will pay for it..."

"I just had a thought," Hayes remarked. "Winnie Kilraven's husband is a fed," he added. "And kidnapping is a federal crime. Now we don't actually have a kidnapping yet, but if El Jefe's enemy is looking into the identity of this unknown child, that's a potential kidnapping. So I was thinking maybe we could get Kilraven to get the private detective on the job."

"What a brilliant idea," Zack said with pure admiration.

"Oh, I'm well-known for my brilliance," Hayes assured him. "In fact, I tell people all the time how smart I am." He smiled.

"They must not listen. Nobody's ever said anything like that to me about you.... I'm going!" Zack laughed, holding his hands palms-out.

Hayes just grinned. "I'll let you know what I find out."

"Thanks, boss."

But when Zack left, Hayes was preoccupied. He had a bad feel-ing about the future. He couldn't do a thing until he knew for certain what the drug lords were up to. He hoped Kilraven would be willing to help, and that he had a budget that would allow it.

"You want me to hire a private investigator to find out if a drug lord is planning on kidnapping somebody in Jacobsville?" Kilraven asked, aghast, when Hayes called him. "Hayes, I heard you got shot. Did you get shot in the head?"

Hayes laughed. "No. In the shoulder. Listen, I know this sounds screwy, but I'm pretty sure that El Jefe has a child in the vicinity. And if El Ladrón's boys are trying to find he...it," he corrected quickly, "what better way to get a rival out of the way than to kidnap his child?"

"You said 'her.'" Kilraven was quick. "You don't need a P.I. You already know."

"Damn," Hayes muttered under his breath.

"Don't worry, this is a secure line and I'm as closemouthed as a clam," Kilraven assured him.

Hayes drew in a short breath. "Okay, I do know. But I can't admit that I know. I promised my father."

"Does the child know?" Kilraven asked.

"No. And I don't know how to tell her," Hayes said heavily. "She's in danger."

"Talk to your father and promise him you wouldn't do it unless you were convinced it was the right thing."

"My father's been dead for years, Kilraven," Hayes replied.

"I know that. Talk to him anyway. Listen, I talk to my dad," he said. "And I'm not crazy, despite what Cash Grier might tell you."

"Oh, Grier doesn't think you're crazy because you talk to dead people," Hayes assured him. "He thinks you're nuts because you're always spouting that sixteenth-century Scottish political history to anybody who gets trapped in a room with you."

"There is nothing more exciting or interesting than sixteenth-century Scottish political history," Kilraven scoffed. "Well, except for sixteenth-century British political history," he conceded.

"I like my history like I like commercials on television—muted."

"I'll pretend you didn't say that."

Hayes sighed. "Okay. Then can you pretend you hired a private investigator and that he told you who El Jefe's child is, so you can tell me and I won't have to break the promise I made to my father, right?"

"Talk about convoluted reasoning," Kilraven began.

"Just do it. Please?"

"Okay," Kilraven said. "Here you go. El Jefe has a child. He moved to Jacobs County to find out more about his child. El Ladrón knows, and he may try to snatch the child. Will that do?"

"Nicely. I'll leave you a nice piece of land in my will," Hayes promised. "I've got a twelve-foot-by-twelve-foot plot covered in stinging nettle.... Hello?"

There was a chuckle on the other end just before the line went dead.

Hayes looked up at the ceiling. "Sorry, Dad. I know. But it's for her own good. She has to know."

He couldn't quite find the words to tell her. He decided that a shower might help him think, so he took one.

He was still pretty weak. He managed to get into his underwear and his burgundy pajama bottoms, but he had to sit down on the closed toilet lid until his head stopped swimming. He really did feel his age. He wasn't mending as fast as he wanted to. His arm was still really sore, and he couldn't use it much. He hoped that the impairment would be temporary. Coltrain was noncommittal, and that nurse at the rehab wouldn't tell him anything. She just kept smiling and telling him he was making great progress.

Some progress, he thought huffily. At this rate, by next summer he might be able to bathe himself without danger of passing out!

He got up a minute later and toweled off his hair with one hand. He looked in the mirror. It wasn't encouraging. He looked drawn and pale. His thick blond-streaked brown hair could use trimming. At least he was clean-shaven and there wasn't any stubble marring his square jaw. There were dark circles under his eyes, though.

He glanced down at his chest and winced. Visible through the thick mat of blond hair that covered the muscles, the newest of the three pockmarks was very noticeable. The wound was healing, but it was unpleasant to look at. There was another one marring his shoulder in back. He grimaced as he studied himself in the mirror, which was foggy because of the heat from the shower. On his side, under his arm, was the scar from where they'd put in the tube to drain his lung just after he was shot.

No woman was going to find that body attractive, he concluded. He wished he'd felt like putting on the clean white T-shirt he brought in here with him, but it hurt to raise his arm. Was that indicative of a new problem? He didn't know. He was going to have to talk to Dr. Coltrain. He was getting worried about his lack of progress.

He slung the towel over one shoulder, and, with his T-shirt between his fingers, he went out into the hall. Just in time to step right in front of Minette, who was coming down the hallway.

Without thinking, Hayes smoothed the towel across his chest, to hide the wounds that he was self-conscious about.

Minette gaped at him. Her face colored. She bit her lower lip.

"What?" he asked belligerently.

"You're trying to hide your chest? Hayes, are you wearing...a bra...or something?" She burst out laughing, almost doubled over.

His lips made a thin line. He slammed the T-shirt to the floor. "Damn it!"

She sobered at once. He was really angry. She stared at him blankly.

He swept the towel away from his chest and dropped it to the floor alongside the T-shirt. Then he just stood there, glaring at her.

"Oh. I see, now..." Her dark eyes were apologetic. "I'm sorry. It just... I mean..." She winced. "It must hurt a lot," she said.

That was the last, the very last thing he expected her to say. It took the fire off his temper. "I thought you were going to say how distasteful it was to look at," he replied, his voice deep with irritation.

"Distasteful?"

Her surprise made him even more self-conscious.

He rubbed a hand over the thick hair beside the newest wound. "I didn't realize how bad it looked until I saw myself in the mirror," he said, averting his eyes.

"It doesn't look bad at all," she assured him.

He thought she was bluffing. His black eyes met hers, but she didn't look as if she were trying to be polite.

"It doesn't?" he echoed.

She shook her head. "No."

He moved one shoulder. "I guess I'm more self-conscious than I realized."

She smiled. "No need to be." She leaned down and picked up his T-shirt and the towel, and handed them to him. She flushed a little as she stared at the broad, muscular chest in its nest of thick, curling dark blond hair. "I'm not used to meeting half-dressed men in my hall."

He smiled back. "Oh."

Her eyes went back to the wound. "It still looks a little red. Is that normal?" she asked.

"I don't know. I was going to call Coltrain." He sighed. "I'm not getting better as fast as I thought I would."

"Are you in a hurry to leave?" she asked.

"Sure. I can't wait to rush home to bouncing biscuits and overdone bacon and burned toast," he agreed at once.

She laughed.

"I just don't want to be in the way here," he said.

She shook her head. "You're not. The kids are having a ball watching movies with you," she confided. "They do whatever I ask now, without any argument, as long as I agree to let them pester you for another cartoon movie every night."

"I don't mind," he confessed, laughing. "They're super kids."

"Thanks."

He drew in another breath. "Listen. We need to talk. There's something I have to tell you."

She raised both eyebrows. "You really do wear a bra?"

He glared at her. "Stop that."

"Sorry. It just slipped out."

He rolled his eyes.

"Okay, I'm serious. What is it?"

He searched her eyes slowly, hesitantly. He didn't want to have to tell her. It was going to be painful, in more ways than one.

He moved a step closer. One big warm hand went to her soft cheek. She was a tall girl, but the top of her head only came up to his nose. He looked down into her dark, soft eyes with utter fascination.

She felt her heart shaking her with every beat. She could feel the warmth of Hayes's breath on her nose. She could feel the heat from his powerful body. Involuntarily her cool hands went to his chest, pressing just above his diaphragm, sliding into the thick, soft hair that covered the hard muscles.

"You're...very tall," she blurted out, for something to say.

"Runs in my family," he murmured. Both hands were on her cheeks now, tilting her face up to his. She had a pretty mouth, shaped like a bow, naturally pale pink, parted, her white teeth just barely visible.

Her nails contracted against the hard muscle and he groaned, but it wasn't from pain.

"Sorry," she whispered, and started to lift her hands.

"Do it again," he said through his teeth, holding her eyes.

"W-what?"

"I said, do it again," he whispered, and bent his head.

She pressed her hands against his broad chest and lightly grazed the muscles while his hard mouth poised just above her soft one. She could taste his breath, feel the growing heat of his powerful body as they stood so close together in the hall. The only sounds were their breathing and, distantly, the steady rhythm of the grandfather clock against the wall in the bedroom Hayes was occupying.

"Your hands are cold," he whispered against her lips.

"Yes," she managed. Her eyes were on his mouth. She could almost feel it, taste it, touch it. For years, she'd dreamed of being in his arms, of having him want her, need her, love her. So unexpectedly, she was right where she'd wanted to be ever since she knew what she felt for Hayes was more than infatuation.

His nose rubbed against hers. She smelled of roses. His eyes closed. His mouth brushed lightly, so lightly, over her parted lips. She hung there, her breath suspended, her half-closed eyes riveted on his sensual mouth while she waited, waited, waited…

His big hands contracted as they framed her face. "What the hell," he groaned softly, and his mouth suddenly crushed down over hers.

She shivered with pure delight. Without thinking of consequences, her arms went under his and around him. She held on for dear life while his mouth slowly, hungrily devoured her parted lips.

She pressed closer, vaguely aware that he was becoming very aroused and that she didn't mind at all.

But he didn't move closer. If anything, he put space between them, so that he didn't make her feel threatened by his masculinity. His hands contracted on her oval face, his mouth hard on hers, his arms gathering her up so that her breasts flattened against his chest.

The pleasure almost countered the pain, but not quite enough. He groaned, and this time it wasn't from pleasure. He lifted his head. He looked anguished.

"Damned…shoulder," he gritted.

"Oh, dear," she stammered.

But she didn't move, and neither did he. She looked up into his eyes, hanging there like a drop of water suspended on the very tip of a green leaf.

"It's like eating popcorn."

She blinked. "Hmm?"

He smiled slowly. "Never mind. Come here."

He bent and kissed her again, this time with less restraint and more hunger. His mouth crushed down over hers until she moaned softly. She felt his hands in her thick hair, tangling in it, savoring its length, its smooth richness, while he fed on her mouth.

Her hands slid up and down his long, muscular back, delighting in the warmth and strength of him, so lost that she didn't even protest when his hands found her hips and pushed them hard into the changed contours of his body. He groaned, and so did she.

Hunger like tongues of flame bit into her untried body, made her feel swollen all over, hot and hungry and desperately in need of something she didn't even understand.

"Hayes," she groaned into his mouth.

"Shhh," he whispered. "Don't fight it. Just relax...."

His ardor drugged her into absolute submission. She'd never felt such pleasure in her life. She wanted to keep on kissing him until the world ended, never stopping. She clung, shivering, as the need overcame all her scruples and she hoped against hope that he'd drag her into the bedroom and lock the door, and take off every piece of clothing on her aching body!

"Minette!"

They broke apart suddenly at the sound of her name echoing from downstairs. They stared at each other in utter shock.

"Minette?" Aunt Sarah called again from downstairs. "Honey, can you come help me change out the light on the hood fan on the stove? I can't get this...stupid...bulb out!" she raged.

"Of course!" Minette called back in a voice that didn't even sound like her own. "Be right there!"

She stared up at Hayes. He didn't know whether to be sad or happy about the interruption. Things had started to get complicated. He was aching from head to toe, and not just in his wounded shoulder.

He eased her away from him, hoping she wouldn't look down. His body was proclaiming its secrets to any eyes willing to look. He could have groaned at his inability to conceal his hunger.

"Your poor shoulder," she said huskily and grimaced when she recognized the discomfort lining his face.

He wanted to say that it wasn't his poor shoulder, it was his poor... He stopped the thought and laughed huskily.

"It's okay," he said. He pursed his lips, which were slightly swollen from the long, sweet contact with hers. "And it was worth it," he whispered with twinkling dark eyes.

She flushed. "Yes. It was."

"Minette?"

"Coming!" she called. She turned, hesitated, turned back. "You were going to tell me something," she began.

"Later," he said. And he wasn't sure if it was a reprieve or not. "Don't worry about it. Go help Sarah."

"Okay."

She left, with a last, secret smile.

7

Hayes was wearing the T-shirt with his pajamas and he was under the covers when Minette brought him a tray for supper.

"I should be coming downstairs for meals," he said apologetically.

"Next week," she said. "Right now, you concentrate on getting better. I know it's slow, but Dr. Coltrain told you it wouldn't be an overnight process."

He grimaced. "I'm not working. That's a first. I haven't had a vacation in five years."

"I know. You're overdue." She smiled at him in a different way. There was an intimacy between them now that was new and exciting. She felt possessive about him.

He saw that. It made him tingle. He grinned up at her.

She flushed, and then laughed.

"What were you going to tell me, earlier?" she began.

"Hayes!" Julie ran into the room, with Shane right behind her.

"Not on the bed!" Minette said urgently. "Hayes is trying to eat, babies!"

"Oh, sorry," Julie said, coming to a sudden stop at the bedside. "We wanted to know if we could watch the dragon movie with you after supper. Please? We'll be ever so good!"

"You've seen the dragon movie ten times," Minette groaned.

"Six," Julie pouted. "Only six, Minette!"

Minette rolled her eyes.

Hayes just laughed. "I've only seen it twice, so I have to catch up. Sure it's okay, if Minette doesn't mind," he told the children indulgently.

"Minette doesn't mind," Minette said heavily. "It wouldn't do any good if I did," she laughed. "I'm outnumbered!"

"You can watch it with us," Julie offered, big-eyed.

"Sure," Hayes mused with a wicked twinkle in his eyes. He patted the bed beside him. "Plenty of room."

"Uh, I need to make a few phone calls," she said, smiling a little self-consciously. "Maybe another time."

"Another time then," he agreed gently.

"I'll be back for the tray. Apple pie for dessert," she added as she went out the door, shooing the kids ahead of her.

She was in the middle of a call with one of the daily newspaper reporters she knew about a rumor going the rounds.

"This man, El Jefe," she told Ginny Ryan, a colleague, "the word is that he's moving to a horse ranch here in Jacobsville. I can't find anybody who knows anything definite."

"Neither can I," Ginny agreed. "It's odd, isn't it? I mean, he was relatively safe across the border, but in the United States, he's under investigation by the DEA, or so we hear. Doesn't Cy

Parks know some of the DEA agents personally? Maybe you could pump him for information."

"I don't know him well enough to presume," Minette said sadly. "I wish I did."

"Sheriff Carson is living with you, and he knows Cy," Ginny prodded. "Couldn't you ask him?"

Minette hesitated. "I suppose I could."

"And then please share with me?" Ginny wheedled. "You weekly reporters know so much more than we daily ones do."

"A likely story."

"No kidding, you do," Ginny protested. "You live in the small communities where people know everything. I only get gossip up here in San Antonio."

"I'll tell you what I find out," Minette laughed.

"You're a pal. I'll share with you, if I turn up anything."

"Deal! I'll call you when... Oh, I've got another call. Sorry."

"No problem. Have a good night." Ginny hung up.

Minette answered the second call. "Minette Raynor," she said into the receiver.

"Minette." It was a man's voice, deep and slow, speaking clipped English with only a trace of a Spanish accent. "She always said it was her favorite name, if the child was a girl."

Minette's heart stopped. "Who are you?"

"I am your father," came the reply.

She didn't know what to say. Her mother had only spoken vaguely of her father, and she'd died before Minette had a chance to ask for more information.

"Are you still there?" the voice asked.

She swallowed. "I'm here."

"I know this must be a shock for you," he said. "And under

normal circumstances, I would never have presumed to force myself into your life. But there are complications which may involve you in great danger."

"Complications." She felt like a parrot. She couldn't even think.

"Yes. I have an enemy. He had your sheriff stalked by a professional assassin, because he dared to arrest one of his enforcers. He believes that if he kills enough people, he will be beyond the reach even of law enforcement. This is a stupid thing, but, then, he is a particularly stupid man." He laughed softly at his own joke.

"Who are you?" Minette asked, and she was certain she wasn't going to like the answer.

"My name, my real name, is Diego Baroja Sanchez," he said. "But most people just call me 'El Jefe.'"

She caught her breath and sat up very straight in her chair. "You're the drug lord...."

"Ah, *mi hija,* please, no stereotypes," he groaned, using the Spanish for *my daughter.*

"Don't call me that," she pleaded.

He laughed. "Too much, too soon, huh?" he chuckled. "All right, then, Minette."

She swallowed again, hard. Her hand, holding the receiver, was shaking. "You bought property next door to Cy Parks...."

"Yes, the infamous mercenary," he laughed. "Where I will feel particularly safe, because most of his men are also veterans of many foreign conflicts."

"He doesn't like drug lords," she bit off.

"Ah-ah," he said, his voice making the equivalent of a shaken finger. "Stereotypes again. I am a dealer in illegal substances, not a potentate. But Cy Parks will like me," he promised. "Because

I am the worst enemy El Ladrón ever made." His voice hardened as he said his competitor's name. "He is just Pedro Mendez, and he calls himself the king of drugs, but everyone who hates him—and there are legions of these—call him the Thief. He steals men's lives in pursuit of wealth. He carries with him a gold-and-diamond-plated pistol, in a holster also layered with gold. Can you imagine such a sight?" he laughed.

She was listening, but her life was crashing down around her. She was the daughter of one of the most notorious criminals in the world. Hayes was going to hate her. And just when things had been going so well between them!

"Ah, you don't want to talk about guns, I can tell. You know, I only recently found out about you. My wife—excuse me, my ex-wife—was told never to try and communicate with me. I also never sent investigators to attempt to find her. It was the only protection I could give her. Even then, El Ladrón was dangerous to anyone close to me, while we were both climbing the ladder, so to speak, of our mutual trade. I loved her more than my life," he added quietly. "There has never been another woman. I grieved for her. I never knew that she was pregnant when she left for the States."

She was really listening now. "You loved my mother?"

"Of course, just as she loved me. I heard of her death, but I dared not send flowers or condolences. I had also heard that she remarried and had a child with her husband. I never knew the child was mine, not until my enemy started paying curious attention to a woman across the border who ran a newspaper. Even then, I thought his interest was because you are known for your fearless publication of drug-related crimes."

"Why did you hire a private detective to find me?" she asked.

"Because my enforcer gathered information that your mother's child was not the child of her husband, but my child. El Ladrón discovered the truth, just before I did," he said curtly. "He wants to kill you, to get to me. But first he would kidnap you and do, shall we say, unthinkable things to you and record them for my benefit." He groaned. "It grieves me that I only now know about you. I would have done so many things differently, if I had known before. You are in grave danger, all because of me."

She swallowed. "You know that I run a newspaper?" she pointed out. "Nothing safe and quiet about my business."

"I found that out, along with your identity, and the information that your business had been firebombed when you attempted to report drug activity in your county by El Ladrón," he said. "Very dangerous. The man is completely insane, and this is not just my opinion. I deal in an illegal substance, yes. But he is obsessed with the thought of becoming the sole trafficker in Mexico, and to that end, he has decided to eliminate the others. His primary target is me, because I am second only to him."

"He wants you dead," she said, and it wasn't a question.

"Of course. As I want him dead," he said, and cleared his throat. "But my motives are, shall we say, slightly more noble than his, because I do not kill people."

"There was a border agent shot just recently," she began.

"Yes. He stumbled onto two of El Ladrón's mules with an SUV full of cocaine. The outcome was predictable. El Ladrón does not hesitate to shoot anyone in his way, and if you do not believe this, look again at your houseguest."

She gasped. "Do you know everything?"

"Of course. One of my men is an expert at intelligence gathering. His former employer in the Middle East met an untimely demise at the hands of some of your countrymen," he added. "His loss, my gain."

"Then why hire a private detective?" she wondered.

"The method of intelligence gathering done by my colleague lacks finesse," he said.

"He can't use a phone?"

He laughed. "He practices his craft more usually with a knife."

"You don't kill people, you said," she shot back.

"Yes, but I never said I didn't injure them," he pointed out. "You must not trouble yourself over this.... I do not disfigure them or leave them with desperate injuries. Most will give the information I wish with very little coaxing, which they later describe as the most horrible torture to save face."

"I see."

"Niña," he continued gently, "I go to mass every Sunday, I contribute to the various welfare agencies, I adopt families at Christmas and flood them with presents, I even maintain a chapel on my property for my workers. I may be a bad man, but I am not without decency."

"You still break the law," she replied solemnly.

"Well, of course. I have to make a living so that I can afford to be charitable," he laughed.

She sighed.

"I know, this is very hard for you," he said. "Losing your mother was the worst thing that ever happened to me. You are my only child, the only really good thing I have ever done. I..." He hesitated. "I wish to know you, just a little, and to protect you to the very best of my ability while I find a way to remove El Ladrón permanently from our lives."

"Murder him, you mean," she said coldly.

"Not necessarily," he replied. "I can provide enough evidence to have him put away for life, if I can get someone with one of the letter agencies to help me."

"Letter agencies?"

He laughed again. "CIA, FBI, DEA, NSA, DHS," he explained. "We call them 'letter' agencies because their names are most often abbreviated."

"You can get evidence against El Ladrón, but he isn't in this country," she said. "He lives in Mexico, from what I hear. . .just across the border in Cotillo."

"Yes, he does, but now that I am here, he will also be here," he said, and his voice became thick with concern. "I cannot let him kill you. So there will be people watching you, always. They will be discreet," he interrupted when she started to protest. "I know that your houseguest will do what he can, along with his friends, but it might not be enough. The assassin El Ladrón sent after him was dealt with quite harshly for missing. And it was only the unexpected movement of the sheriff that saved his life. Otherwise, he would be very dead. The assassin was one of the best of his kind."

"Oh, dear." The worry she felt was much more for Hayes than for herself. "He said he was going to send another one."

El Ladrón laughed. "Yes, he is. In fact, he has already deposited the requested amount in the assassin's Swiss bank account."

"It's not funny," she said with bitter anger.

"It is, if you know who he actually hired," the man told her with gentle affection. "It is one of my own men, posing as the best assassin in Europe. So do not worry. Your houseguest is perfectly safe for the moment. And if we can find a way to deal

with El Ladrón before he suspects the truth, he will be safe forever. At least, from that quarter."

She was silent for a long time. It was so much to get used to.

"Your sheriff, he knows about me," El Jefe said suddenly.

"What? How do you know that?" she burst out.

"I have listening devices in some very odd places," he said. "He
spoke to someone recently about me. He was very upset that he
could not tell you who I was, because he made a promise to his
own father. He is quite famous for keeping his word. So many
people today find it inconvenient or old-fashioned. I consider it
a point of honor. I never break my word, once I give it."

"He knows." She was feeling chills all the way to her feet.
"He knows."

"Yes. It surprises me that he will associate with you, because
he blames me for his brother's death. And you, of course, are my
child. My child," he added softly. "How sweet that word sounds
now that I can put a name and a face behind it."

"Hayes hates me," she said unsteadily. "He always has, ever
since Bobby died. I never understood why. I thought he meant I
was connected with the local drug dealers, but I don't have anything to do with them. I was too young and too naive to ever
hang around people like that when Bobby and I were in school
together." She groaned. "I never knew!"

"I am deeply sorry," he replied. "We choose our paths through
life without considering that each pebble thrown into a still lake
makes ripples that eventually touch everything around it. I chose
to be on the wrong side of the law, and even though you knew
nothing about it, I still influenced the people around you in a
sad way. I am sorry for that."

She bit her lip. "Well, at least now I know why he hates me," she said heavily.

"You have…feelings for him." There was a long sigh on the other end of the line. "So I am sorry once more. But it is always good to know the truth. Even when it hurts. We do no service to others by lying."

"You are one very strange drug dealer," Minette said.

He laughed. "I am just a man." A voice was muffled in the background. He put his hand over the receiver and mumbled something back. "I must go. I have a visitor." He laughed. "I think it is my neighbor. This conversation should be quite interesting."

"Cy Parks?" she asked, shocked.

"The same. Do not worry. I have never yet killed a guest."

"Promise me," she returned.

"Ah, you know me so well already and we have only just met. I do promise. And I promise that El Ladrón will never touch you," he added quietly. "All the same, be careful of your surroundings. And keep a careful eye on your little brother and sister because, believe me, he will not hesitate to harm them if he can. He considers that any member of an adversary's family is fair game."

"I will." She paused. "Thank you, for telling me."

"It was not a pleasure, except that it pleases me very much to have a child. I am sorry that the news gives you less pleasure than it does me. We will speak again. Farewell."

He hung up.

Minette put the receiver down. Idly she noted a spot of coffee on the desk and grabbed a nearby paper towel to mop it up. Her father was a drug lord. Her father was a drug lord. Her father was…

"Minette! Can we watch another movie, please? Please?" Julie called from the staircase.

She swallowed, got to her feet, picked up her cupful of cold coffee and walked out into the hall. "No, sweetheart, tomorrow's a school day. You and Shane have to go to bed now."

"Awwww, do we have to?" Julie moaned.

"Yes. Go on, get into your pj's and tell Shane," she added. "I'm going to heat up my coffee in the microwave and I'll be up to tell you a story and tuck you in. Go on, now."

"Okay!"

She ran back up the staircase. Minette heated her coffee. She wanted to go into Sarah's room and cry on her shoulder, but the poor woman had gone to bed earlier with a headache and she hesitated to wake her.

So she went upstairs, sipped coffee while she read a Dr. Seuss book to the kids and then put them both to bed.

Then she went out into the hallway. She hesitated at Hayes's door. But it would do no good to put off this confrontation, she told herself. She had to deal with it, and the longer she waited, the worse things would get. She had to protect Julie and Shane and Aunt Sarah. She wasn't worried for herself.

She knocked on the door.

"Since when do you have to knock on doors in your own house?" Hayes asked amusedly.

She closed the door behind her, but she stopped at the foot of his bed. Her face was drawn and pale.

"What's wrong?" he asked at once, and his concern was obvious.

She moved one shoulder. "I just got a phone call."

"Let me guess, they know I'm here and they're going to try again," he guessed.

She shook her head. "No. Actually," she said, taking a deep breath, "I just got a phone call from my...father."

Hayes sat very still against his pillows. "Your father."

She nodded. "El Jefe. Isn't that what they call him? My father, one of the most famous drug lords in the country. Maybe in several countries."

He winced. He'd promised his father that he'd never tell her the truth. He'd blamed her, because her father had supplied the drugs that killed his brother. He'd hated her. But since they'd become so close, his feelings were in flux. He certainly didn't hate her. And now he felt very guilty that he'd let her find out that terrible news all by herself, without any warning.

"I should have told you," he said heavily. "I'm sorry."

Minette's eyebrows lifted. "He said you knew. He said you promised your father that you'd never tell me," she said with sad eyes.

"I did. How the hell did he know that?" he burst out.

"He has listening devices. One of his enforcers used to work for some Middle Eastern leader who was killed."

"I'll bet I know the one," he replied. "That late Middle Eastern madman's top aide has a degree from MIT and he's the most dangerous man on two legs with an automatic weapon. They say he's handsome and personable and if you met him on the street, you'd never guess what he did for a living."

"Some combination."

"You bet it is. And he's here, with your father, about to start a drug war."

"It's much worse than that," she said. The anguish she felt was visible on her pale, drawn face and shimmering eyes.

He held out an arm. "Come here, sweetheart," he said in a tone so tender that it made her cry.

She didn't even hesitate. She dropped down onto the bed beside him. He curled her into his body with his good arm and held her pillowed against his chest while she cried as if her heart would break.

"I've never even gotten a parking ticket," she sobbed, "and my father is the worst criminal in the country!"

"Now, now," he said, soothing her back with his big hand. "He's definitely not the worst. Even our best people can't hang any murders on him. Although," he added thoughtfully, "we could hang a few on people who have worked for him over the years. And there are many lives lost by people who overdose on illegal drugs," he added grimly.

"Rub it in."

He held her closer. He felt her pert breasts very firm against his chest, soft under the firmness. It aroused him, and he shifted just a little under the covers so that she didn't feel it. He genuinely wanted to provide comfort, not sex. Well, right now, anyway.

"I'm not," he protested softly. He kissed her beautiful pale golden hair, just at her forehead. "Listen, criminal behavior can come in many forms. Some who bend the laws are just like other people. Most of them pay taxes, love their families, give to charity, even go to church. Except they make money illegally."

Her small, curled fist hit his chest gently. "He's not normal. And I'm his daughter!" she groaned. "What if those qualities are in me, too? What if I end up on the wrong side of the law?"

"Bull," he replied easily. "Environment and upbringing have a lot to do with that."

"So does genetics."

He shrugged. "We could argue forever. It won't change anything. You're not a criminal."

"My father is."

"Why did he call?"

She sighed and wiped at her eyes with the back of her hand. "He says his worst enemy decided to target me. That's why he moved here. He's going to have people watching me, he says, to keep me safe."

Hayes chuckled. "Well, they'll be in good company. I have it from a reliable source that some of Cy Parks's men are also watching you." He leaned closer. "So is Zack, but you're not supposed to know that."

"Great. I'll be at the head of a parade!"

"Not a visible one."

"When my father hung up, Cy Parks had just walked in his door," she added.

"Good Lord, he's got guts!" Hayes caught his breath. "I guess, considering his past, it's not so surprising. He always was one to wade into trouble. Did anyone ever tell you what he did in Africa?"

"No."

"An orphaned African child he loved was killed in the country where he and the others in his group were working. The men who did it started firing with machine guns. Cy walked right into the gunfire and got to them. He avenged the child."

"How did he live through that?" she asked, aghast.

"No clue. History says Wyatt Earp did the same thing in a

shootout with some of the Clanton gang after the O.K. Corral gunfight. Guy was firing a shotgun, Earp walked right into the fire and shot the man, never was scratched. In fact, there's no evidence that he ever suffered a gunshot wound in all his time as a lawman. He lived into his eighties."

"My goodness. Didn't he hang out with Doc Holliday?"

He chuckled. "Did you ever watch that movie *Tombstone* with Kurt Russell and Val Kilmer?"

"I don't think so."

"You should. Except for the 'red sashes' the rustlers wore, it's very true to the historical record. And, in fact, Val Kilmer's portrayal of Holliday is right on the money, down to the pale face and coughing sprees and drinking. You know, ragged little kids followed Holliday around in every town he visited, because he'd feed them. They asked him once if his conscience didn't bother him, because of all the men he killed. Know what he said?"

"No," she replied, fascinated.

"That he coughed that up, along with his lungs, long ago. He was only thirty-six years old when he died, with his boots off, of tuberculosis in Glenwood Springs, Colorado. Two years older than me."

That put things into perspective. She snuggled closer, careful not to jar him too much. "Very young."

His arm contracted.

"I'm so sorry," she said after a minute.

"For what?"

"For what my father did," she said heavily. "For Bobby..."

He winced. He felt the pain of what he'd done to her over the years, hated her, persecuted her, for something she didn't even know about. And now that she did know, it seemed so futile, so useless, all that hatred. "No, Minette," he said quietly. "I'm sorry. For blaming you, when you never had a part in it."

"You don't...hate me?"

He shifted, so that her head fell back against his shoulder on the bed. He looked straight into her black eyes. "I don't hate you." His gaze fell to her soft mouth. "I'm not sure that I ever did, really."

The way he looked at her made her heart race. She stared at him with fascinated delight, loving the strong lines of his tanned face, the way his thick hair fell naturally into a wave over his left eye, the thickness of it. Her hands longed to tangle in it, the way they had when he'd kissed her...

"Looking for trouble?" he asked huskily.

"Pardon me?"

He chuckled. "I look that way at a steak when I'm hungry," he mused.

"Oh!" She averted her eyes and flushed.

"No, don't do that. I like it," he whispered, tilting her face back so that he could look into her embarrassed eyes. "I like it a lot."

"You do?"

He nodded. His head bent. He brushed his lips over hers softly, slowly, parting them so that he could catch the upper lip in his teeth and nibble at it.

She had no experience of such things. Her life had been devoted to the two children she'd inherited from her stepfather and stepmother, to the newspaper. But Hayes didn't seem to mind that she came with a ready-made family. He smiled against her lips, shifted and kissed her again, with hunger but also with restraint.

She relaxed. She hadn't realized how tense she was. She hoped

Hayes wasn't going to ask for more than she could give. She was a person of faith. She believed certain things were right and others were wrong, and she wasn't going to change her beliefs because of anyone else's opinion.

"You think I'm just out for a good time, don't you?" he whispered as he kissed her.

"I…don't know."

He lifted his head and searched her eyes. "We live in a goldfish bowl. I can keep a poker face, but you can't. If we get involved, everybody's going to know about it."

"That wouldn't be a good idea, then?"

He pursed his lips and studied her with smiling eyes. "Oh, I didn't say that. I'm thirty-four. I live with a giant iguana. Women won't date me because they think Andy will eat them. On the other hand," he pointed out, "you have two little dependents that you're not about to jettison because some guy thinks you're more attractive without them."

"Fair assessment," she had to agree.

"I like kids."

She smiled. "I like iguanas."

His eyes opened wide. "You what?" he asked.

"I like iguanas," she said. "I had one for a pet when I was about sixteen. I kept him for two years, but one morning I found him dead in his cage. I begged my stepfather to have him autopsied, because I was afraid it was something I'd done wrong. It wasn't— he had something wrong with him, internally. I never quite understood what. But the vet said that animals in the wild try to hide things that are wrong with them because it can be fatal to show weakness. The thing is, an iguana's metabolism is so slow that by the time you see something wrong, it's too late to save the animal." She sighed. "I just never saw anything wrong. He seemed perfectly fine. He was eating and drinking..."

"And sometimes animals just die. So you like iguanas. How about that?"

"Andy doesn't like women," she reminded him.

"He doesn't like most women."

"So there's hope?"

He laughed and bent to kiss her again. "There's always hope. It's the last thing we lose."

She touched his lean cheek, and slid her hand into the thick hair at the back of his head. "Hope is good."

He kissed her harder. "Yes."

"What are we going to do?" she asked against his mouth.

"I can think of a few things..."

"About my father?" she qualified.

He lifted his head with a sigh. "I can't think of a few things. But I'll work on it." He bent and started kissing her again, with more insistence this time, and she went under like a person on chloroform.

"Minette! I'm thirsty! Can I have a drink of water?" she heard through a veritable fog of passion.

Hayes lifted his head. He stared at her blankly.

"Be right there!" Minette called back. She sighed. "Sorry."

He managed a smile. "Think of it as home-based, verbal birth control," he mused.

"Hayes!" She thumped him, but gently.

"Sorry. Couldn't resist it."

She smiled. She leaned up, bravely, and kissed him very softly. "I have to go."

"I know. We'll talk again in the morning, and see what decisions we can make," he replied. His face grew harder. "I think I need to have a little talk with your dad myself."

"You'll ask Coltrain first," she informed him when she was back on her feet.

"Yes, Mom," he returned.

She shook her finger at him. "I am not your mother."

"I'll say." He gave her a long, deep appraisal. "Nice. Very nice. If you ever cut that hair, I'll wear mourning for a year," he added softly. "I love the way it feels in my hands."

She flushed. "It's a lot of work..."

"I look terrible in black," he pointed out.

She laughed. "Okay." She went to the door. "If you go to see him, I'm going with you," she said. "I want to know what he looks like."

"There used to be a Wanted poster in the post office..."

"Stop that."

She went out and closed the door.

8

Minette told Aunt Sarah over the breakfast table about her real father.

Sarah grimaced. "I had a feeling he was someone on the outside of the law," she said. "I only got bits and pieces from your mother, but they did add up." She shook her head. "I was very fond of her, you know. She gave me a home when I had no place to go, after my husband died. I lost everything. He was a gambler," she said heavily. "He gambled away everything we had and then drank himself to death because of it. He was a good man. He just had this habit he couldn't break."

"What a shame."

"Yes. I couldn't get him to go to a counselor to talk about it. He said people would think he was crazy. What a terrible way we used to treat people with mental problems," she added. "Now, there's a treatment for almost anything. It wasn't the way of things twenty years ago and more," she added.

"I know. I'm so sorry. But having you here is wonderful for me," Minette said. "I couldn't make it without you."

"Thank you, sweetie," Sarah said. "I love being part of your family." She hesitated. "Have you spoken to Hayes?"

"Yes."

"He was very quiet when I took his breakfast up, while you got the kids to school," she said.

"He knew about my father," Minette said.

"I'm so sorry. If I'd known, I'd have told you."

"I know that. Thanks." She smiled. "Hayes said he promised his father he'd never tell me, but he knew. That's why he blamed me all these years for Bobby. It wasn't what I'd done, it was what my father had done—supplying the drugs that killed his brother."

"I think Hayes blames himself, too," Sarah said very quietly. "I know I blamed myself when my husband died. I thought maybe I could have done things differently and maybe he wouldn't have gambled so much."

"We can't change the past," Minette said. "No matter how much we'd like to. We have to go on living."

"You're right."

Minette finished her coffee. "I have to call Bill at the office and get him to take over for me today. I'm going to be busy."

"Doing what, or should I ask?" Sarah wondered.

Minette smiled. "Something crazy, and don't you dare tell Hayes. I'm going to see my father...."

"Not without me, you aren't," Hayes assured her, coming into the room fully dressed. He was wearing his uniform. He was still pale and a little wobbly, but he looked almost normal. His hair was neatly combed and he smelled of sexy, spicy aftershave.

"This isn't a good idea," she began.

"Copper said it was fine. He thinks it won't hurt for me to move around a bit, keep my lungs clear."

"Did you tell him where you were planning to move around to?" she asked.

"What he doesn't know won't hurt me," he said with a grin.

She laughed. "You're incorrigible."

"Totally. Shall we go?" He gave her a speaking look when she hesitated. "You're not going to sneak over there by yourself. And shame on you, when I told you last night I'd go with you."

She grimaced and averted her eyes, coloring just a little as she recalled what the two of them had been doing the night before. Hayes saw that, and laughed softly.

She got up from the table, all flustered. "Just a sec, I have to call Bill," she said.

"Okay. I'll wait."

"Won't take but a moment." And it didn't, she called him on her cell phone, told him what she'd like done and hung up. "See?"

"Nice. I like delegating, too," he said. "Saves time."

"Bill can handle anything I can handle. It's just sending Jerry around to get ads and having Arly assign our two reporters to the top stories." She grimaced. "Mostly it's just high school sports. I hate most sports, but local people love them."

"I like soccer," Hayes remarked.

Her eyes brightened. "So do I!"

He grinned.

Sarah looked from one of them to the other with her lips pursed. They probably didn't realize it, but their expressions were telling her things.

"We should go," Minette said after a minute. "Should we let him know we're coming?"

Hayes glanced around the room. "Oh, I expect he knows already. Come on. Who's driving?"

"I'm driving," she assured him. "You'd put us in the ditch with your shoulder in that kind of shape."

"Spoilsport. Where's your sense of adventure?"

"I'll look for it later. I'm still driving."

She stopped at Cy Parks's house on the way, because Hayes wanted to talk to him. Cy's wife, Lisa, let them in with a big smile. She was blonde, like Minette, with pale eyes and she wore glasses. But she was pretty. The Parks had two children, both of whom were now in school.

"The house is a wreck," Lisa said apologetically. "We've got wall-to-wall toys because the power went out last night and we had to keep the kids occupied somehow!"

"It didn't go out at our place," Minette said.

"Yes, well, one of your ranch hands didn't get drunk and run into a utility pole, either, did he?" Cy drawled as he joined them. He was tall and dark haired, with green eyes. He favored his left arm, and the hand that peered out from under the shirt showed signs of having suffered burns in the past. Most people knew that he'd run into his burning house in another state in a vain attempt to save his wife and child. A drug lord, the late Lopez, had sent an assassin. Cy had more reason than most to hate drug dealers.

He put an arm around Lisa and bent to kiss the top of her head. "That cowboy will be looking for work today, too. I don't tolerate alcohol here."

"I thought everybody in Texas knew that," Hayes chuckled.

"Apparently one man didn't." Cy motioned them into the living room.

"Coffee?" Lisa asked.

"Yes, thanks," Hayes said.

"Love one, thanks," Minette said. "I didn't get my second cup at home this morning because somebody was impatient to leave home," she looked pointedly at Hayes.

"I'm always in a hurry," he mused, grinning.

"I heard you were staying with her," Cy remarked as Lisa went to make a fresh pot of coffee. "I thought my ears were going."

Hayes glanced at Minette apologetically. "That was my fault. I've been trying to make up for things."

Minette averted her eyes. "We've...I've," she corrected, "had some pretty shocking news."

"Yes, El Jefe's your dad," Cy said grimly.

"Does everybody know?" Minette cried, throwing up her hands.

"Depends on your definition of everybody," Cy returned with a gentle smile. "It's my business to know things. Eb Scott's, too. We're providing some high-tech security for you. El Jefe approves. He's got someone in the woods at night, keeping an eye out. Word is that Hayes, here, has got a guy watching you, too." He sighed. "I hope they don't all stumble into each other one dark night and start shooting."

"Me, too," Hayes agreed, "but we have to do what we can to keep her safe. More people means more security."

"I agree."

"Why did you go to see El Jefe?" Hayes asked.

Cy pursed his lips. "Friendly neighborly visit?"

Hayes gave him a bland look.

Cy shrugged. "I wanted him to know that I knew who he was."

"He knows who you are, too," Minette replied. "He said so when he called me last night to tell me he was my father."

Cy grimaced. "I can imagine that it came as something of a shock," he replied.

"That's an understatement," she said.

"No doubt. Well, I wanted him to be aware of how I feel about drug trafficking and having it next door to my prize Santa Gerts. He was shocked that I would think he'd expose his prize-winning thoroughbred horses to such things."

"Excuse me?" Hayes replied with a stunned expression.

"He said that his business and his private life are kept quite separate. He's broken no laws in the United States and has no intention of doing business here." He leaned forward. "He says that he has people on his payroll across the border who do all the legwork for him. He doesn't want any legal complications from the DEA. For whom, it seems, he has a great deal of respect."

"So do I," Hayes replied. "I've known several of their agents. They're very good."

Cy nodded.

Lisa came in bearing a tray laden with coffee, mugs and all the accessories. "Don't fight over it," she laughed. "I can make more."

"I never fight over coffee. Well, unless it's latté," Minette informed her. "And I make my own at home." She grinned. Lisa laughed.

Hayes stared at her. "I'm hurt. You know I love latté and you've never offered me a cup of it."

"Lies," she said. "I gave some to you and I even tried to make Zack drink it when he came over to talk to you."

"I'd forgotten. Sorry. I absolve you from all guilt."

"I should hope so! I treat my houseguests with great care, I'll have you know."

They smiled at each other. So did Lisa and Cy. The attraction between Hayes and Minette was very obvious.

"Ahem," Hayes cleared his throat, because Cy was giving him a knowing look, "back to El Jefe, then."

"Anyway, he gave me some information about El Ladrón's connections. I'll gladly share them."

"Mind sharing them with Rodrigo Ramirez and Alexander Cobb?"

"Our friendly local DEA." Cy nodded. "Of course." He glanced at Minette. "I'm sure this has been traumatic for you."

"Very," she replied. She took a breath. "Very upsetting."

"We aren't responsible for what people we're related to do," Cy instructed.

She grimaced. "Bad blood is bad blood."

"There are worse criminals than your father," Cy replied. "He is, in a sense, a prince among thieves."

She managed a wan smile. "Thanks."

"He'll know you're coming, I imagine," Cy sighed.

Minette finished her coffee and stood up. "In that case, I hope he knows that I like latté!" She emphasized the last word, looking around the room for invisible bugs.

The men just laughed.

They pulled up at the front door of the house that was just getting the finishing touches on the property adjoining Cy's. It had a steel structure and had been erected in an incredibly short amount of time with many prefab materials. It was huge and glorious, painted a pale sand color, with elegant arches and an enormous fountain at the semicircular front driveway that led to the front door.

"No porch swing," Hayes murmured. "How can people build a house without a front porch?"

A tall man with graying thick black hair, black eyes, a mustache and a big white smile came out onto the driveway. "The front porch is in the back, *amigo*," he chuckled, "where an assassin would have a hard time trying to hit me! I am Diego Baroja Sanchez. El Jefe." He held out his hand, and Hayes shook it. "It is good to meet you, Sheriff."

"I wish I could say the same," Hayes mused.

Diego looked at the child he'd never seen with a myriad of expressions. He moved closer, his eyes becoming teary. "You are the image of her," he said huskily. "You look just as your mother did at your age, except that you have my eyes instead of hers. She was beautiful. But of all her beauty, it was her hair that I loved most, next to her warm heart. She had hair like a princess in a fairy world. Hair like yours."

Minette was stunned. She hadn't expected this reaction.

"I am your father," he said quietly. "And I am most honored to meet you, face-to-face."

She didn't know what to say. "I...it's nice to meet you, too," she stammered.

He sighed. He smiled. "Please. My house is your house." He motioned them inside. "And also," he whispered, "I have latté."

She burst out laughing.

They sat down in an elegant living room, swathed in satin and white carpet, with exquisite hand-carved furniture in Mediterranean shades, leather-covered chairs and a grand piano.

"You play?" Minette asked, aghast.

He nodded. "I am most fond of classic blues, but I can also play the masters," he chuckled. "Music is my passion. Your mother, also, was musical."

"She was?" Minette asked dubiously.

"But, of course. She could play the stereo. Also several radio stations." He grinned.

Minette laughed. Her mother couldn't carry a tune. She did remember that, at least.

The older man studied Hayes Carson. "The wound, it is healing?"

Hayes nodded. He sat back, wincing a little. "Slowly, however. It seems age has a part to play in healing."

"Ah, but you are still young."

"Only in terms of mountains," Hayes sighed. "I'm young for a mountain. Ancient for a fruit fly. On the wrong side of thirty for a human."

The other man smiled. "Age is part of the process. We learn to adjust." He indicated himself with an elegant, well-groomed hand. "I can no longer beat my men on the soccer field, but I have learned to be a very good referee. And they have learned better curses."

They laughed.

Minette studied him, looking for similarities. She had his nose and eyes. She was tall, as he was.

He noticed her doing that, and smiled with real affection. "We resemble each other, yes? That pleases me very much. But you are still the image of your beautiful mother. I miss her every day, as I always will. She was my heart."

"She was mine, too," Minette said sadly.

"And so you have the little brother and sister, who are not

even of your blood, but you care for them as though they were your own." It was a question.

"My stepmother, Dawn, was a wonderful, loving person. After my mother died, it was just me and my stepfather. He was very good to me. I always knew that he wasn't my real father, but he said that when you raise a child, it's yours, blood or no blood."

He nodded. "I am most grateful to him for the very good job he did of bringing you up," he said with sincerity. "I had heard that your mother bore a child to her husband, but your mother did not share with me the fact of her pregnancy before I got her out of Mexico. In truth, it was a terrible time. I sent her away, sent people to make arrangements for her safety, for a place to live, and to insure that she would never be connected with me in any way." He shook his head. "The worst part, the hardest part, was that I had to divorce her in Mexico, where we were living at the time. I am Catholic, you see, divorce was frowned upon at the time, as it still is, in many ways."

Minette's heart leaped. "You were legally married to her?"

He glowered. "I am a decent man," he said quietly. "Honor is everything to me. I would never have compromised an innocent young woman without offering her the sanctity of marriage. It goes against my faith."

She smiled warmly. "Now I know that being a dinosaur is genetic," she said, amused.

"*¿Qué?*" he asked, uncertain of the meaning.

She laughed. "I am very old-fashioned," she explained. "I don't move with the times."

"Ah, I see," he said, smiling. "You are not as many of these modern women who think it is good to enjoy many men without benefit of clergy." He nodded. "In my youth, this was a trend that had just begun, in California, with the 'hippies.'"

"My mother always talked about 'flower children,'" she laughed. "She didn't like their morals, but she loved the feeling they had for the earth and nature and growing things. We always kept a garden while she lived, and she planted flowers in every available space. After she died," she said sadly, "my stepfather continued the tradition. And now I keep it, in memory of her. She loved sunflowers, so I plant them everywhere."

His eyes were sad. "Yes. Sunflowers. I often brought her bouquets of them when I came home. She said they smelled of happiness."

"Yes!" she laughed. It was a wonderful, shared memory.

"It broke my heart to let her go. But if she had stayed with me, she would have died. I had no idea she was pregnant. She never told me. That would have been like her, to protect me. It was so painful, the thought of never seeing her again." He winced. "You see, I did not dare to contact her, or send investigators to find her, even after the danger was over. Because by then, I was very deep into the international underworld, and I had involved myself with the trade in South America, where I went to live. Inquiries cause comment, which can provoke action. Anyone close to me is in danger." His dark eyes narrowed. "And that includes, unfortunately, the daughter of whom I was unaware of until very, very recently. My worst enemy sent investigators to find you, which is why I hired my own." He shook his head. "You see now what would have happened with your mother, God rest her precious soul, if I had attempted to locate her after she left. One investigator can invite much trouble, because I am always watched now."

She looked around nervously.

El Jefe laughed. "No. Not here. I have a most amazing enforcer." He glanced toward the door and let out a dialogue of Spanish toward an elderly woman in a beautiful white dress that came to her knees, embroidered in bright colors. It was the prettiest dress Minette had ever seen, she couldn't help staring.

The woman, whose gray-streaked black hair fell to her waist like a thick curtain, saw her interest and grinned. She said something to the boss.

El Jefe burst out laughing. "Lucienda says you like her dress, is this so?"

"Oh, yes, it's so beautiful. Forgive me, I didn't mean to stare," she said, self-consciously.

"This is the costume of my people. I am Mayan. I come from Cancún in Quintana Roo. Quintana Roo is a state in the Yucatán Peninsula of Mexico," Lucienda explained in very precise English. She smiled, turning around for Minette's benefit. "I am very proud of my heritage. It pleases me that you like my clothes. I did the embroidery myself."

"It must have taken weeks," Minette said.

"Oh, yes, but this is a labor of love." Lucienda moved closer so that Minette could see the exquisite detail of the embroidered flowers, mostly red, and the accompanying leaves and swirls and stitching.

"I've never seen anything quite like it," Minette sighed. "It is just so beautiful!"

"Thank you."

El Jefe was studying his daughter with keen eyes. "So many of your people in these difficult times are hostile to our culture. You are not."

Minette's eyes were soft. "I learned long ago, from my mother, that we measure people by character and kindness, not color or race or beliefs. She said that the earth is like a gigantic flower garden. We are the flowers. We come in all shapes and sizes and colors, and God loves us all." She laughed. "That's what I think, too."

"And I. You are very much like your father," Lucienda said gently. She glanced at Diego. "I will go and fetch Señor Lassiter."

Minette's eyebrows lifted. "Lassiter?"

"Yes. An American. From a small town in Wyoming, I believe he said," Diego told her. He shook his head as he stared at Minette. "Two weeks ago, I was an aging bachelor. Today, I am a father. It is a magnificent alteration."

Minette smiled. She was beginning to get used to the idea. Well, a little.

There were muffled voices coming from the hall. Lucienda came in first, slightly flushed and laughing.

Just behind her was a tall, broad-shouldered man with thick, straight black hair. He had olive skin and jet-black eyes, like Diego Sanchez. He had high cheekbones and a chiseled, sensual mouth. He was wearing jeans and a T-shirt with an odd red symbol on the front and lettering that read, Alliance, Beware!

Minette paid more attention to the shirt than the man. "Alliance?" she asked.

He gave her a long look, and then grinned, showing snow-white teeth. "I'm Horde."

Minette glanced at Hayes Carson, who rolled his eyes.

"Another 'World of Warcraft' fanatic," Hayes sighed. "I ought to know, I work with one."

"World of…what?" Minette asked, confused.

"It's a PC game, what they call a massively multiplayer online role-playing game, or MMORPG," Hayes explained. "There are two factions, Alliance—that's the good guys—and Horde, the bad guys."

"Hey, we aren't bad," Lassiter said haughtily. "We're only misunderstood."

"My mistake," Hayes mused, and chuckled.

"He plays the game in his spare time," Diego said with a smile. "Which he has precious little of, I might add."

"My chief deputy, Zack, is my ongoing authority on the game," Hayes said. "Since the new Pandaria expansion came out, he comes to work every day like a zombie from lack of sleep."

"I know the feeling," Lassiter told them.

"This is my daughter," Diego introduced Lassiter to Minette.

"Yes, I know, I have a file devoted to her life," Lassiter said. His black eyes twinkled as he approached Minette. "It's a great pleasure to make your acquaintance."

"Thanks," she said. She was studying him. "MIT?" she murmured.

"Ya. MIT. I did a double major, physics and Arabic languages."

"Nice to meet you," Hayes said, "and do you have time to explain the concept of vortex mathematics and the spatial interaction of dark matter and black holes...?"

Lassiter gave him a speaking look. "Not nice."

Hayes grinned. "Sorry. Couldn't help myself. I don't often have the opportunity to meet a real live geek."

"I have a card somewhere that entitles me to two consecutive episodes of nerd rage," Lassiter said, laughing.

"Nerd rage?" Minette was all at sea.

"It's a gamer thing," Lassiter said. "We have all sorts of abbreviations and in-jokes."

"She doesn't game," Hayes said.

"I do so," she retorted. "I play Animal Farm on Facebook."

Lassiter rolled his eyes.

"When Julie and Shane get a few years older, you're probably going to know more about gaming than you want to say," Hayes told her.

"I expect so. Julie's best friend has a PlayStation and she goes over there to play some of the newer children's games. She's getting a PlayStation of her own for Christmas so she can play arcade games. Shane has an Xbox 360, but he only plays wrestling games. They're too violent for her. And he shares, but very reluctantly," she laughed.

"I am always available to give advice on gaming systems, and even to help install them," Lassiter said with pursed lips. "If he promises not to shoot me, I'll hook up the whole system for you." He jerked his head toward Hayes, who was looking suddenly hostile.

"Why would Hayes mind?" Minette asked.

Lassiter just laughed. Hayes didn't.

"Back to the matter at hand," Diego said, quickly defusing the tension. "I have Lassiter watching your house for signs of covert activity." He glanced at Hayes. "You, also, have a man in the field, I believe?"

"Yes," Hayes said, calming a bit. He didn't want Lassiter around his girl. His girl. He felt the words all the way into his heart as he glanced at her with pure possession. Yes. She belonged to him, and he wasn't sharing. Especially not with some intellectual gaming geek.

The gaming geek was giving him amused looks. "And Cy Parks also has a man watching your ranch at night," Lassiter told Minette. "It might not be a bad idea for all of us to coordinate these efforts, in the interest of safety." The smile vanished. "I tend to shoot first. I imagine your deputy and Parks's man have the same mindset."

Hayes nodded. "The potential for confrontations is a bit upsetting."

"I agree," Lassiter replied. He glanced at his boss. "I've got electronic surveillance pretty much everywhere, but there's nothing that can replace human eyes and ears in the field. I'm a hunter," he told Hayes, and his expression became hard and dangerous. "I can hear a mouse walk across cardboard at a hundred yards in the dark. And I can track."

"So can Zack," Hayes replied. "He likes venison."

Lassiter was amused. "So do I."

"Zack says his father taught him. They still go hunting together."

Lassiter's smile faded. "My father and I aren't speaking at the moment. He didn't approve of my choice of employment."

"Employment?" Minette asked.

Lassiter averted his eyes. "It's a long story."

"Considering who you worked for," Hayes remarked, "I can understand his position."

"I don't invite public comment," Lassiter said with cold steel in his tone.

Hayes quirked an eyebrow. "Hit a nerve, did I?" he asked, and he didn't apologize.

"A few years ago," Lassiter told him very quietly, "you'd have been hanging from one thumb off a tall building for a remark like that. However, I've mellowed a great deal since the loss of my previous employer. Now, I'd just hang you from both hands." He smiled blithely.

Hayes glared at him. "You're welcome to try that. At your convenience."

"I never attack a man when he's down. It's an honor thing."

"We can have this conversation again when I'm back on my feet," Hayes replied. And his smile was ice-cold.

"Do you think we could attempt to get along?" Minette asked the men, exasperated. "I mean, the object of this collaboration, El Ladrón, is a man who once threw his own uncle into a vat of acid in a rage, if I recall properly?"

Lassiter and Hayes tried to stare each other down, but it didn't really work. With mental shrugs, they turned their attention back to Minette and her father.

"Yes, he did," Diego spoke for them. "He has a bad temper and he doesn't mind killing people, even relatives." He seemed worried. "I wish to prevent something similar happening to you. Which brings us to the subject I want to address."

"What would that be?" Hayes asked.

Diego leaned back against the sofa. "I have a small journal. It was obtained, at great cost, from one of El Ladrón's most trusted lieutenants. It is written in code, which I have no means to break."

"Totally untrue," Lassiter said with a grin, dropping his elegant length into an easy chair beside the sofa. "I could break the code if I had enough free time."

"Yes, but time is the thing." He turned to Hayes. "I am willing to turn this information over to the DEA. I understand that you know at least two agents personally."

"I do," Hayes said. "And they'd be grateful for the intel. Which doesn't mean that they won't be looking for a way to arrest you, I might add."

Diego shrugged and smiled. "If they can find any evidence of wrongdoing in this country, I will go willingly and without handcuffs." He leaned forward. "They must find means to stop Mendez before he goes after my daughter," he added urgently. "Toward that end, I will do anything within reason to assist them."

Hayes looked impressed. "That's quite an offer."

"Will you carry the request to the appropriate people?"

"I will," Hayes said. "Today."

"I am in your debt."

"So am I. For that, at least," Lassiter added. He was looking at Minette again, with an expression that made Hayes's face clench.

"We should go," Hayes told Minette.

She grimaced. She didn't really want to leave.

Diego saw that, and he smiled. "It pleases me that you want to stay," he told her as he rose. "But your companion is right. You will be safer away from here. Wait." He took a pencil and jotted down a number on a slip of paper. He handed it to her. "This is a private cell phone. No one has the number. It is a, how do you say, throwaway phone."

"I imagine you have a box of those," Hayes chuckled. "They're pretty much untraceable," he added to Minette.

"Business," Diego replied easily. "Just business." He took his daughter by the shoulders and kissed both her cheeks. "It is an honor, and a great pleasure, to have you in my life. But I wish to spare yours. So we should keep meetings like this to a minimum.

You can call me whenever you like, though," he added, smiling. "Very often would be my preference. I want to get to know you."

"I'd like that." She went to the door, followed by the three men. Outside, a man was leading a beautiful thoroughbred down the path to the enormous barn. The horse's coat was black, brilliantly shinning, with white socks on all four legs.

"He's beautiful!" Minette exclaimed.

"These are my children." Diego gestured toward the paddock nearby and the barn. Three other horses grazed in the paddock. "One of the mares will drop a colt in the spring. I have high hopes to continue the bloodline. We won the Preakness in Kentucky this past season."

"I read about that," Hayes said. "Your horses are magnificent."

"They are. I raise palominos," Minette said. "But mine don't have any super bloodlines. They're just pets. I love every one of them."

"Now, that is genetics at work," Diego exclaimed. "You see? Horses are really in the blood!"

Everyone laughed.

9

"I don't like that guy," Hayes said as they drove off the property.

"My dad?" Minette asked, turning her head briefly to meet Hayes's irritated eyes.

"No. His enforcer. Lassiter."

"Oh. I thought he was rather charming," she remarked.

"Charming. Like a snake with a haircut."

She burst out laughing. "Hayes!"

He sighed. "Well, maybe that's not the best description I could have come up with. But you get my meaning. He's very slick."

"Very smart, too." She glanced at him. "And he's not the only one," she added when he looked even more irritated. "Black holes? Dark matter? Vortex mathematics?"

"I subscribe to two science magazines," Hayes confessed. "I don't have a degree in physics, but I do love the subject. Well, that and quantum mechanics."

"Over my head," she remarked. "I'm more of a car mechanics sort of person. Not that I can do much more than check the oil and kick the tires."

He laughed. "That's about the size of it, with me, too. But I can keep things running around the ranch. I just don't have time to do a lot of tinkering. I suppose your father's enforcer does have a little free time when he's not killing people to indulge his mechanical skills," he added with stinging anger.

"You really don't like that guy. Why?"

Hayes's black eyes narrowed. "I don't like the way he looks at you."

Minette accidentally jerked the wheel and the truck headed for the ditch, but she corrected it at once. "Sorry, hand slipped," she lied.

He wasn't buying that. His eyes twinkled. "Uh-huh."

She concentrated on getting the truck to the stoplight. She didn't look at Hayes. Her high color might have revealed more to him than she wanted him to know. She was flattered that he minded how an attractive man looked at her. It was, well, sort of possessive. She liked it a lot, but she didn't want to make her pleasure obvious.

"Do you have physical therapy today?" she asked suddenly.

"Tomorrow," he said.

"Oh. Okay. I was going to offer to drive you."

"I think I should be driving myself," he began.

"Dr. Coltrain said not until he tells you it's okay." She looked at him. "You don't want to do something to set back your progress."

He grimaced. "I guess not." He sighed and looked out the window. "I'm getting cabin fever, is all."

"You don't like having to stay in one room," she translated.

"It's a very nice cage, with great food and company," he replied. "But I miss Andy."

"Want to swing by and see him?" she asked. "It's on the way."

He brightened. "I'd love to, if you don't mind."

"Not one bit." She frowned. "Do we need to go by your office and get your house key from Zack?"

"No. I keep a spare hidden, just in case."

"Good thinking."

He smiled. "I try to plan for emergencies."

"I noticed."

She pulled up at his front porch and they both got out of the vehicle. Hayes went around the corner and came back with a key.

He turned it in the lock, and invited her to go in first.

"Hey, Andy!" he called. And he whistled.

"He comes when you whistle?" Minette exclaimed.

"Usually. I don't know.... Andy!" he exclaimed as his huge scaly roommate came scampering out of the kitchen. "Hi, buddy!" he said enthusiastically. "Haven't forgotten me yet?"

The big lizard blazed its eyes and shook its head enthusiastically.

"That's what they do when they like something, or when they're courting," Hayes explained helpfully.

"Oh, I see. He really likes you," she teased.

He made a face. "Now, don't get too close, just in case," he said. "Andy has some problems with women."

"I've heard all about that," she agreed.

The big reptile cocked its head as it looked at Minette. But, strangely, he didn't attack her. He just watched.

"Gosh, he's beautiful," she said, her voice soft with feeling.

"I didn't realize they were quite so colorful. He's almost turquoise in places."

He smiled. "They change color—well, just a bit—depending on a lot of factors—heat, light, things like that."

"What does he eat?"

"Fruits and veggies," Hayes said. "But he likes shredded carrots and spring salad mix best." He reached down and picked up the huge reptile. Andy put his front feet on Hayes's chest. "No, no, old fella," Hayes laughed, turning him slightly. "No climbing today, I'm afraid. Let's see if you've got carrots."

He put the lizard's belly on his hand and carried him gently under his arm into the kitchen.

"I can't believe he lets you pick him up," Minette exclaimed.

"Tell you a secret," he said with a grin. "They're cold-blooded. I'm warm. See the connection there?"

"Yes, I do, but he's also blazing his eyes and shaking his head," she laughed. "So I'm betting he likes you, too."

He put Andy down on the floor and looked in the refrigerator. "Bless Zack's heart. A whole tub of shredded carrots."

He pulled out the fixings and made Andy a nice iguana salad, placing it on the floor in a paper bowl. "Less cleanup," he told her with a grin.

"Look at him eat!" she laughed. The big animal's nose was completely buried in the bowl of salad. Next to it was a long, deep ceramic bowl of water.

"He's a big guy, so he takes a lot of feeding. Look here." He took her into the next room, which looked like a study, complete with desk. Except in one corner there was a dead tree on a stand, a shelf next to it and a heat lamp suspended over the shelf. On the shelf was a long, flat thing that looked like a rock except that it plugged into the wall.

"This is where Andy lives. He's got a view——" he indicated the window that the shelf gave access to "——and a heat lamp, and even a hot rock. See, they're cold-blooded so they have to have an outside source to heat them up so they can digest food. Otherwise they get something called 'belly-rot.' It's usually fatal."

"Gosh, there's so much to learn," she said.

He nodded. "It's sort of like the setup Cag Hart used to have for his snake, except he kept the snake in an aquarium. Tried that. Andy just moped. So I potty-trained him and he has the run of the house."

"He's just amazing."

He smiled warmly. "You know how to make friends."

She laughed. "No, I'm not trying to flatter you. I really like him." She studied him quietly. He was so handsome. "Hayes, why don't you have a female iguana?" she asked, curious.

"The females tend to be more aggressive," he explained. "Not all the time, but the ones I've encountered have been. This guy who owned a pet shop a few years ago in Jacobsville had a female, a big one, about five feet long in a custom cage. Every time a man came near it, she'd whip the glass with her tail, drop her dewlap and start hissing. Eventually, I think he gave her to a breeder. He couldn't sell her."

"Goodness!"

"It's the same with anoles, a smaller green lizard," he laughed. "The males are very docile and don't mind being handled."

She pursed her lips. "Are you very docile and don't mind being handled?" she teased, and then she gasped and went red with embarrassment for saying such a forward thing. "Gosh, sorry, I don't know where that came from!"

He moved toward her, took her gently by the waist and brought her close to him. "I'm not always docile," he whispered. "But I don't mind being handled. Not at all." He bent his head and brushed her mouth with his.

It was like starting a brush fire. He caught his breath, slammed her body against the length of his and his mouth became insistent and demanding all at once.

Minette couldn't even protest the very intimate hold. She slid her arms under his and around him, her hands flattening on his long, muscular back. She moved even closer, shivering a little as she felt him become immediately capable.

He whispered something under his breath, but she didn't hear him. She was blind, deaf, dumb, desperate to keep his warm, hungry mouth on her lips. She moaned helplessly and stood on her tiptoes to get even closer to the source of all that incredible pleasure.

His hands slid down her back and caught her upper thighs, grinding her against the hunger that was almost bending him double with need.

"Oh, God, this was a mistake," he ground out against her mouth. "Minette, we have…to stop. Right now!"

"Okay." She kissed him harder.

"Listen…!"

Her mouth opened.

"Oh, damn it…" He lifted her higher against him, groaning because it really hurt his shoulder, but something else was hurting even more. He caught the back of her head and his tongue went into her mouth, thrusting hard and deep.

She thought she might pass out, the pleasure was so deep and throbbing and wild. She shivered against the powerful length of him. There was nothing in the world. Nothing except Hayes and the silence in the room and the intense, unbearable tension that was growing and growing and growing…

The sudden sound of glass hitting the floor broke them apart.

Hayes looked up. Andy was standing on the desk with his dewlap down. He'd just used his long tail to knock a glass onto the floor. Now he whipped it again and knocked over a cup full of pencils.

"Are you sure he's a he?" Minette asked breathlessly as she stared at the giant reptile. She was still plastered against Hayes, her body throbbing in time with her heartbeat.

"Well, no…" he had to admit. It was hard to breathe and talk when his body was urging him to drag her to the nearest bed. "The guy who sold him to me swore he'd been checked and neutered, and he was a male. That's why I named him Andy."

She looked up at Hayes. "Well, I think the guy who sold him to you lied."

Hayes looked at the big lizard. "Andy?" he asked aloud.

Andy knocked over a photo of Hayes's father with his tail.

Slowly, very slowly, Hayes let Minette go. Andy's dewlap retreated and his posture changed. He stood there, unchallenging, just staring at Hayes.

Hayes looked down at Minette. "I see problems ahead."

"You do?"

He nodded. He was looking at her mouth. "I don't intend to stop kissing you."

She smiled dreamily. "I'm so glad you said that. Because I like it very much."

He nodded again. He smiled. "It does seem to be addictive."

She laughed. "I'll have to learn to make salad. Maybe Andy can get used to me."

"As a last alternative I'll have him checked again by a vet and if he's a female, I'll get him a boyfriend."

She chuckled. "What an alternative."

He bent to her mouth. "Let's tempt fate one more time."

She opened her lips and kissed him back with unbridled hunger. He was absolutely delicious to kiss. His mouth was firm and soft and very expert. She didn't even want to know how he learned how to kiss that way. It was enough to know that he wanted her. She wanted him very much. Her body was telling him so.

Crash! They looked over toward the desk. The telephone in its cradle had gone over the side. Andy's dewlap was down again.

"Either we move to another room and lock the door or we give it up for now," Hayes said with a long sigh. "I think it's probably a good idea to give it up. I'm not really in any condition for what's supposed to come next."

She laughed again. She didn't want to say that she wasn't about to go that far with him unless they were in a committed relationship, but she didn't quite know how to put it. He should know by now that she had old-fashioned hang-ups. But she knew men could be devious after a long dry spell. And from what she knew of Hayes, he hadn't had a special woman in his life for years. Being the sheriff of the county, it would be hard to hide a relationship from all the prying eyes.

He released her slowly. She moved away and turned her attention back to Andy. He was calm again, his dewlap relaxed, his eyes steady, his head cocked as he watched his human interact with that odd-looking thing with so much hair.

"Andy," Hayes said, drawing in a deep breath, "bad lizard. Bad!"

Andy just stared at him.

"You can't reason with reptiles," Hayes muttered.

"It's his house and you're his human," Minette explained. "Or her house. Maybe."

"A jealous iguana." He shook his head and grinned. "Now I've seen everything."

Minette looked up at him with pure adoration. "I like your big dangerous lizard, all the same. He, or she, really is beautiful."

"Thanks." He went to the desk and stroked Andy behind his ears, along the narrow band of raised scales that ran all the way down his back. The ones along the end of his tail were as sharp as razor blades. "Okay, pal, you get your way, temporarily. Now, Andy, I want you to clean up this mess you made and stop knocking stuff off my desk. Bad iguana!"

Andy cocked his head.

"Fat chance, huh?" He leaned over, picked up the landline phone and started to put it down when he noticed something. There was a scratch along the case of the phone. He looked at Minette and put his finger to his lips. He pulled out an odd little tool from his desk drawer and opened the phone. There, embedded in the wiring, was a foreign object. He pursed his lips, unhooked the foreign object and put the phone back together. With a laugh, he put the little device on the floor and stomped on it, violently.

"I hope your eardrums burst with that," he muttered as he

picked up the tiny pieces. "Damn. I probably should have saved it and given it to my investigator."

"Temper, temper," Minette said, wagging her finger. "Curses, too? You're losing it, Hayes."

He glanced at her and made a face. "Seems like it, yes."

She moved closer. "Do you think it was El Ladrón who put it there?"

"I don't know. We'd better go." He stroked Andy again. "You behave. And eat anybody who comes in here who wasn't invited. Got it?"

Andy's eyes blinked.

"An attack iguana?" Minette mused.

"Why not? He looks terrifying."

Minette stared at the big lizard and smiled. "I think he's pretty."

Suddenly Andy dropped his dewlap and started shaking his head and blazing his eyes.

"Well!" Hayes exclaimed.

"That doesn't look threatening at all. Do you think he'd let me pet him?" Minette asked.

"I don't know...."

"Can I try?" She really wanted to make friends.

"Just be careful. His tail is like a whip. It can cut."

"Okay." She moved a little closer. "Sweet boy," she purred to the iguana. "What a pretty baby you are!"

Andy was still blazing his eyes.

Very, very slowly, she moved her hand toward his head. He watched her. Then, just as her hand reached toward his back, he arched and brought his tail up and stared at her.

"Move back," Hayes said.

She did, at once. She knew a threatening posture when she saw it.

"It's early days yet," Hayes said, waiting until the iguana dropped the threatening posture before he picked him up, gently, and set him on his hot rock on the shelf. Andy spread out at once.

Minette laughed. "Would you look at that? Mr. Leisure!"

Hayes grinned. "He has moods. But you made a good start with him."

"I'll keep trying," she promised.

He caught her hand in his and linked their fingers together. "He'll get used to you."

"I know."

They walked back out the door and locked it. Minette was worried by the listening device Hayes had found.

"You should call somebody about that bug," she said when they were in the truck, driving away from the ranch.

"I think you're right. I'll do that, when we get home."

It made her feel warm all over, the way he said that, as if he thought of her house that way. She smiled to herself.

She glanced at him, and a worrying thought nagged at the back of her mind. "Hayes...you don't mind, that my father turned out to be a notorious drug lord?"

She drove with her left hand. The right lay on the seat between them. He picked it up, and linked his fingers with hers.

"You can't choose your relatives," Hayes said. "Your father supplied the drugs that killed my brother. But he didn't intend to kill Bobby. Intent is everything, in law. I don't approve of the way he makes his living. He feeds on the addiction of people. It's not a good thing. But it isn't as if he held a gun to my brother's head and forced him into an overdose." He drew in a long breath. "I've thought a lot about what you said, about guilt. And I think you're right. It's like a sole survivor of a plane crash or train derailment, feeling guilty that he lived when so many others died. But God does have a hand in what happens to us, and I think there's a purpose behind every single bad thing that occurs."

"I must be contagious," she mused.

He chuckled. "Not so much. My father was religious. He took me to church every Sunday when I was a boy. When I got into my teens I didn't want to go, and he didn't force me. But I've got that foundation, you see. When things go wrong in my life, when bad things happen, I have that bedrock of faith to hold on to. It gets me through the daily disasters."

She nodded, and he glanced at her. "Actually we're both in businesses that see the very worst of humanity. But even in that darkness, there's the occasional soft light burning."

"I guess." She drew in a breath. "I just hate the coldness in our society, the meanness, the lack of respect."

"It's not taught anymore," Hayes said. "Maybe information overload is the problem. You know, you can't even watch a television program now. They flash ads for upcoming shows right on the screen during the show, so you can't concentrate on what you're trying to watch. The whole world is going to have some form of attention deficit disorder and everyone will wonder why!"

"Too true. I guess I'm guilty of the texting thing. Not when I drive," she pointed out firmly. "That's insane, to try to type while driving. But it's easy to send Aunt Sarah a text if I'm going to be late, or I have to make a stop—she's not always near her phone, but she checks her messages constantly."

"Hey, there's this thing called voice mail," he said humorously.

She made a face. "I can't figure out how to set it up, so I just text."

"I can teach you."

She smiled. "Okay."

He laughed and squeezed her fingers.

Thanksgiving was a riotous affair. The kids were out of school and Sarah and Minette spent the whole televised Christmas parade cooking.

"You know, I've never seen this parade," Minette commented, standing in the doorway in an apron with a spoon in her hand. "I'm always cooking. Have the Rockettes performed yet?"

"Ten minutes ago, sorry," Hayes said. He grinned. He was sitting in the big armchair with a lap full of children. He had Shane on one side and Julie on the other. He looked like he'd won the lottery.

Minette smiled at them warmly. Her family. Her brother and sister, and her...she wasn't sure what Hayes was. But he belonged here. She knew that.

"What are you cooking?"

"Everything," she chuckled. "And I'd better get back to it before I burn up the sweet potato casserole that's in the oven."

"All of us here appreciate your efforts," Hayes said. "Furthermore, before you say that I'm not contributing to the workload, they also serve who only stand and wait. Or some such thing. Sit and wait, maybe." He smiled, showing snow-white teeth.

Minette loved the way he looked, in jeans and boots and a red plaid flannel shirt. He looked elegant, even so.

She was wearing jeans, too, with a bright red pullover shirt that had reindeer trying to push an overweight Santa onto a roof. It was hidden under the holly and mistletoe apron she was wearing.

"Okay. I agree that you're contributing. But let me know when Santa Claus comes, I never miss that!"

"We'll come get you, Minette," Julie promised. "Cross my heart." And she did cross it and grin.

Minette laughed on her way back to the kitchen.

A short time later, the summons came.

"Santa Claus!" Julie called from the doorway. "Santa's on TV!"

"On my way," Minette said.

She put down the knife she'd been using to slice turkey, covered the turkey in aluminum foil and rushed into the living room.

"Oh, it's Santa!" Shane exclaimed. He got out of the chair and joined Julie on the floor, as close to the television screen as they could get, which wasn't very close because it was on a raised black entertainment center.

Minette laughed, wiping her hands on a wet paper towel. "The star of the parade," she mused.

"You've been on your feet all morning," Hayes said with a wicked grin. "Time to sit down, honey."

While she was digesting that, he reached out and tugged her gently down onto his lap. He grimaced. His shoulder was still sore. He shifted her, so that she was lying against the good one.

She almost melted into him. She felt safe and secure with all that warm strength so close to her. She leaned her head against his chin and watched television, feeling warm and tingly all over.

Hayes contracted his good arm and took a deep breath. "You smell like turkey and cranberry sauce. Careful that I don't take a bite out of you. I'm hungry."

The others thought he was talking about food, and they laughed. But Minette looked up into his eyes and knew that he wasn't. His hand slid up and down along her side, just barely brushing the outside of her breast. It was very stimulating. Involuntarily she leaned toward him, just a little, tempting that exploring hand closer...

"Minette, do you want me to put the turkey on a platter?" Aunt Sarah called from the kitchen.

Minette gasped and sat up on Hayes's lap. She looked toward the kitchen, but her aunt was nowhere in sight. "No, I'll...I'll do that. Be right there."

Aunt Sarah looked out the door, caught her breath and died laughing. "Sorry, sorry," she chuckled and vanished back into the kitchen.

"Caught," Hayes whispered at Minette's ear, and kissed it.

She laughed self-consciously. "Sort of, yes." She sighed as she looked down into his handsome face. "I have to go."

He shook his head. "I'm devastated."

"Are you, really?"

"Really."

She sighed again and her smile widened.

"I have to go," she repeated.

"You said that." He cocked his head. "Well, have a nice trip."

She burst out laughing as she got to her feet. Hayes was grinning.

"Gosh, Minette, you're all red! Are you sick?" Julie asked suddenly.

Minette cleared her throat. "The kitchen, it's hot in there," she explained.

"Oh. Okay. Look at Santa's reindeers!" she exclaimed. "Minette, does Santa have real live reindeer where he lives?"

"Of course he does, sweetness," Minette replied gently.

"And can they fly?" he persisted.

"That's what we're told," she replied.

"This boy at kindergarten says that there isn't a Santa Claus. He says it's all phony," Julie muttered.

Minette got down on one knee. "Well, you tell him that in this house, there is a Santa Claus and he's bringing you all sorts of presents on Christmas morning!"

Julie beamed. "Okay!"

Minette got to her feet and glanced at Hayes with a frown. "I get so tired of people who think they need to force their opinions on the rest of the populace."

"Tell me about it," Hayes said.

"I'm going to finish carving the turkey," she said darkly.

"Now, listen, you be careful with the knife," he cautioned.

She made a face. "I'm only going to vent my frustrations. Remember, the turkey is deceased," she reminded him.

"I remember." He gave her an amused look. "Just watch where you cut, okay?" His expression softened. "I don't want you to hurt yourself."

She almost melted onto the floor. "You don't?"

"Of course I don't. What a question!"

She smiled slowly. "I'll be careful."

"You do that."

She went back into the kitchen, warm all over.

10

The meal was delicious. Minette was proud of the way it turned out. Cooking for the holidays was special, and she'd tried very hard to produce the sort of dishes that had been in her family for several generations. She had her great-grandmother's cookbook with its recipes, and even a few that had been handed down from her great-great-grandmother.

Great-Aunt Sarah remembered some by heart and had taught Minette how to make them. All in all, the food was some of the best Minette had ever cooked. She loved watching the kids and Hayes wolf it down.

"This dressing is unique," Hayes said. "I usually just get a box of it and follow the directions." He shook his head. "As for giblet gravy, forget it. I don't think you can even buy a can in the grocery stores."

"Not that I'm aware of," Minette laughed. "You have to have

the giblets to do it with. A lot of people throw them away and never even cook them."

"And the rolls," he exclaimed, studying one. "Homemade rolls with real butter! The only place I ever even see these is at Barbara's Café. I usually get extras to take home and put in the freezer."

"I can make them anytime you like," she said, pleased by the praise. "I love making bread."

"I like turkey," Shane said, grinning.

"Me, too!" Julie said.

Minette smiled. She wasn't big on turkey except in sandwiches. She had a very small piece on her plate. She liked vegetables much better than meats.

"You aren't eating much," Hayes commented quietly.

She sighed. "After you spend so much time cooking it, you just don't really have a lot of enthusiasm for eating it," she chuckled.

"I see."

She exchanged a long look with him that set her whole body tingling.

Aunt Sarah chuckled.

They averted their eyes and pretended a great interest in the food.

Minette finished a bite of sweet potato casserole. "Hayes, you really need to tell somebody about that bug you found," she said unexpectedly.

"You found a bug? Can I see it?" Shane asked. He was fascinated with insects. Minette had purchased several picture books of them for him.

"Sweetheart, it's not that sort of bug," Minette said softly.

"It's an electronic bug," Hayes explained. "I'll tell you all about them one day, okay?"

"Okay."

Sarah grimaced. "They put a bug in your house?" she asked Hayes worriedly.

"Apparently," he said heavily. "I'll call Zack after we eat."

"We should have invited Zack over for dinner," Minette said sadly. "He's all alone."

"Barbara made a plate for Zack and took it over to him," Hayes told her. "She thinks he needs pampering."

"Good for her! Barbara's such a good cook." She frowned. "Is she going to marry her daughter-in-law's father, you think?" she added.

He shook his head. "She likes General Cassaway very much, and he is head of the CIA, but she said no man could ever compare with the husband she lost." He laughed. "And you're not the only person who ended up with a notorious father—remember that Barbara's adopted son, Rick, turned out to be the son of Emilio Machado, now president of the South American nation of Barrera, but formerly involved in kidnapping across the border."

"I had forgotten that," she said. "We never really know a lot about our parents."

"True."

Hayes finished his pumpkin pie and sighed. "Oh, that was delicious, honey!" he said.

Minette beamed and flushed. He didn't seem to even notice the endearment, which was interesting because Hayes never, ever used them.

"Thanks," she replied.

He glanced at her. "If I stayed here long, I'd be on a diet. I swear, this is the most wonderful meal I ever had. Even my mother couldn't cook this well."

"I'm flattered."

He shook his head. "I don't flatter people," he said honestly. "I say what I think. It's not a good thing, from time to time," he added with a chuckle.

"Oh, I like honesty," Minette replied. "The truth is always best, in the long run."

"I totally agree."

"It was lovely, dear," Sarah told Minette.

"You helped," she replied. "Pat yourself on the back, too. I couldn't do anything around here if I didn't have you to help me."

Sarah, flattered, had a nice color on her high cheekbones. "You're just saying that."

"I'm not." Minette smiled.

Sarah got up, went around the table and hugged her great-niece. "Well, I couldn't do much without you," she said, and cleared her throat. "Now before we start crying and embarrass Hayes, I'll get the dishes in the dishwasher."

"I'm very hard to embarrass," Hayes assured her with a grin.

She laughed, started picking up plates and headed for the kitchen.

"Can we watch a movie, you think?" Shane asked, and he was looking at Hayes.

"Not the dragon movie again," Minette groaned.

Hayes glowered at her. "What's wrong with the dragon movie? I love the dragon movie."

"Me, too!" Shane exclaimed. "Please? Please?"

"Yes, please?" Julie asked, looking up at Hayes with big, soft blue eyes.

Hayes looked at Minette. "Tell me you could say no to them?" he dared.

She waved a hand. "Go!"

"I'll go get the movie, Hayes!" Shane exclaimed, and ran for the staircase.

"Before you watch a movie, please call Zack," Minette said quietly.

He stared into her worried eyes and nodded. "I suppose I better."

He went into the living room, dropped into the easy chair he'd claimed for his own and got out his cell phone.

"Zack. Is this a bad time?" Hayes asked.

Zack made a harrumphing sound. "I'm all by myself eating cold turkey. There is no bad time."

"Cold turkey? Why?" Hayes asked.

"Because my damned microwave gave up the ghost just as I was putting the plate in to heat it up," he muttered.

"You've got a stove, haven't you?"

"The stove came with the rental house," Zack said. "But just because I have a stove doesn't give me the instructions I need to actually use it!"

"Oh, gosh."

Minette stuck her head in the door. "What's wrong?" she whispered.

"Zack's microwave died. He's eating cold turkey."

She went to Hayes and held out her hand for the phone. "Zack? Minette. Come on over here. Hayes needs to talk to you and we've got a kitchen full of hot food and no way to save it all."

"You mean it?" Zack asked, aghast.

"Of course I mean it. Come on."

"You sweetheart," Zack said. "Thanks a million. I'll just put the plate Barbara brought me in the fridge and get a new microwave tomorrow. Not much hope of an open appliance store on Thanksgiving Day."

"See you in a bit then," she said. She handed Hayes back the phone.

"I'll save what I was going to say until you get here," Hayes chuckled. "This is wonderful food. You're in for a real treat."

"I know that. She's a doll, isn't she?"

"Yes, she is, and she's spoken for, so don't get your hopes up," Hayes said at once, and with a nip in his tone.

Minette stared at him, wide-eyed. He looked back at her with warm, evident affection and something else—something like possession.

"What was that? Yes." Hayes chuckled again. "Okay, woman-hater, come on over. We'll see you then."

"What did he say?" Minette asked.

Hayes grinned. "He hates women."

She did a double-take. "He doesn't seem to hate me."

"No, he doesn't hate women in general," he emphasized. He shook his head. "He just said that he's got some scars from a relationship he had years ago."

"Poor guy. He's so nice, too."

"I did wonder why he didn't date, but you don't press issues like that these days." He leaned forward. "It's very politically incorrect."

She glared. "You have no idea how sick I am of those words."

"Yes, but it's the times we live in," he sighed.

She made a face. "I spend my life trying not to offend anyone in print." She narrowed her eyes. "We have too many people living too close together, sticking their noses into everybody's business."

"Well, the only remedy for that problem would be catastrophic and politically incorrect," he said, tongue-in-cheek.

She glared at him.

He chuckled. "Sorry."

She wrinkled her nose and smiled. "You're a nice sheriff. I can't imagine you being politically incorrect with anybody. You don't even cuss. Well, mostly."

"I do my best."

She sighed. She loved looking at him. He looked back, his eyes soft and quiet and hungry. While they were staring at each other, Shane came flying into the room with a DVD in its jacket.

"Hayes?" Shane tugged at his pants leg. "The dragon movie!"

He snapped out of it, blinked his eyes and smiled sheepishly. "Okay. The dragon movie. I'll put it in the player."

"You will not." Minette pushed him gently back into the chair. "You're recuperating. I'm not."

She fed the movie into the Blu-ray player and smiled. "Have fun. I'll go get the plate ready for Zack. But," she added to Hayes, "I want to know what he says about that bug."

"Would I have secrets from you, even if you are a nosy, spying little newspaper reporter?" He said it as if it were the greatest compliment, and with affection in his eyes.

She flushed. "You'd better not."

"Never again. I promise." He crossed his heart. Twice.

She sighed and went back to the kitchen.

Zack was still irritated when he arrived. He really was good-looking, with thick black hair and deep-set dark eyes and a silky smooth light olive complexion. He was built very much like Hayes, with a lithe but muscular rodeo rider's physique. He had big hands and big feet and a big nose. But they just made him even more attractive.

"Here, Zack," Minette called from the kitchen doorway. She handed him a full plate, with a fork on top, and a hot mug of black coffee. "No sugar or cream, right?"

He laughed, shocked out of his bad mood. "No sugar or cream," he agreed. "Thanks, Minette."

"There's a price for that," she said sadly. "You have to sit through the dragon movie while you eat it."

His eyes opened wide. "Excuse me?"

She led him into the living room and offered him a seat on the sofa where he could put his mug and plate on the wide wooden coffee table. The movie was blaring away. The kids, lying on their bellies on the carpeted floor, were spellbound. Hayes, drinking his second cup of coffee, grinned at Zack.

"Sorry," he said quietly. "It's their favorite movie."

Zack chuckled. "No problem. I survived *Attack of the Killer Tomatoes*. I guess I can get through this one."

Hayes pursed his lips, glanced at Minette and winked. She flushed, laughed and went back into the kitchen.

Far from being bored, Zack sat through the movie with the greatest apparent interest, and was actually laughing when it came to an end.

"Hey, that wasn't bad at all," Zack said enthusiastically.

"I told you animated films weren't just for kids," Hayes reminded him.

Minette stuck her head in the door, noted Zack's empty plate and picked it up. "Seconds?" she asked.

"Just coffee, thanks, but I'll come get it. Hayes, another cup?"

Hayes held out his empty cup. "Thanks."

Zack went back toward the kitchen. Minette, on her way to the living room, watched him walk with open curiosity.

"Something wrong?" Zack asked, pausing. He towered over her.

She shook her head and smiled sheepishly. "It's just that you remind me of someone when you walk."

His eyebrows arched, asking a silent question.

"Cash Grier," she replied. "I don't know him well, I've only spoken to him a few times, but I've seen him walking down the sidewalks in town. He moves in a very strange way. I can't really explain it."

"You want to know what it is?" Zack replied.

She nodded.

"It's the way a hunter walks in the woods," he replied. "A soft, gliding, irregular motion. You see, animals are alert for rhythmic patterns, because only humans walk like that. A hunter learns to adapt his gait so that he doesn't frighten his prey." He grinned, showing perfect white teeth.

She was studying him. "A hunter? Deer hunter?"

He pursed his lips. "I have hunted deer once or twice."

He wasn't saying it, but she knew what he meant. Cash Grier had been a sniper in his mysterious past. Zack had been in the military, too. She looked up at him for a long time and her eyes narrowed.

"Ah, yes," she said softly. "I know that look."

"What look?"

"Don't they call it the 'hundred-yard stare'?" she asked.

His face closed up, even though he still had a faint smile on his lips. "Men who know combat share it."

"Yes."

"Side effects of the skill," he replied.

"Sad ones."

He hesitated. He nodded. Then he closed up like a flower. "Coffeepot?"

She laughed. "In the kitchen, on the counter. I just made a new batch."

"It's good coffee."

"I would have made you some latté, but I'm out of the pods," she said apologetically.

"I'm not much on fancy coffee, remember. I like any sort, as long as it's strong enough to keep me awake."

She stared. "Late night?"

He grimaced. "Ya. They just released the new 'Halo' game for Xbox 360," he sighed. "I'm worn out and I haven't gotten to the end yet!"

She burst out laughing. "You gamers," she chuckled, shaking her head.

"I don't drink, smoke or gamble," he pointed out. "Gaming is a permissible vice, and it isn't illegal."

"I guess so."

He laughed.

But he wasn't laughing when he and Hayes sat in Minette's office discussing the bug Hayes had found in his telephone.

"Sophisticated," Zack pronounced when Hayes described it to him. "Pity you didn't bring it here with you."

"Sorry. There wasn't much left. Made me mad, so I stomped it."

"There are probably more," Zack replied. "I should go over

there and do a complete sweep." He looked around. "It wouldn't hurt to check around here, either."

Hayes groaned. "Is there no privacy left in the world?"

"No," Zack said shortly. "We've traded privacy for pseudo-security. There's a neat saying, that if we protect everything we protect nothing."

"Who said that?" Hayes asked curiously.

Zack laughed. "Holman W. Jenkins, Jr., in a *Wall Street Journal* editorial following the Hurricane Katrina disaster. He said, and I quote, 'to protect everything is to protect nothing.' Wise man."

"I guess we don't have the resources to protect everything, even if we want to."

"But we can still afford security cameras everywhere to spy on everybody, laws to regulate who has access to information and government rights to stick their noses into people's private bank accounts...!" Zack was on a roll.

Hayes held up a hand. "We're officers of the law."

"Sure we are. But we're turning into a nation of paranoids, spying on each other to make sure nobody's infringing on our rights. Meanwhile, we're losing privacy and independence by the hour!"

"I can't argue that," Hayes said. "However, in my county, we're not approving spy tactics. So let's find out who thinks they have the right to spy on us!"

"Got my vote. I'll get my equipment and bring it over this afternoon. After I've swept your house from top to bottom."

Hayes sighed. "Better sweep the outbuildings as well, I'm afraid."

"I had that in mind."

Hayes drew in a deep breath. "I hope to be back at work within the next two years."

Zack laughed. "Copper will let you go soon."

"I hope so. I feel better. I just can't lift anything."

"Including a riot shotgun," Zack reminded him. "So wait it out until you're a hundred percent before you go back to work in the field. And even then," he added curtly, "stop rushing into things without backup!"

Hayes grimaced. "Crackers and milk!"

"Cussing doesn't change facts."

"It helps."

Zack laughed. "If you say so. I'll get my gear and start working."

He waved a hand and went back down the hall. "Thanks for the great meal, Minette," he said. "And the coffee."

"But I've got pumpkin pie with homemade whipped cream," she groaned. "I was just about to bring it out!"

"I'll be back. I'm going to sweep your house."

Minette blinked. "I have a vacuum cleaner...."

"For bugs," he muttered.

"Oh. Bugs. Bugs?" She looked around, aghast. "Surely not here...!"

"Hayes is here, and they're after Hayes," he reminded her. He moved in and lowered his voice. "They're after you, too, sweet woman," he added quietly. "We have to make sure they don't get access to any information that would help them nab you or Hayes."

She put down the knife she was using to cut the pie. "My life used to be so calm and quiet."

"It never was," he replied. "You work for a newspaper."

"It used to be a little calmer," she said doggedly.

He laughed. "You have friends," he pointed out. "And you're being watched even when you don't know it. But bugs are not allowed. So we're getting rid of them."

Minette looked around. "Well, if they're listening, you've just given them advance notice."

"I doubt very seriously that they've bugged your kitchen," he said, and his dark eyes smiled. "Or the bathroom. The rest of the house, however, would be fair game. Which brings to mind a question. Have you had any utility people inside the house lately?"

She thought. "Not really. Oh. Wait. The phone company said there was a problem on the line and they checked the phone in the office and my bedroom." She went pale. "Darn!"

"I'll go over the phones when I get back. Meanwhile, don't call anybody unless you use your cell phone. They didn't touch that...?"

"No. I have my wireless contract with a different provider," she said.

"Good thing. You can make calls that aren't monitored. I won't be long."

He left. Minette made a face. This was getting tedious. She hated the idea that someone was spying on her, especially people who might want to kill Hayes. She tried not to think that her own life was in jeopardy. Her father's worst enemy would love to have her in his power, to hurt her father.

"Imagine me, in the middle of a turf war," she mused aloud.

"What, talking to yourself again, sweetie?" Sarah asked as she came back inside from emptying the kitchen garbage can. She was busy getting out a new liner for the can.

"I'm always talking to myself," she laughed. "I was thinking about my father...my real father, and his enemy."

Sarah straightened up. Her face was solemn. "I'm so sorry about that. I would have told you, if I'd known."

Minette hugged her. "I know that." She sighed. "I'm not worried about me. I'm worried about Hayes. They almost killed him once. Sooner or later, El Ladrón is going to figure out that his new hit man actually works for my father. What if he hires someone who never misses? What if...?"

"What if tomorrow never comes?" Sarah inserted. "You can't live your life on 'what-ifs,' my darling. You have to take one day, one hour, at a time and get through it."

"I suppose you're right." She shook her head. "It's so hard!"

"Life is hard. We just put one foot in front of another and keep walking."

"Okay." She let her great-aunt go and turned back to the pie. "I'll keep walking down the hall with a slice of pie for Hayes and the kids," she laughed.

"Great idea. Cut us one while you're at it. I'll get the whipped cream out of the fridge. Where's Zack?" she added after she peered down the hall into the living room.

"Bug hunting. Don't ask." She held up a hand. "I'll explain it all to you later." And she started cutting pie.

"This is delicious," Hayes said, closing his eyes to savor the pie as Minette sat next to him eating hers. They were watching a new cartoon movie about Rapunzel. It was hilarious.

"Thanks. This is a great movie," she added.

He chuckled. "It's one of my favorites. I like the horse."

"Me, too!" Julie exclaimed. "He's so sweet!"

"Sweet." Hayes rolled his eyes. "Well, I guess he is, at the end. Right now, though, he's after the hero."

"I want my hair to grow long like that so I can pull people up by it. Can I grow it long, Minette, please?" Julie pleaded.

"We'll see," Minette said.

"Okay!" Julie went right back to her viewing.

Hayes looked at Minette curiously.

"Pick your battles," she said under her breath. "In five minutes she won't remember asking. Trust me."

He chuckled again. "You've got this child-raising thing down to an art, haven't you?"

"Years of practice." She grinned.

"You really love it, don't you?"

She nodded. Her eyes went from Shane to Julie and back again, who were intently watching the movie on the floor in front of the TV. "They're the most precious things in my life. I can't imagine not having them here."

"I noticed. You know, I've never been around kids much. They come in the office to get candy on Halloween and I see them when I help hand out presents at the orphanage. But I've never gotten to know any. Not like this." He was studying the children. "They're...fascinating," he said, trying to find the right word. "They come out with the most incredible questions. What makes the sky blue? Why do fireflies light up at night? Why doesn't the moon fall down? Stuff like that. They keep me busy on my iPhone looking up answers," he confessed, laughing. "I'm learning with them."

She smiled warmly. "They like you, too."

He shrugged. "It feels natural somehow, being around them." He frowned. "Never felt like this before."

Minette was awed by the feeling that admission gave her. It showed in her softened features, her warm dark eyes.

He looked at her and his heart seemed to burst with emotion. He could barely breathe for the force of the hunger he felt.

His hand slid to hers and gripped it firmly, locking her fingers into his. "I wish I could take back the past few years. Start over with you," he said huskily.

She searched his eyes. "We can't go back. We can only go forward."

"Yes. Forward." His fingers contracted into hers, caressing and possessive. "Together."

Her heart jumped up into her throat. She colored prettily.

He leaned toward her, his eyes on her parted lips.

She lifted her face, entranced. The world around her dissolved, and she didn't notice the movie had come to an end and the children were changing the channels to find another cartoon show. There was only Hayes and that sensual, chiseled mouth coming closer and closer and closer...

"...said today that he was delighted to be assuming the office of mayor after the terrible and unfortunate shooting of his colleague, the former mayor. Mendez has been linked with one of the family drug cartels locally, but he said in an interview that this is a standard tactic of the other parties to denigrate the candidate. In Mexico, special elections are rare because two candidates are elected at once, insuring that the office will be occupied in case the elected official is unable to serve, or dies in office. A member of a drug enforcement agency in the United States said that Mendez's ties to the drug cartels were an open secret, and that evidence points to him as the source of the elected mayor's shooting. Mendez denies all allegations."

The blaring of the news shook Minette and Hayes apart.

"Aw, there's no cartoons on," Shane muttered, holding the controller.

"Try another channel, Shane," Julie encouraged.

"No!" Hayes said quickly. "Wait!"

He got off the sofa in a burst of energy and gently took the controller away from Shane. "Wait. I know that guy!"

"What?" Minette exclaimed.

"That guy!" Hayes was pointing to the photograph of the new mayor of Cotillo, a small town across the border, a hub of area drug trafficking to the United States. "He's the so and so that I arrested for narcotics trafficking! And he's just become mayor of Cotillo? Good Lord, he'll turn the whole state into a narcotics empire!"

Minette's jaw fell. "Hayes, the man who hired someone to kill you…do you think it could be Mendez, because he's afraid you might see him on the news or in a paper and remember who he is and what he did?"

Hayes looked at her, stunned. "Bingo," he said shortly. "Mendez…Mendez." He stared at the television with his mouth open. "Pedro Mendez—El Ladrón!" he exploded.

11

"Imagine that," Hayes exclaimed when the kids found a show they liked and went back to watching television. "A drug lord, becoming mayor of a town by killing the current mayor."

He was sitting in a chair in the kitchen while Minette put dishes in the dishwasher.

"You said he was El Ladrón...."

"No! I said his name was Mendez. Charro Mendez. Pedro Mendez is El Ladrón's real name. A cousin or a brother, he has to be a relative," he pointed out.

"Sorry, I misunderstood. But what a coincidence, to have them air his photograph on the news." She hesitated and glanced worriedly toward Hayes. "He'll know there's a chance that you've seen him."

He nodded grimly.

"Oh, dear. Just when I thought things couldn't get worse." She had a thought. "What if he's mixed up with my father?" she worried. "I mean, I don't have many feelings for him, I hardly know him, and I don't approve of how he makes his living." She sighed. "But he is my father."

"I've been doing some covert intelligence gathering on your father's 'associates,'" he said. "He won't hire murderers, and he has nothing to do with drug addicts or gamblers. The people he has working for him are ethical, in their criminal way. They never hurt women or children, and they don't deal drugs around grammar or middle schools." He shrugged. "It doesn't mean he's not a drug lord. But he's not as nasty as some of them are. His rival, for instance, burned down a house where a widow and her five children were living. Her husband had wronged him. He'd already killed the husband, but his vengeance extended to even the youngest member of his family."

She shook her head. "What a monster."

"He's done worse things. I won't tell you what they are."

She lifted an eyebrow. "I've covered murders, fires, floods, you name it. I've seen bodies in all manner of unspeakable conditions. You can't shock me."

He studied her with new respect. "I'd forgotten that. You understand things that most people don't even know about."

"Or want to know about," she agreed. "We don't talk to 'civilians,' ordinary people I mean, about a lot of the things we see." She sighed. "But we carry the memories around like extra baggage, all our lives." She had that same look she'd seen on Zack's face. The hundred-yard stare.

"For someone who's never been in combat," Hayes said gently, "you have the demeanor of a war vet."

She smiled. "Thanks."

"It bodes well for the future," he murmured, "that I can talk to you about things I'd never be able to discuss with most other women."

"Don't expect that I won't ply you with questions you might want to avoid answering when you're investigating crimes. I may own the paper, but I'm still a reporter at heart. I love scooping the big dailies."

"You take chances, too," he recalled. "Like the way you went after one of our local drug suppliers and got your paper fire-bombed."

"Oh, that was our late great employee who had his eyes on a Pulitzer," she said. She could laugh about it now, but it hadn't been in the least funny at the time it happened. "He found some shady underworld contacts he thought he could trust and tracked the supplier down to a little border town, where he arranged a meeting. And, come to think of it, the town was Cotillo, where Mendez is now mayor!" She whistled. "Anyway, the informant could apparently be bribed, because he had a heavy drug habit. So he told our guy a lot of things he didn't remember later. You can't really get confirmation on secondhand information like that, but I let the reporter publish his notes because I thought it might flush out some local talent." She rolled her eyes. "Boy, was I right! We had thousands of dollars worth of repairs, I slept with a pistol under my pillow and the ace reporter took a pow-der and went back East looking for work. It seems that he didn't expect death threats because of what he uncovered."

"Naive," Hayes replied.

"Naive, and deadly. Someone actually shot at him and broke the windshield of his car. He was in it at the time. He ran like a scalded dog." She made a face. "I never run. I just published more of his notes and the DEA started investigating the allegations. They made about five arrests and we never had any more threats. I guess the publicity made them back off."

He shook his head. "Sorry. It wasn't the publicity."

She widened her eyes. "What?"

"Eb Scott, Cy Parks, Harley Fowler and Cash Grier paid a friendly visit to the source of the firebombing."

Her lips fell apart. "What?"

"It seems that Cash has some, shall we say, very dangerous contacts in a certain major eastern city. Contacts who could, for a price, take down even the head of a large drug distribution center. I do believe the supplier who had your business firebombed went on a permanent vacation to South America, where he still sleeps with a loaded gun and a bodyguard." He chuckled. "Cash Grier is unique."

"Terroristic threats and acts..." she began.

He waved a hand. "Good luck proving that in a court of law. I did make some sort of veiled threat, but decided that it was in my best interests not to rock the boat. I was very angry with you at the time," he confessed sadly. "For stupid reasons. You aren't your father. I blamed you for Bobby's death and you had absolutely no part in it. I'm sorry for that, as I've said a lot lately. But I was ticked off that Cash removed a threat that could have gotten you out of the newspaper business."

"I see. You wanted me shut down."

He moved a shoulder restlessly and averted his eyes. "I thought you might sell up, if things got hot enough. Not that I would have allowed anyone to harm you, even so," he added curtly. His eyes searched her wan face. "I felt protective about you, even when I thought I hated you." He smiled sadly. "Odd reaction, don't you think?"

She smiled back. "It's been a rocky road, all around."

He nodded. He looked deep into her eyes and she felt herself tingling all over. She hesitated with a dirty cup in her hand and stood just staring at him.

"You are incredibly handsome," she blurted out, and then flushed at her own boldness.

He stood up, took the cup away, pulled her gently against him and bent to kiss her with barely curbed hunger.

She reached under his arms and pressed close, aching for a closer contact, for his arms to crush her, his mouth to devour hers. He must have felt the same way, because he obliged her. They rocked together, burning for each other, clinging in something like anguish as they kissed harder and harder.

The sound of a knock at the front door didn't penetrate the fog of delight they were sharing. But a loudly cleared throat at the doorway finally did.

Hayes and Minette stared at Zack blankly, still locked in each other's arms and breathing erratically.

"The bugs?" Zack remarked, holding up a detector.

"Bugs." Hayes looked blank.

"Bugs, right," Minette echoed.

Zack just shook his head. "Carry on. I'll find the phones all by myself. If I get lost, I'll come back and ask for directions, even though I'm a guy, and guys hate to ask for directions...." He sounded plaintive.

Minette gently drew back from Hayes and cleared her throat. "The phones. Right. Come on, Zack, I'll show you where they are."

"Wait for me. I'll come along in case you get lost." Hayes

caught her fingers in his, grinned at her and they led Zack down the hall, past the living room, to her office.

On the way, they told Zack about the recent unfortunate accident that the mayor of Cotillo met with, and his shady successor.

"Charro Mendez." Zack's lips made a thin line. "Boy, do I know that name! We arrested him for narcotics possession, and had to cut him loose for lack of evidence. But before then, I worked a case in tandem with a DEA agent. There was a kidnapping. Remember the Fuentes brothers?"

"Yes," Hayes said, frowning.

"Well, Charro Mendez is their first cousin." He shrugged. "The drug trade is pretty incestuous, it runs in certain families and they try to keep it that way. Meanwhile, poor helpless victims are tortured, murdered, threatened, hunted…and they wonder why so many people come sneaking across our border. Guess what, nobody shoots them here because they had a bad day, or because they might speak to a police officer. Nobody threatens to burn down their houses." He shook his head. "They should be political refugees."

"The Yaquis are, did you know? The only Native American tribe in the history of this nation to be given refugee status when they came over the border of Mexico to escape intolerance." She laughed self-consciously when they stared at her. "Sorry. History major. I'm full of irrelevant facts."

"That's a good one," Zack replied.

"Thanks."

"So we have a drug dealer running a city. He'll give his friends all the help he can. Probably El Ladrón is his best buddy." Hayes glowered.

"Actually he's Mendez's second cousin," Zack laughed hollowly. "It's all in the family, I told you so. But why would he put out a hit on you for what's public information?"

Hayes stared at Zack. He hadn't considered that.

"Unless," Zack continued, "he's trying to protect someone over here that he needs, badly, for his distribution network. Do you remember the DEA agent telling us that they still had a mole inside the agency, one who's never been found, but who's on the payroll of the Zetas, the biggest drug distributors in Mexico?"

"Yes. But they don't know who it is. Neither do I," Hayes said. "Couldn't it just be that I hassled Mendez and he wants revenge for being arrested? You know how these guys think, they live in the cult of machismo. An insult is punishable by death."

"That's possible, of course," Zack agreed. "But I think there's something more going on here. Perhaps," he added, "you should go see her dad." He jerked his head toward Minette.

She gave them both a long look. "Isn't there a bug in here?" she asked.

They exchanged glances.

"Well, so much for my great reputation in law enforcement." Zack picked up the phone, opened the back with a small screwdriver and took out a bug. "Can you hear me now?" he yelled into it.

Seconds later, the phone rang.

Minette picked it up, frowning.

"Could you please tell your guest not to yell in my ear?" Lassiter asked with incredible courtesy. "That hurt."

"It was you?" Minette exclaimed. "You bugged my phone?"

"Yes, I bugged your phone. Put me on speakerphone, please."

She didn't bother asking how he knew she had one. She sighed and pushed the button. "Sheriff Carson?" Lassiter continued.

"Yes," Hayes returned curtly, glancing curiously at Minette.

"Lassiter," the man replied. "I thought you might like to know that the bugs you're busily dismantling are mine. I replaced the ones El Ladrón's 'telephone repairman' installed."

"Eavesdropping?" Hayes Carson asked. "I hope you have a federal warrant to go with it," he added in a cold tone.

There was laughter. "In fact, I do. But that's the only information you'll get out of me."

"Who are you?" Minette asked abruptly.

"I work for your father, Miss Raynor," Lassiter said, sounding amused. "You know that."

"Who do you work for, when you're not working for my father," she asked slowly.

"Oh, now, that would be telling too much. Let's just say that I'm involved with an agency that has a vested interest in El Ladrón's local activities and leave it at that."

"Lassiter. Why does your name sound so familiar?" Hayes wondered.

"You might know of my father. He has a detective agency in Houston."

"Dane Lassiter is your father?" Hayes exclaimed.

"That's right. My mother is one of his chief investigators. My sister works for Houston P.D. as an intelligence specialist."

"What a connection," Hayes laughed. "I've spoken to your dad several times on cases we've been involved in here. He's one of the best in the business."

"Thanks. I do agree."

"But my father said you worked for some Middle Eastern madman..." Minette said.

"Actually I did, very briefly," he replied. He chuckled. "Who do you think gave his movements away to the proper authorities?"

"My gosh!"

"However, back to our own little problem," he added. "I've turned up some activity near Cy Parks's property, and not your father's activity, Miss Raynor. There are at least four heavily armored SUVs parked on a back road there."

"It wouldn't be on Burns Lake Road, would it?" Hayes asked at once. He glanced at Minette and Zack to see if they got the connection.

"It's where we've found most of the bodies that are dumped around here," Zack answered for them.

"Yes, actually, that's where they are. I found them on aerial surveillance, they're quite well concealed."

"Aerial surveillance?" Hayes exclaimed.

"I have access to satellite data," Lassiter told them. "Don't ask, I can't tell you."

"I could send my deputies out there...." Hayes began.

"And do what? Arrest them for parking in the woods? They've done nothing illegal. Yet."

"But you think they will," Hayes mused. "Why?"

"Just a hunch. I think they're gearing up for a kidnapping attempt on Miss Raynor."

Hayes pulled her protectively close. "Over my dead body."

"That's the idea," Lassiter said with a cold laugh. "If you get in the way, you're their new target. El Ladrón's looking for a way to get at her father for ruining one of his most lucrative drug deals. It cost him about four billion in narcotics and he wants revenge."

"Four...billion?" Minette exclaimed.

"Oh, yes, big money," Lassiter replied. "Under the Rico statutes, federal agencies could go to town on new and better equipment if we, if they," he corrected himself, "could get their hands on it."

None of the three listening said anything about the slip of the tongue, but they did exchange knowing glances.

"Anyway," Lassiter said. "About those bugs. It might be very wise to leave them in place for now."

Zack looked at the small device in his hand and glanced at Hayes. He looked at Minette. She grimaced, but she nodded.

"I guess he's right," she said. "If anything happens, he'll find out before our bodies are cold."

Hayes chuckled. "No cold bodies are appearing on my shift, I assure you."

"Mine, either," Zack replied.

"That's the plan. And if you could replace the listening devices you removed at Sheriff Carson's house, Zack, isn't it?" he added.

Zack let out a breath. "The big lizard's mad at me, at the moment. That's going to take a little work, getting into the office past him at Hayes's house."

"Ah, yes, Andy." Lassiter chuckled. "He's partial to bananas. I offered him two slices and he followed me around like a puppy."

"Yes," Hayes agreed. "He's nuts about bananas."

"I'll go buy a bunch and get busy," Zack said with a harassed look.

"I'll ask the county commission to authorize a raise in pay for you," Hayes said with a grin.

"Yeah, they'll do that about the same time they declare us a province of Canada," Zack said sarcastically. "Never mind. I can pay the bills and eat out once a month. I'm happy."

"Thanks, Zack," Hayes said.

"All of you, keep your eyes open," Lassiter cautioned. "Even I don't have total access to what these guys are doing."

"Yes, and my daughter must be safe, no matter what," came a deep, concerned voice. "*Mi vida,* you take care, yes?"

"I will. Thanks," she added, because she recognized her father's deep voice.

"It was never my wish to involve you in something so dangerous." He sighed. "I believe the large drug families are truly gaining more power than they should in political arenas. It should not be so. We run a business. Politics should be the will of the people, not the will of a few."

"As I recall," Hayes said, "Thomas Jefferson, one of our presidents, said that the price of freedom is eternal vigilance." He pursed his lips. "I wonder if he was talking about surveillance devices...?"

"Bite your tongue," Minette said with a laugh.

"Hey, don't knock the tools of the trade," Lassiter replied. "You may be very grateful for them one day. I'll talk to you later."

"Be safe, my child," El Jefe added.

The line went dead.

"Well," Hayes said, "we learn something new every day, I expect."

"I just learned to never let a utility repairman in my house ever again," Minette said with irritation in her tone.

"And I learned to carry bananas when dealing with giant lizards." Zack grinned at Hayes.

"I put more money in the petty cash jar on the dining room table," Hayes told Zack. "Buy Andy some more eats."

"Already did," Zack chuckled. "Except I forgot bananas. On my way now to get some. I'll phone you later."

"Watch your back," Hayes advised.

"You do the same."

"Lassiter's father is a P.I.?" Minette asked, curious.

"Oh, yes. And that's a long and interesting story that I heard from one of our DEA agents who had dealings with him," Hayes replied. "Lassiter worked for Houston P.D. until he was almost killed in a shootout. He was left with injuries that he thought wouldn't let him return to the job he had, so he opened a detective agency and staffed it with some of his former colleagues on the force."

"My, my."

"He made his reputation by taking on cases no other detective agency would touch. After a few years, he was the first name people thought of when they were pursuing dangerous people. He was involved, peripherally, in the bust of a very nasty international child pornography ring some years ago."

"I remember reading about that. One of the principles in the case wrote a bestselling novel about it. Cord Romero's wife, as I recall."

He chuckled. "Yes. Cord was a legend in merc circles. He worked with some of our local soldiers of fortune on cases until he and his wife had kids. He keeps a lower profile now. I understand he gave up the demolition work he specialized in."

She shivered. "I can imagine that his wife would have locked him in a room without a key if he'd even mentioned going back to it."

"No doubt."

"Which still leaves us with the question of why my father's adversary is sending hit men after you," she said. "I don't think it's because you know that a crooked mayor was mixed up in drug smuggling." She frowned. "Hayes, do you remember seeing anybody else when that drug bust went down?"

He hesitated. "Not really. Things were pretty confused. I was out there with two DEA agents, a couple of my deputies, a Texas Ranger and some assorted local law. It was at night, too, which didn't help."

"Who were the DEA agents?"

He thought back to the hectic arrests. "One of them was Rodrigo Ramirez," he recalled. "He married Jason Pendleton's stepsister, Glory, who now works as a part-time district court prosecutor on district attorney Blake Kemp's staff."

"And the other one?"

The frown deepened. "Now that's a good question. I don't remember actually being introduced to him. He came with Rodrigo."

"You could call Rodrigo and ask if he remembers who it was."

"I guess I could." He smiled at her and pulled out his cell phone. "Maybe his memory is better than mine."

But Rodrigo didn't remember, either.

"Now that's very odd," Rodrigo said in his faintly accented tones. "I remember the bust, I remember being there. But I don't remember the agent who came with me. He wasn't one of our regulars, like Sarina Lane or even Alexander Cobb," he added, naming his former partner and the local head of the DEA office.

"It would be on the arrest report, I imagine," Hayes said. "I'll pull up the file. Don't worry about it. How's that new son?"

Rodrigo chuckled. "Glory and I are over the moon. He's the

most fascinating little miracle you ever saw. You should come and visit."

"Time would be a wonderful thing," Hayes sighed.

"I heard about the shooting," Rodrigo said, solemn now. "We know who hired the hit man. We've got people working on an arrest."

"Me, too," Hayes said, "but this is going to be a long, slow process. In the meantime, I'm making some very unlikely allies," he chuckled.

"Like your former nemesis, Miss Raynor?" Rodrigo asked, tongue-in-cheek. "We heard you were staying with her."

Hayes looked at Minette with warm affection. "My former nemesis turns out to be the best thing that ever happened to me," he said softly, watching Minette color prettily. He drew her to him and looked down into her eyes. "We're not enemies any longer."

"Glad to hear it. About this other unlikely ally..." Rodrigo continued.

Hayes blinked. "Okay, now, that's top secret."

"If you say so." Rodrigo's deep voice was amused. "Consider it an open secret in our bureau, however. You're walking a very thin line there, Sheriff."

"I know. The problem is, he has access to information that I don't."

"Miss Raynor's house is bugged," came the droll reply.

"Crackers and milk, do you know everything?" Hayes burst out.

"Not everything. I still don't understand the unified field theory that Einstein was working on, or why bears hibernate or..."

"I get the picture."

"Who put the bugs in, and why are they still there?" Rodrigo persisted.

Hayes sighed. "We're sort of doing a back-scratching thing."

"You and the biggest drug lord in northern Mexico, you mean."

"He's one of the biggest, and not the worst by a long shot. The worst is his archenemy, who seems to be planning a kidnapping."

"With you as its object?"

"Not me. Minette."

Rodrigo was quiet. "Just a minute. I'll call you back."

He hung up. A minute later, Hayes's cell phone rang.

"This is a secure line," Rodrigo said. "Why is El Ladrón after your host?"

Hayes glanced at Minette, who looked sad and embarrassed. "Because her father is El Jefe."

"Oh, good God!" Rodrigo burst out.

"Yes. It's complicating things. She didn't know until he moved in behind Cy Parks's property a little while ago and started stocking it with his purebred racehorses. He knows Minette's in danger, and he's got his people protecting her."

"Along with some of Cy Parks's people, your people and, rumor has it, the police chief of Jacobsville."

"That would be largely correct."

Rodrigo sighed. "One night we'll read about a massive shootout in the dark when one side mistakes the other for the enemy."

"God forbid!" Hayes exclaimed.

"I won't add to the problem by putting any of my people in the field," Rodrigo promised. "But this could get complicated very quickly, especially if El Ladrón's agents manage to get their hands on Miss Raynor. He has a reputation for dealing very harshly with prisoners, and he has no respect whatsoever for human life. He kills women and children as handily as he kills men."

"Even the late, great and unlamented Lopez drew a line at killing children," Hayes recalled.

"His only saving grace, and not much of one at that. But he died and the Fuentes brothers took over. Now it's El Ladrón running the cartel, and his cousin Charro Mendez who just became mayor of Cotillo through assassination. They'll take over the drug trade in northern Mexico if they can. Nature does abhor a vacuum."

"I'd like to take a vacuum to every drug dealer in Texas and dump them all in the deepest part of the ocean," Hayes said.

"I don't blame you. So would I." Rodrigo hesitated. "Can you have a look at those logs and see if you can dig out the name of the DEA agent who was with me? I've got babysitting duties today while Glory's taking a deposition," he chuckled.

"Not a problem."

"Odd that I wouldn't remember who it was," Rodrigo added. "It must have been an agent from one of the satellite offices. I know the people I worked with in Houston, and I know most of the agents in San Antonio."

"It was a hectic night," Hayes said. "I wouldn't worry about it."

"I have to." Rodrigo was somber. "We know we've got a high-level mole in our organization. We don't know who he is, or where he is."

"I doubt very seriously that he'd be somebody in a satellite office," Hayes commented. "It would need to be someone with access to sensitive information."

"Every office has a computer, and they all contain high-level data," Rodrigo told him. "But I do agree that it's unlikely we'd have some low-level person dealing with a drug lord. We found one deep-cover agent working with the Zetas. He was fired, and prosecuted. But we learned that he wasn't the only one. We've never been able to uncover the remaining mole."

"Send Cobb after him," Hayes chuckled. "That man has a talent for digging."

"Don't remind me," Rodrigo replied. "I had a couple of run-ins with Cobb myself before I knew him well."

"You might ask him if he has any ideas."

"If he did, he wouldn't share them. He plays his cards very close to his chest. If you find out anything, let me know, will you? But don't talk on an open line. I'll call you back on a secure one, as I did this time."

"Will do. Take care."

"You, too."

Hayes glanced at Minette. "I need to check some records. Want to come down to the office with me?"

She smiled. "I'll get my jacket."

12

They stopped by Barbara's Café for lunch. Barbara grinned broadly when they walked in. "Nice to see you out and about again, Hayes," she told him.

"It's nice to be out," he replied.

"You look a little glum," Barbara noted.

"She won't let me drive," he grumbled, wrinkling his nose at Minette, who grinned.

"Dr. Coltrain won't let you drive," she corrected. "I'm just his mouthpiece."

He chuckled. So did Barbara.

"I made a nice lemon cake for dessert today," Barbara said as she handed them the lunch menu.

"My favorite," Hayes replied.

She grinned. "And homemade rolls with butter."

"Now, I've been having those nightly," he mused with a warm glance at Minette. "She's an incredible cook."

"Don't you put me out of business," Barbara chuckled again, wagging a finger at Minette.

"No worries, I'm just a temporary setback," she said with a grin.

"Oh, I'm not so sure of that," Hayes mused, and he looked at her long enough to make her blush.

They had a tasty lunch and then drove over to Hayes's office. Zack was rummaging through a drawer, muttering when they arrived.

"What can't you find?" Hayes asked.

"The stapler," Zack sighed. "It's the one most essential piece of equipment in this whole office, and the one thing I can never lay my hands on! It's got legs. It walks!"

Hayes gave him a long-suffering look. He reached into the "in" tray, lifted the top sheet of paper and uncovered the stapler. "I do that to keep Yancy from carrying it off. He never brings it back."

Zack laughed. "Okay. Now I know how to hide it, too. Thanks. What are you doing here today?"

"Looking for the name of a DEA agent who showed up at the drug bust, the one where the new mayor of Cotillo was holding a gun on me. I disarmed him and arrested him. But he got out on bond and went over the border."

"Oh. That one." Zack gave him a long look. "I had the same thought about that bust, so I pulled up the file."

His expression wasn't comforting. "And?" Hayes prompted.

"It's not there."

"What?" Hayes sat down at the desk, pulled up his confidential files and tried to open the one dealing with the successful drug bust.

"It's empty," he said, stunned.

"Yes. Erased, unless I miss my guess," Zack said grimly. "I was going to call you after lunch."

"Who had access here?" Minette asked.

"All the deputies," Hayes said.

"All the deputies, the investigator, the clerk and the sheriff."

"The clerk?" Minette pounced on the one person out of the loop. "Don't you have a new one here, because the last one got sick?"

Hayes and Zack exchanged glances.

"Yes, but she's related to John Hulsey," Hayes pointed out. "He's one of our more prominent attorneys. He gave her a wonderful reference."

Minette just stared at him.

Hayes flipped open his phone, pulled up a list of attorneys and called John.

"Hi, Hayes, you getting better?" John asked.

"Somewhat. Listen, John, that reference you gave your niece…"

"My what?" John asked blankly.

"Your niece, Beverly Sands…"

"I have a nephew named Charles and a niece named Anthea. Nobody named Beverly…"

"She gave you as a reference," Hayes said, feeling stupid, "and presented me with a letter, written on your letterhead stationery with what I could have sworn was your signature."

"Should have called me, Hayes," John said gently.

"Yes. Yes, I should have," Hayes said heavily. "Good Lord, I feel stupid!"

"We all make mistakes," John said. "But you should fire her."

"If I ever see her again, I swear I'll not only fire her, I'll have her up for fraud," Hayes muttered. "Thanks, John."

He hung up. He let out a long breath. "Of all the dumb, idiotic things to do. Me, of all people!" he exclaimed. "I always check people out. But she seemed so naive and trusting. So honest."

"She had me fooled, too," Zack confessed. "I liked her. She made coffee." He glanced at Minette and laughed self-consciously. "Listen, I love to drink it but I can't make it. It was a selling point in her favor."

"Where is she, would be my next question," Hayes said grimly.

"She didn't show up for work this morning," Zack replied. "Called in sick." His eyes narrowed. He went over to the communications desk. "Hey, Bob, will you run over to Beverly Sands's house—" he paused, looking at the address she'd given on her application "—24 Oak Street, and see if you can get her to the door? That's right. Yes. Thanks. Let me know. Okay.

"I sent Bob," Zack said. "He'll find her."

But Bob didn't find her. And, in fact, 24 Oak Street was the address of a small coffee shop that had opened just recently. No Beverly Sands there. Despite the size of Jacobsville, even the sheriff didn't know the street address of every single house or business in it. But the mistake was painful.

"Why didn't I check that address?" Hayes asked, aghast, when Zack told him. "I'm the sheriff!"

"You're not perfect," Minette replied gently. "Jacobsville is a small town. People trust each other."

"Yes, but I know better."

"I got pulled in by her, too, boss," Zack reminded him.

"So, now what?" Minette asked.

"Do we have fingerprints, at least?" Hayes asked.

"I was about to do that when we got mixed up with El Jefe and things heated up in the investigation," Zack sighed. "I'd put it off as one of those things that wasn't absolutely essential to be done in a rush…"

Hayes threw up his hands. "Crackers and milk!" he cursed.

"Doesn't Eb Scott have some wild-eyed, unbelievably skilled computer tech in his employ?" Minette asked the men.

They looked at her.

"Information can't be completely erased unless the whole drive is reformatted, and yours obviously hasn't been. Right?"

Hayes dug for his cell phone again.

By late evening, the computer tech was starting to re-create the lost file. It was taking time, because the information was fragmented. But the young man was certain he could pull it up. It was late, though, and he told the others they might as well go home.

So, Hayes went back home with Minette and walked up on a very odd gathering in her backyard.

"What in the world is going on?" Minette exclaimed when she and Hayes got to the back porch.

Four men were facing each other. Three of them were yelling. They stopped at the sound of her voice. Suddenly they looked very sheepish.

"Uh, hi," one of the men said slowly. He attempted a smile.

"Who are you guys?" Minette wanted to know.

"Good question," Hayes said, and he looked every inch a lawman.

"That's what we're sorting out. Trying to sort out," the one who'd spoken said. "Okay, that's one of El Jefe's men over there."

He indicated a taciturn man with dark hair and eyes. "That's one of Sheriff Carson's volunteer deputies, I think." He indicated a man that Hayes recognized as a part-timer. "I'm sort of working for Cash Grier," the spokesman added with a self-conscious chuckle. "And nobody can get *him*—" he indicated a tall, cold-eyed man with long, black unbound hair down to his waist "—to say who he is or even who he works for."

"I don't have to say," the man replied haughtily. "I'm a tourist. I was looking around for points of interest and I got lost."

"In the middle of the night on private property?" Hayes pointed out.

The man, wearing jeans, shrugged and looked around. "I don't see a single sign identifying this as private property."

"Who are you?" Hayes persisted icily.

The tall man looked directly into his eyes. "Carson."

"I'm Carson," Hayes shot back.

"My name is Carson, too," the man replied. "That's all I'm telling you."

"Wait," the first man who spoke broke in, "I know you. You're the guy who went with Emilio Machado to South America to take back his country. You work for Cy Parks when you're not off somewhere with Eb Scott's group."

The man named Carson shrugged. "Maybe I do. Maybe I don't. Maybe I'm just a lost tourist."

"The points of interest are that way," Hayes said, pointing toward the road that led to Jacobsville. "Start walking."

"Unfriendly place," the tall man huffed. "No wonder it's so small."

"You just go back and tell Cy Parks we have enough madmen out here running into each other. We don't need any more cluttering up the landscape. And thank him," Hayes added reluctantly.

"Boss sent me here to do a job," Carson replied. He folded his arms and stared belligerently at the other men. "Not leaving until I've done it." He looked at Hayes, daring him to do anything about it.

"Son of a..." Hayes started.

"Now, Hayes," Minette said gently as he took a step toward the other man. "More people, less problem."

"Sure, unless they shoot each other!" Hayes exclaimed.

"I'm not shooting anybody," the man named Carson replied curtly. "I don't carry a gun."

"What, you talk people to death, do you?" the first man scoffed.

Carson shifted his weight. "Don't need to talk."

Hayes was noting something the others seemed to have missed: a huge bowie knife in a sheath at a strange angle on the tall man's belt.

"That's an illegal weapon," Hayes pointed out, indicating the knife. "I could have you arrested just for carrying it."

"I have a permit."

Hayes glared. "A knife permit? Who the hell gave you that?"

"Cash Grier," Carson replied. He didn't smile, but he looked so smug that Hayes wished he was in some condition to slug that expression off his smooth face.

"I don't believe it," Hayes said.

"Don't care," Carson replied. "Arrest me if you want. I'll prove it in court." He did smile then, coldly. "My first cousin is married to the senior U.S. senator from South Dakota," he added.

It was a powerful threat. The gentleman in question was well-known in the media for his bad temper and his great concern for Native people.

"Well, my second cousin works security for a bank in San Antonio," Hayes shot back.

Minette barely smothered a giggle.

"Listen, we're all out here for the same reason, to protect Miss Raynor," the first man interjected. "Why don't we just divide the property up into four sectors and each take one to patrol?"

"You should run for public office," Carson told the man. He pointed toward Hayes. "Against him."

"Not me," the man chuckled. "I know this county. Trust me, he's unbeatable unless he barbecues a tourist over an open fire."

The man named Carson, posing as a tourist, pursed his chiseled lips. "I would taste terrible," he assured Hayes.

It broke the ice. Hayes burst out laughing.

"Oh, hell, get out of here," he chuckled. "And could you guys please stop arguing and get back to work?" Hayes asked. "We're never going to keep this place secure at this rate."

"Not our fault, really," the spokesman apologized. "The tourist there——" he indicated the man named Carson "——tackled him——" he pointed to El Jefe's man "——and things went downhill from there."

"I was trying to protect her." The drug lord's man indicated Minette.

"Me, too," Carson returned. "You looked like a drug dealer to me," he added, tongue-in-cheek.

"Maybe I am and maybe I'm not," El Jefe's man snorted. "You got a warrant?"

Carson actually smiled at him. The smile made the man back up a step.

"I'm very grateful, for all the help," Minette added. "But coming out in the open isn't going to help matters."

"She does have a point," the spokesman said to the other three. "Shall we get back to work, gentlemen?"

"A sound idea," El Jefe's man said, and the other man agreed. Carson didn't speak. He pointed out the sector he claimed and walked off toward it.

Minette and Hayes left them to it.

"Well, I do feel safer," Minette commented on the way into the house. "It was nice of my...father...to watch out for me. And Cy Parks and Cash Grier and you," she added, so that she didn't sound ungrateful.

"And me," Hayes said. He grinned at her, linked his fingers with hers and walked her into the house.

By morning, the computer whiz had found something. He called Hayes but was unwilling to give out the information even on what seemed like a secure line.

"Can you meet me at your office?" he asked Hayes.

"Sure. I'll be right over."

Minette drove, against Hayes's wishes. "I'm much better," he reminded her with a grimace. "I can drive, at least."

"You can undo all the recuperation, too, Hayes," Minette argued. "It won't be much longer before you're back at work. Dr. Coltrain said you're making great progress."

"I'm impatient," he said, glancing out at the passing scenery. "I'm not used to inactivity." He glanced at her and smiled. "Not that I haven't enjoyed watching movies and doing stuff with the kids. And with you. I've enjoyed the food and the company very much."

She flushed and laughed. "Thanks. I've...we've...enjoyed the company, too. None of us is used to having a man around the house."

He pursed his lips. "Do you think you could get used to having a man around the house?" he began.

She caught her breath. She was so busy staring at Hayes that she didn't notice the sudden acceleration of two pickup trucks behind them.

Hayes looked up and started to say something, but before he could even get the words out, one of the trucks rammed the left front fender and forced the truck off the road. It barely escaped a roll. When it came to a stop, before Hayes could get his pistol out of the holster, two men with automatic weapons pointed at his head prevented any thought of resistance.

"So, Miss Raynor," one of the small men said with a flash of white teeth, "someone we work for would like to meet you."

"Over my dead body," Hayes began.

The pistol was cocked. The man looking at him didn't seem angry or even disturbed. "You lived despite our boss's best efforts, Sheriff. If you wish to stay alive even for a day longer, resistance would be quite unwise."

"Come with us," the man near him said, taking Minette roughly by the arm. But when Hayes stepped toward him, defying the man with the pistol, he eased his grip. He spoke to the other man in a language that wasn't Spanish. They grimaced, looked at their prisoners and the other man nodded irritably.

"Let's go," the older of the two men said.

They separated the prisoners. Hayes was bound and placed in one truck, Minette in the other.

Minette had a pretty good idea of what was going to happen

to her. She hoped that Lassiter had been monitoring the phone, and that he'd bugged her truck, as well. If he had, there was just a glimmer of hope that she and Hayes wouldn't be found lying in a ditch in some unspeakable condition. If not...well, everybody died at some point, she supposed. She had to hope and pray that it wasn't Hayes's time, or her time. Not just yet.

Much later, they were blindfolded and placed in the backseat of a powerful, expensive SUV and driven somewhere across the border at night.

Hayes was chomping at the bit, embarrassed and furious that he hadn't been paying attention to their surroundings, that he'd let this happen. He knew that Minette was the target of the kidnapping, knew who was behind it, too. He had to hope that their friends were somewhere watching, waiting, in a position to do something to get them out of this mess that he'd helped land them in.

He couldn't move. He was bound and gagged and blindfolded. He was aware that they'd put Minette in the backseat with him, but he couldn't communicate with her. They'd taken his cell phone and smashed it before the prisoners were transferred into the SUV. His hands were cuffed, with his own damned hand-cuffs, and the pain was pretty bad. At least they hadn't locked his hands behind him, which would have potentially undone all the uncomfortable physical therapy he'd been having for weeks in an attempt to stop the muscles from atrophying. He still wasn't recovered from the gunshot wound that this very group of bad guys had given him in the first place. He was furious. But he had to keep his head, if he was going to help Minette escape being killed. He hoped, he prayed, there was a way to do that.

* * *

It was dark and cold in the small house they were taken to. Hayes had been keeping track of time while they were driving, and he guessed that they were being transported across the border to Cotillo. These men belonged to one of two rival factions trying to gain sole ownership of the small Mexican state, what was left of the Fuentes crime family, now headed by El Ladrón, and the forces of El Jefe. It was a prime location, with mountains for cover and easy and quick access to the United States, with no border patrol or other federal law enforcement nearby. Presumably the winner would face off against the Zetas or some other powerful narcotics cartel in a bid for even more territory. It never seemed to end.

The house was dark. Apparently it had no electricity, because Hayes heard a match strike and then a radiant glow penetrated even the darkness of the blindfold he was wearing.

The blindfold was removed. He looked first for Minette. She was standing beside him, still bound. Her expression was one of quiet resignation. Her blindfold, also, had been removed. They looked at each other with visible pain, knowing that it might be the last time.

"Put them over there," the man who'd kidnapped them said, indicating two cane-bottomed chairs near a window.

Hayes protested when the man undid his cuffs and started to pull his arms behind him.

"Wait." Their captor pursed his lips. He smiled haughtily. "The sheriff's wound is troubling him, no?" he chuckled. "Tie his hands in front of him and bind them to his ankles," he told one of his henchmen. "That way, if he decides to act, he will inflict his own punishment."

Minette wasn't accorded the same courtesy. Her wrists were tied together behind the chair, although they made no attempt to bind her feet. In her mind, she was going over possibilities, ways to escape, ways to save Hayes.

He was doing the same, but with little hope. He cursed his injury, which was nowhere near healed. Even when it did heal, he was going to have to deal with months of rehab and even after a year, there would still be some loss of mobility and function in the shoulder where the bullet had penetrated.

He cursed these drug traffickers, cursed his own stupidity in letting himself be captured, letting her be captured. Whatever they did to him, please, God, spare her!

"Now, we wait," their captor said with a chuckle. "You will be honored. My boss himself, Charro Mendez, is coming to deal with the two of you. He is the mayor of Cotillo, but also the second cousin of Pedro Mendez, the leader of our drug cartel." He smiled coldly. "Charro has told us to treat you with great care and respect. He does not want a hair on your head to be harmed." He moved to Minette and leaned close. "He is bringing with him a man who is expert with camcorders," he whispered, loud enough that Hayes could also hear him. He smiled from ear to ear. "So that we can record for your papa all the things that we plan to do to you."

The insinuation made Minette sick to her stomach. The kidnapping had been terrifying. But the look in that little weasel's eyes was so explicit that she wished they'd just shot her in the first place and put her out of her misery. But of course, that wasn't the plan at all. They wanted her father, the father she'd

never known, to see her torment and know that he was responsible for it.

Minette raised her chin. She didn't smile, or blanche, or
flinch. "My father," she said quietly, "will hang your employer
up by his thumbs and cut him to pieces."

"Yes, my lady, but you will be long dead if that ever happens,"
he chuckled, standing erect. He looked at her with malicious
pleasure. "I will ask for the privilege of having you first, for the
benefit of the cameras."

She stared into his eyes, aware that Hayes was muttering
curses nonstop beside her. "Bring weapons," she advised softly.

The man thought that was hilarious. "I like a woman with
spirit," he chuckled again. He turned away and tossed orders to
his men. "Pepito, you keep watch. Don't talk to them, okay?"
he said in Spanish.

"No, of course not," the very young man agreed. He stuck his
pistol in his belt. "I will be most careful."

"And no toying with the woman," he added coldly. "You understand?"

"She is too pale for me," the boy laughed, but the laughter was
hollow. He seemed very nervous.

"Yes, you like your girls big and round, like your wife, yes?
You remember your wife and children, Pepito," he added softly,
and the young man shifted nervously. "We will not be long.
Charro has said that he will come later today." He gestured the
other two men toward the door, speaking to them again in that
language Minette couldn't comprehend.

The door closed behind them.

"God, I'm sorry, Minette. I'm so sorry!" Hayes said heavily.
"This is all my fault."

"No. I should have watched where I was going. I'm sorry," she replied. She stared at him hungrily. "We were too careless." She looked at the boy, Pepito. "If you have one ounce of mercy in you, please kill me."

"Minette!" Hayes groaned.

Pepito sighed. "Señorita," he said gently, "we are none of us free to do anything except what our boss tells us. I have a wife and two little girls," he added, his face drawn. "They are kept in Cotillo, in a small house, in a village where there are armed guards. If I do anything that the boss does not like, they will be tortured and killed."

"Dear God!" Minette exclaimed, horrified.

"It is the way they control us," Pepito continued in a dull, heavy tone. "My brother was one of the head men in our organization. He works for Charro Mendez, who is our boss. My brother brought me into this. I would make lots of money, he said. So I was tempted and I agreed." He glanced around the bare room. "My brother was killed by Mendez for losing a shipment of cocaine. So I sold my soul to the devil." He crossed himself. "I am not even allowed to go to mass or to confession. Charro Mendez is afraid I would tell a priest things that might be discovered."

Minette had always assumed that people got into the business of drug dealing because they liked the danger and the wealth. She'd interviewed at least two men who told her they would never give up the trade because it paid so well. But this was a very different story.

"Are your parents alive?" she asked the boy.

"Only my mother," he replied. "My father protested what my brother was doing, when he persuaded me to join him. My brother had my father...killed, before he himself was killed."

"Monstrous!" Hayes said curtly.

"Yes. Monstrous. They hanged my poor father, right in our village, as a warning." He swallowed. "So I am sorry for your trouble," he added. "But I cannot help you. To do so would be to forfeit the lives of my wife and our children."

"I understand," Minette said with true sorrow.

"Your boss should be brought up on federal charges and put away for life," Hayes said with cold contempt.

"Chance would be a fine thing, yes?" the boy replied. "He has been arrested many times. But even people in law enforcement can be bribed. I have heard of a man who works for your DEA. He has been on the boss's payroll for many years."

"Who?" Hayes asked.

"Ah, that I do not know. And even if I did know, telling would get my family killed."

"Not if we could get them out of Mexico," Minette was thinking out loud.

"That is a fairy tale. Charro, or worse, his cousin Pedro Mendez, can hire assassins to find me even in *Los Estados Unidos,*" he pointed out. He looked at Hayes. "As the sheriff can attest, yes?"

"Well, El Ladrón's assassin missed, didn't he?" Hayes asked belligerently.

Pepito sighed. "Yes, he did, and he was killed for it." He winced. "They say another one was hired, but since you are here, his services will not be needed." The allusion wasn't lost on Hayes or Minette.

"They mean to kill us both?" Minette asked.

Pepito shrugged. "I am just a mule," he said, using the slang for a drug transporter. "I know nothing of the boss's plans except what you have heard earlier. But I think they mean to kill both of you. Miss Raynor will die to torment her father, but you—" he indicated Hayes "—will be killed because you are with her, and also because you humiliated Charro by arresting him in your country. It would be too dangerous to permit you to escape."

Escape. Minette thought of it, hungered for it. The ordeal that was facing her would be infinitely worse than anything she'd endured in her life. She thought of Shane and Julie and Great-Aunt Sarah. She thought of her newspaper, her home. She'd taken safety and family for granted. If she got out of this alive, she promised herself, she'd never take anything for granted again.

"Well," she said after a minute, glancing at Pepito, "I think Hayes should read you your rights."

Pepito blinked. "Señorita?"

"Your rights," she emphasized. "You know, so that you're aware of what they are before he puts you in jail."

Pepito laughed. "Lady, you and the sheriff are our captives in Mexico, where neither of you has any powers of arrest or even escape."

Minette looked at Hayes with a faint grin. "Go on," she said. "Do your duty."

He smiled, too, and shook his head. "Pepito, you have the right to remain silent," he began. "Anything you say can and will be held against you in a court of law...."

Minette burst into laughter at the sheer audacity of the statement.

13

"What do you mean, you lost them?" El Jefe raged at his man.

The man winced. "They were going to the sheriff's office. He called me—" he indicated Lassiter "—and said to follow them. But my damned truck wouldn't start," he said furiously. "Of all the times...and I just had it in the shop!"

"So I told Marist to go instead," Lassiter told the boss. "He was going to pick them up at the sheriff's department and follow them. But they didn't show up in the time he figured it would take for them to get there, so he backtracked and found Minette's truck on the side of the road."

El Jefe wiped his face with a spotless white handkerchief. "My daughter, in the hands of that...barbarian," he groaned. "You know what will be done to her!" he raged.

They did. They were silent. It was a failing that struck them to the bone.

"We must get her back, we must do something!" El Jefe raged again.

The front door opened. A tall man walked in. He had long hair down to his waist, black as night, silky and thick. He approached El Jefe without a second's hesitation.

"I need to borrow a few things," he said.

Muffled groans accompanied the entrance of two men who looked as if they'd been dragged behind a pickup truck for a mile.

"He overpowered us...!" one of them raged.

"I will shoot you!" the other one threatened and came close.

The intruder fell into a balanced, leisurely stance. "Be my guest."

"Enough!" El Jefe commanded. He waved his bruised men away. He turned back to the intruder, who straightened up, oblivious to the angry men nearby.

El Jefe gaped at him. "Who the hell are you? Borrow a few things? My daughter has just been kidnapped...!"

The newcomer held up a hand. "Turn the page, I've read that one," he said. "I know where she is. I need a helicopter, a good radio, a few hand grenades and him." He pointed to the man standing beside El Jefe.

"Him?" El Jefe stared at the stocky, impassive man beside him. "Ruy? What for?"

Carson pursed his lips and grinned. "He's going to sell you out to El Ladrón."

"El Ladrón has my daughter, he doesn't need me!"

"Wait." Carson smiled. "I have a plan. Just listen."

El Jefe groaned. His distress was evident.

Lassiter's black eyes twinkled. "I'd hear him out, if I were you," he advised.

Carson's eyebrows arched. "Do I know you?"

Lassiter chuckled. "No," he replied. "But I know about you. Word is," he drawled, "that you were assigned to take care of a man who tortured a female journalist when Emilio Machado retook Barrera in South America. You helped a mercenary named Rourke dispose of him, I believe?"

"I might have," Carson replied coolly.

"And?" El Jefe prompted Lassiter, curious.

"I believe they found him later, distributed among at least three crocodiles."

Carson's expression didn't change. "Poor crocodiles were starving," he commented. "I felt sorry for them."

El Jefe smiled. "In that case," he said, "it will be my pleasure to put my finest helicopter in your hands, complete with pilot."

Carson smiled back. "Thank you."

"Just save my daughter," he replied. "Please."

"I'll do my best," Carson assured him.

There was a little trouble at the border. DEA agent Rodrigo Ramirez, along with senior FBI agent Garon Grier, were arguing with a border patrol agent who was determined not to let them through the checkpoint that led across the border with Villa Montaña, the state where Cotillo was the capital.

"Listen," Ramirez said, moving a step closer, "this is official government business. There's been a kidnapping."

The agent shrugged. "No surprise there. Cotillo is famous for harboring captured Americans for ransom."

"We need to get through to speak to the mayor."

"Border's closed. Sorry." The man smiled coldly, daring them to do anything about it.

They moved away a few steps. "Hardball?" Grier asked Ramirez.

"Definitely hardball." He pulled out his cell phone and started making calls. After the fourth one, Ramirez walked back to the border agent and handed him the telephone.

"What do you want me to do with this?"

"Speak to the person on the other end of the line, of course," Ramirez replied.

The border agent put the phone to his ear. He gasped, looked at Ramirez and went pale. "Oh, yes, sir," he said in Spanish. "Yes, definitely. Yes, I am sorry. I did not realize...no, no, sir, of course, I will do it immediately. Yes, sir. Yes! And, sir, congratulations on your great victory.... Yes, sir, at once!" He closed the phone. He handed it back to Ramirez. He was very pale. "You may go at once, *señores,* and many apologies for this delay! If I may be of any service," he added hopefully.

Ramirez looked as if he might suggest something patently off-color. Grier bumped shoulders with him.

"Don't rock the boat," he advised under his breath.

Ramirez gave him a harsh look. "Spoilsport."

They got back into the bucar, the bureau car that Grier had taken for the trip, and passed across the border into Villa Montaña while the Mexican border guard stood at attention and saluted.

Pepito was getting nervous. He was also hungry. He went into the kitchen and fixed himself a sandwich. There was no fresh bread. He missed his wife's tortillas, so lovingly filled with good fresh beef and fine European cheese, not to mention imported coffee that he was given as part of his perks for the work he did. Those things were a luxury, but he had become used to having them with his new job. It would be difficult to go back to the old days of planting crops that were always at the mercy of the weather, to carving out a tiny living on the land which never fed the empty bellies of his growing children.

There was, of course, the horrible jobs he had to witness and sometimes help with. Like what was going to be done to that brave little American woman in the next room. It turned him inside out to see such tortures as his boss inflicted for betrayal. Just recently several men who opposed his authority in Cotillo had been mercilessly tortured and then hanged on the side of the road. He wanted everyone to know that he, and not El Jefe's bunch, held power here.

Not two days later, a third smaller cartel had performed a similar act by beheading four men who belonged to El Ladrón's camp. It never seemed to end. Somewhere in the mix was El Jefe, on the sidelines, watching. Pepito was certain that he, El Jefe, would wait until one faction or the other was victorious. Then, while the victors were weakened by the cost of their victory, El Jefe would strike and take over the state. It was the way of drug politics.

Pepito told himself that he would not mind working for El Jefe. At least the man was religious and provided a chapel and a priest for his workers.

He wandered back into the living room where the sheriff and the woman were speaking in whispers.

They stopped talking when he approached.

Minette searched his face. "Pepito—excuse me, may I call you that?" she added respectfully.

Pepito had been called many things in his young life. But it was touching to be addressed with such care by a woman like that, who had wealth and power in her country. "Yes, of course," he stammered.

"Pepito, I have been here for many hours and I need, I have to—" She broke off and lowered her eyes, seemingly embarrassed. "Is there a bathroom?"

He looked hunted. "Señorita, this is a poor place. We have no, how you say, indoor plumbing here. Only the finest families in Cotillo have bathrooms." He hesitated. She did look desperate. "There is a—how you say in English?—an outhouse," he said finally.

"Could I..." She indicated her tied hands.

He hesitated. Surely she wouldn't try to escape. She was thin and slender and worn down by her capture. They would kill him if she got away. But she had to go to the bathroom, such was obvious. They might kill him if she soiled herself and was not presentable when the men came to, well, to kill her.

"I can't wait much longer. I'm so sorry," she said huskily. "Please?"

He could never resist a woman's pleas. "Of course," he said after a minute. He laid the heavy AK-47 across a table and helped her stand up. "Come with me, *señorita*."

Hayes felt his heart jump as the gun was placed almost within reach of his hands. If only he could get them free, even for a few seconds! But while he was tormenting himself with possibilities, Pepito casually picked up the rifle and escorted Minette out the door.

That made it worse, because Hayes couldn't see what was going on. What if that little worm decided that he wanted Minette before his boss got back? What if...

He swallowed, hard. He was completely helpless. No cell

phone, no gun, no knife, nothing to get him out of this damned predicament. He cursed his own idiocy for letting them be kidnapped in the first place. But there was nothing he could do about their situation. He was going to have to sit here and watch Minette die. Unless he could come up with a plan, something, anything, that would get him free of his bonds!

While Hayes tormented himself, Minette walked toward the outhouse, her posture slumped, her head down.

She stopped at a rude, tall, narrow shack which smelled of terrible things. She saw white powder under it in back and realized that quicklime was used as a sanitation measure to control the odor and break down the byproducts of human elimination. She shivered delicately as she noted that quicklime was also used to help bodies decompose faster. There were two bags of it leaning up against the outhouse. For her and Hayes, afterward? she wondered.

She swallowed her fear. She paused at the door and looked at Pepito pleadingly. "I can't...well, I can't do what I have to do with my hands tied..."

"Señorita, I cannot release you," Pepito said sadly. "I am most sorry, but if you were to manage to escape, my wife and children will surely die."

"I understand." She sighed. She opened the door with her hands bound and pulled it closed behind her, grimacing as she prayed that rattlesnakes hadn't denned up under the structure. It was almost winter, she reminded herself, and cold even in northern Mexico. Surely snakes would be hibernating?

She had to go. She maneuvered her jeans down enough to allow her to use the foul-smelling toilet. She was going to die, she knew it. Hayes was bound and there was no way to free him. He would die, too.

No! There had to be a way, something she could do, a way to save him! She looked around desperately. There was a magazine with explicit photographs of women, crumpled and lying on the ground. There was, incredibly enough, toilet tissue on a roll dispenser. The dispenser was made of gold and had jewels embedded in it. She had to force herself not to laugh at the irony of the valuable item in a place like this. But then, she noted that some of the jewels looked like diamonds...

"You must hurry, *señorita,*" Pepito urged at the door. "They will return soon. You must not be seen missing from the house!"

"I'm almost through!" she called back.

She fumbled the toilet tissue out of the holder. She turned the cylinder in her hands and began to rub it against the nylon cord with which she was bound. Thank God it wasn't the handcuffs Hayes was wearing or this would never have worked! She moved the cylinder feverishly, delighted when she saw it quickly fraying the nylon. Those stones were really diamonds, and they would cut through anything! She only needed to get one...hand...free! There!

She was free! She had the use of both hands now. Pepito was young and strong, but she had the element of surprise on her side. And she was trained in martial arts. She wasn't expert, but she knew enough to, hopefully, get the advantage of an unsuspecting opponent. She felt a brief sorrow for his family, but Hayes was her first, her only concern. She had to save Hayes. And she was going to.

She went over the scenario in her mind. How she would approach him, what she would do. Her heart raced like mad. Her breathing was so quick she felt as if she was smothering. Her mouth was dry, her hands clammy. She pulled up her jeans.

"Señorita!"

"Just another minute, please, I can't help it…something I ate," she pleaded.

"Oh. I see. Okay. But hurry."

"I will."

She gripped the jeweled toilet-roll holder in her hand. Through the gaping crack in the door, she saw Pepito staring toward the horizon.

Okay, girl, she told herself. *Now or never.*

She threw open the door so hard that it knocked Pepito down. Grasping her advantage, she jumped over him, retrieved the AK-47 and held it on him.

"Get up," she said in a tone that threatened death.

"Señorita, please, do not kill me! My family…!"

"You should have thought of your family before you got into this damned racket," she raged at him. Her dark eyes were blazing with anger and indignation. "Get going!"

She gestured toward the house with the barrel of the gun. "Now!" she demanded.

She prodded his back with the barrel, but took care to stay far enough behind that he couldn't turn suddenly and disarm her. In a struggle, he might win. She only had the advantage while she held the rifle.

"Unfasten his cuffs!" she directed Pepito.

"But, *señorita,* I do not have the key!" he exclaimed.

Hayes was laughing. "I don't damned well believe it!" he exclaimed. "Minette!"

She backed away from Pepito. "Desperation drives us in odd

ways," she said. "Pepito, I want you to lie down on your stomach with your hands behind you. Over there."

"They will kill my family!" he wept.

"I will kill you if you don't do what I tell you to!" Minette exclaimed. "Do it!"

"*Sí,*" he groaned. "Very well."

With an audible sigh, he spread out on the floor with his hands behind him. Minette searched for something that would do the job. She found a piece of discarded duct tape, which had been used to gag her. She twisted it into a long string, knelt over Pepito, who hadn't moved, and quickly tied his thumbs together. It was a neat and simple but effective way of binding a prisoner.

"How the hell did you learn that?" Hayes asked with admiration.

"I interviewed this merc," she explained. "God, how do we get you loose before they get back?" she exclaimed.

"Mendez's enforcer took the key with him," Hayes muttered. "These are the best cuffs money can buy. I ought to know. I paid for them."

"Maybe a hairpin," she muttered, looking around frantically. "I've never picked a lock in my life, but..."

"Just get me on my feet," he said heavily. "Leave the cuffs for now. We have to get out of here before his crazy boss comes back!"

"I agree."

She took the jeweled toilet-roll holder from her pocket and went to work on the nylon cord that bound Hayes's wrists to his feet.

"What the hell is that?" he exclaimed.

"Vanity," she explained, and managed a grin. "It brings us all down in the end."

She finished cutting the cord. Hayes stood up and almost fell. "Sorry," he said. "I'm a bit unsteady."

"Not to worry, gramps, lean on me," she teased.

"We have to get going."

"I know."

"Señorita, my family, my poor family!" Pepito was crying openly. "They will kill me but Lido will torture my wife and my babies!"

"Lido?" Minette queried.

"The man who was here, with the gold-plated weapon," Pepito said miserably. "Lido is the enforcer of Pedro Mendez and his cousin Charro, who is mayor of Cotillo." He took in a shaky breath. "Lido likes to do bad things to women...."

Minette looked at Hayes and grimaced.

"Go ahead," he said heavily. "But give me the AK first. I can manage it with the cuffs, I think."

And he did. He held it with some difficulty while Minette got Pepito on his feet.

"I'm not untying you," she told him curtly. "And if you make trouble or try to betray us, I'll shoot you. Deal?"

He hesitated. "Deal. But my family..."

"Pepito, I can't storm an armed camp," she pointed out. "I'm sorry. I can save you. I can't save any more people today, I've hit my quota."

He sighed sadly. He nodded.

"Let's go. Quickly!" Hayes said.

"Provisions," Pepito said. "We must have food and water."

She muttered a curse, but he was right. They were miles from civilization and they had to keep up their strength. Even in cold weather, the desert was dry.

She gathered up what she could find in the kitchen in a knapsack and threw it over her back. She grabbed a couple of blankets off the worn bed and draped them over Pepito's shoulder.

"Now let's go, while there's still time!" she told them.

They followed her cautiously out the door. She took the AK from Hayes, because she could see the pain it was causing him to carry it. She hoped he hadn't done irreparable damage to his shoulder on this unexpected and painful journey. She hoped she wouldn't cause more. But they had to escape. They only had one chance, and this was it.

She looked at Pepito. "I have to trust you. Which way to the border?"

He bit his lip. He was considering his options. Really, he had none, but he knew this country and they did not. Chances were very good that if he didn't speak, they would wander around lost until his boss, who had an excellent tracker, hunted them down. Perhaps the boss would consider Pepito a victim and be forgiving...

"If we get caught," Minette said in a steely tone, "I'll swear on my life and honor that you helped us escape."

"And I'll swear with her," Hayes added coldly.

Pepito ground his teeth together. "They will kill my wife and children!" he sobbed.

"If you survive this, you might still be able to save them," Minette said.

He looked at her through tear-filled eyes. "With what?" he asked heavily. "I have no money, no weapons, nothing!"

Minette was thinking fast. "Pepito, do you know why they kidnapped me?"

"Because they wanted the sheriff and you were with him," he said.

"No. It's the other way around." She lifted her chin. "My father is El Jefe."

He laughed. "It is a joke, no?"

"It is no joke. You heard the boss say that he was going to videotape himself killing me and send it to my father. My father is his worst enemy. El Jefe."

Pepito would have crossed himself had his hands been free. "El Jefe could save my wife, if he would," he ventured.

"And your children," she agreed, nodding. "If you help save me, you could ask for any reward, anything at all. Couldn't you?"

He seemed to come to a decision all at once. He nodded. "It is this way. Through here. Move quickly. It will not take the boss long to get here. He has a tracker who will find us if we are still in the area."

"Stop talking and start walking," Hayes advised.

"Good advice. Take it," Minette seconded.

They walked for a long time, through scrubby undergrowth and across dry stream beds. They walked into the mountains and around for what seemed hours. Hayes was weakened by the ordeal. He was shivering, too.

"How much farther is it?" Minette asked anxiously.

Pepito sighed. "It is very far, *señorita*," he replied. "Miles and miles, and we cannot get there in one day, not when the sheriff is so weak."

She groaned. But when she looked at Hayes, she knew Pepito

was right. Of course, he could also be lying, buying time for his boss to hunt them down.

"Is it really such a long way?" Minette asked the shorter man. "It didn't take us very long to get here in the SUV."

"Yes, it did," Hayes said heavily. "I'd say we were more than thirty miles from the border."

"Oh, dear God," Minette burst out worriedly. "It will take forever to walk that far!"

"We don't have a choice unless we can steal a car," Hayes said facetiously. He looked around. "Good luck finding one in the desert, too."

She groaned out loud. Hayes might not make it that far. He was already moving like an invalid. The trip and the rough physical treatment might have caused him even more problems that weren't visible.

They stopped in the shelter of an overhanging rock.

"Could we risk a fire?" Minette asked Pepito, because Hayes looked bad.

"Yes, if we make one that has little smoke," he replied. "But I cannot gather wood like this."

Minette hesitated. She didn't trust him not to run away and leave them.

He stared back at her, holding out his hands.

"If you betray me," she promised him, "my father will hunt you down."

He swallowed. "I know that, *señorita*. You must trust me."

She looked at Hayes, but he was sitting on the ground, his back to a rock, so exhausted he could barely move. "All right. Give me your word you won't run."

"I give you my most solemn promise," Pepito told her.

She drew in a long breath and finally used the jeweled toilet-roll holder to cut away the duct tape she'd used to bind his hands.

"I will return shortly. I give you my word." He hesitated. "Your father, you are certain he will help me?"

"I am absolutely certain," she replied. "Please, hurry," she said, glancing worriedly at Hayes.

"I will be quick."

He walked away into the darkness. Minette sat down beside Hayes and put her arms around him, holding him close, warming him with her body.

"It will be all right," she whispered. "We got away. We'll make it to the border. I swear we will!"

He sighed and slid his good arm around her. "You are the stuff of legends, lady," he chuckled softly.

"I had this wonderful inspiration…a sheriff who's afraid of nothing and walks right into gunfire," she whispered.

He brushed his lips against her hair. "Thanks. I feel all better now. Hurts my pride that you had to save us. I wanted to save you."

"Next time," she promised. "Here. Lie down."

She coaxed him onto the hard ground and curled into his body, as close as she could get, to warm him with her own body heat.

"Miss Raynor, what *do* you have in mind?" he murmured at her ear. "I'm not that kind of man!"

"Oh, yes, you are," she chuckled. And despite the ordeal of the past few hours and the threat of danger, she was happier than she'd ever been in her life.

He curled toward her. "I guess I am, after all," he mused. His good hand slid into the back of her jeans and down, curving around her hip. "Soft." He groaned, because the cuffs were still on and it pulled the sore muscles in his injured shoulder. "Crack-ers and milk," he muttered as he drew his hand back.

"Isn't this easier?" she whispered, sliding it into the front of her blouse. "This way, it won't pull the muscles in your...oh, my gosh...!" she gasped when he bent his head and worked his way under the blouse, onto her soft breast. His mouth worked on the hard nipple, creating a tender suction that lifted her off the ground. She moaned as his mouth moved up to her lips and he rolled onto her, nudging her long legs apart. They strained together in an agony of need, blind and deaf and dumb to their surroundings.

"Oh, God, I can't...damn this shoulder!" he groaned, when he realized that what he was trying to do was impossible while he was wearing handcuffs.

Minette clung to him, straining to breathe, while she fought down a hunger that threatened to undo them both. "Later," she promised. "I'll get those cuffs off if I have to shoot them off. Then I'll ravish you!" she whispered huskily, pushing her mouth up into his.

"Minette," he groaned.

"Sorry." She managed to draw back. "Really sorry. Depraved virginity," she whispered. "Got the best of me."

"Depraved...virginity," he burst out laughing.

He rolled onto his side, wincing, and looked into her eyes. "That's a condition I would very much like to remedy for you."

"Would you, really?"

"But only if you marry me," he continued, his lips pursed. "After all, I'm a public figure. I have my reputation to consider. I have to set an example."

She wiggled both eyebrows. "Okay. How soon can we get married?"

"If I bribe a public official..."

"You're a sheriff. Can't do that," she replied.

"Damn. Well, we'll get a license and get married at the end of the week. How about that?"

She smiled and kissed him softly. "That's assuming that we last until then."

A loud noise in the distance caught their attention. It was followed by a second. It sounded oddly like explosions. That was when Minette realized that their prisoner hadn't returned with any firewood. Had he found some way to alert the others to his presence? Did he have hidden fireworks with him, perhaps, some way to signal his boss and the men who wanted to do away with the prisoners?

She looked around. "Did you hear those explosions? Pepito!" she groaned. "He's sold us out!"

He frowned. "That didn't sound like gunfire. It sounded like a grenade going off. Maybe more than one."

"Maybe Pepito had one that we didn't know about. I'll bet he's just signaled his boss." Minette sighed. "So much for expecting him to keep his word. He'll lead his boss back here."

Hayes indicated the AK solemnly. "So we make a stand," he said. "And pray for reinforcements."

She searched his eyes. She nodded slowly. "A last stand. Together."

He smiled, very slowly, and with great pride. "That's my girl," he said huskily.

Night was closing in fast. It was cold. Minette huddled together with Hayes, because it was stupid to wander off in the

night in a desert, where anything could be waiting. They knew
that the United States lay to the northeast. If they could find a
constellation they recognized, it might help them navigate.

"I never studied astronomy," Hayes groaned when she suggested it.

"Neither did I," she replied.

"Back to the drawing board."

"Moss grows on the northern side of trees," she said helpfully.

"Good luck finding it in the dark. In fact, good luck finding a
tree," he pointed out. "There are hardly any where we are." He
nodded toward the long expanse to the horizon, barely dotted
with an occasional mesquite tree.

She nodded, despondent.

They were freezing. She wrapped blankets around them and
opened their last bottle of water. They had to drink sparingly.
There was a little beef. They ate some of it, as well. Every minute, they expected armed company to show up and surround
them. But so far, there was no indication of people coming after
them.

"I'm sorry I trusted Pepito," she told Hayes.

In essence, they were trapped. They couldn't go anywhere
because they didn't know where they were. They had a rifle
and a few bullets. Pepito's boss had a small army and the arms
to go with it. Against that might, two lone people, one of them
injured, had little hope.

"I trusted him, too," Hayes reminded her. "What else could
we do? I thought he might wait to see your father before he sold
us out. I guess that was wishful thinking...."

She hugged him gently. "Thanks. So what do we do now?"

"I suppose we try to get a little sleep and then start walking.

With luck, we might find a better hiding place or someone in law enforcement who would help us."

"Okay," she said. She curled up against him with a long sigh. "I wish we'd never gone to your office."

He smiled, closing his eyes. "Me, too. I'm really worried about the computer tech," he added. "Eb Scott won't take that lying down. He'll send men out to find him, and he won't be gentle with his abductors."

"I hope he finds them."

"Well, I do, too, as long as he turns them over to me for prosecution," Hayes stated grimly.

"That's my sheriff," she said, and she closed her eyes, too.

14

"What if Pepito decided to go and try to save his family?" Minette opened her eyes and wondered aloud.

"I suppose, in his place, I might do the same," Hayes replied. "It would be hard to put the lives of children below the lives of people you don't even know."

She smiled, pulling the blanket closer around them. "I was thinking about Shane and Julie," she said softly. "It will be hard for them, if we don't make it back. They've already lost both their parents—"

"Let's just go one step at a time," he interrupted. "We're free, thanks to you." He shook his head. "Imagine using a toilet-paper-roll holder to cut yourself free."

She grinned. "Thanks to Pepito's boss," she chuckled. "Imagine having something like that in an outhouse!"

"I'll have to remember to tell my deputies about that when we get home. It will tickle them, when they remember the guns we

confiscated that were gold-plated and studded with diamonds."
He grimaced. "What a haul. The feds confiscated them. I imagine
they'll put the proceeds to good use, tracking down the people
who bought those weapons."

"I hope they can." She drew in a long breath and looked
around. There was a sliver of a moon. They had no fire. She
heard coyotes howling somewhere nearby.

"Coyotes won't attack people, will they?" she wondered.

"I don't think so," he told her. "Actually Native Americans
have some fascinating stories about coyotes protecting wounded
people alone in the wilderness."

She pursed her lips. "Perhaps we should talk to the coyotes
and see if they'd be willing to give us a hand," she laughed. "Or,
rather, a paw."

He linked her fingers with his and shifted closer. "It gets
damned cold in the desert at night," he said. "I've had to spend
a night or two outside, on the other side of the border, hunting
fugitives."

"You're in a very dangerous line of work," she murmured.

"Yes. I never thought about it before, but I am." He glanced
down at her. "I love my job, but maybe it's time I thought about
putting on a new deputy and paying more attention to administration."

Her heart jumped. "You'd do that?"

"I think I would," he said.

She reached up and kissed him, very softly. "I'd like it very
much if you stayed alive for a long time."

He laughed and kissed her back. "Okay. I'll do my best." He
turned her gently and slid down beside her on the hard ground.
"I don't want our children to be orphans," he whispered.

She pulled him close, hungry for the feel and taste of him. As he kissed her, his hands wandered slowly over her body, making it swell, making it ache for more.

Her mouth opened under his, tempting him. She slid her hands under his shirt, against his back, where the scars were from other wounds. They didn't bother her at all. They were marks of his bravery.

He felt her hands, felt their gentle stroking, and relaxed. She didn't find his scars repulsive. That made him feel really good. He nudged her legs apart, knowing that this was a very bad idea, and lowered himself so that they fit against each other almost as close as possible.

She arched up, feeling him swell, feeling his hunger. "Please?" she whispered, shifting so that he was even closer. She shivered. "Oh, Hayes, please...!"

He moved against her, hurting from the need, aching to do what she wanted. But just as his hands went to the fastening of her jeans, the coyotes started up again. They sounded closer, menacing.

He sat up, pulling her with him.

"What is it?" she asked blankly, still shivering with unsatisfied passion.

"The coyotes. Listen."

They were very loud.

She reached for the weapon and handed it to him. "Just in case," she said.

He nuzzled his face against hers. "Just for the record, I didn't want to stop."

She laughed. "Me, neither."

"We'll have all the time in the world. We just have to live through the next couple of days," he told her.

She smiled. "What an incentive!"

He chuckled. "I was about to say that, myself."

She looked out over the darkened landscape, dotted with a few mesquite trees in the distance. Was Pepito there, gathering wood? Or had he run away to find his boss? She voiced those concerns.

"Either he'll come back, or he won't," Hayes said quietly. "We have to hope that he's like me. If I give my word, I keep it."

"Do you think he will?" she wondered. "He loves his family. He's scared to death that Mendez will have them tortured and killed."

"I know. But you promised your father's help. That will carry weight."

"I hope so," she replied. But she was feeling the cold, separated from Hayes, and the fear and uncertainty came back like a bad dream.

"Come here," he said softly, lying down to cuddle her as close as he dared. "We can keep each other warm while we wait."

She smiled and snuggled close. "Can I take off your clothes while we wait?"

"For shame," he teased. "You'll embarrass the coyotes."

She nuzzled his chest with her cheek. "I don't care. Come on. Live dangerously."

"I already have, and you can see the result. Here we are, lost in Mexico, waiting for people to come and kill us."

"That's not the sort of dangerous I mean." She opened his shirt and put her mouth against the thick hair that covered the warm muscles of his chest. "Ooooh, that feels good," she whispered.

He drew in a shaky breath. "I know something that will feel even better." His hands went to work on her shirt, tugging it over her head. Her bra followed. He pulled her bare skin against his and groaned as the pleasure shot through him like fire.

She moved restlessly. "It really does...feel better."

His arms contracted, but the damaged one hurt. He shuddered as pain followed the pleasure. "Minette, I can't," he whispered when she tried to coax him closer. "God, it hurts...!"

She gasped. "Your shoulder! Gosh, I'd forgotten. I'm so sorry!"

She sat up. In the pale light of a quarter moon, he could see her breasts, pale and hard-tipped.

"Beautiful," he whispered. He bent and caught one in his mouth, tasting it, savoring it with his tongue.

She arched backward and shivered. "Yes," she whispered shakily. "Beautiful."

He laid her down and fed on her soft breasts for what seemed a very long time. Reluctantly he drew back. "Wrong time, wrong place," he breathed, kissing her softly. "We're going to freeze if we keep that up. And besides, I'm not doing so good."

"Shoulder hurt?"

"Like hell," he agreed, sitting up and grimacing as he moved the arm. "And I still can't get the damned cuffs off." He held them up from one wrist. "Sorry."

"No, I'm sorry," she whispered. She kissed his eyes shut. "But it was worth it."

He chuckled. "Yes. It was."

She put her bra and shirt back on and moved close to him. "I am a brazen hussy," she told him. "And proud of it."

He laughed with pure delight. "Shameless. That promises to

be delicious when we finally have the opportunity to really know each other."

She nodded. "I'll be worth waiting for."

He kissed her forehead. "I know." He brushed her lips with his. "So will I. That's a promise."

She felt him shiver and pulled the blanket closer around them. He felt warm to the touch, but she couldn't decide if it was fever or something else. She was worried about his shoulder.

"I wish we had something you could take," she said. "For the pain, at least."

"I'll manage. If we could just get warm, that would be something."

She looked out into the darkness with resignation. "I don't think Pepito's coming back," she said sadly. "He wouldn't be gathering wood in the dark."

"There's a little light," Hayes said, noting the moon. "Think of it logically. Even if he could get back to Cotillo, to his family, how would he get them out all by himself?"

"I suppose Mendez has them well-guarded," she agreed.

"He can't go back to his boss, assuming that Charro knows we've escaped. So where else can he go except back here? Your father is the only hope he has of saving his wife and children."

"They may already be dead," she said, her voice low and soft with compassion. "Mendez is a monster, like his cousin El Ladrón. And that Lido, who said he wanted to hurt me in front of the camera before he killed me..." She shivered.

"Thank God most of the Mexican people are kind and compassionate and devoted to their families," he replied. "We tend to dwell on the criminal element, the drug lords, the drug dealers, the mules. But there are millions of good people down here who don't commit crimes, who go to church and love their children."

"Yes," she agreed. "We tend to forget that."

He drew in a long breath. "It's so damned cold!"

"You're feeling it more because of what we've been through physically," she replied gently. She wrapped him up closer in the blanket. "We'll get out of here. I know we will."

"But not tonight," he sighed. "Let's try to get a little sleep. Maybe when it gets light, we can at least watch the sunrise and see which way east is. Then, we just start walking north. Eventually we'll end up somewhere."

She laughed. "Good idea. I like it."

He kissed her forehead. "Go to sleep."

She closed her eyes with a sigh and relaxed.

The mayor of Cotillo was a particularly unpleasant man. Grier and Ramirez were sitting with ramrod-straight backs in his office while he went on and on about the stupidity of Americans who thought he was involved in drug trafficking.

"Do I look like a drug lord to you?" Charro Mendez concluded finally, giving the men a belligerent glare.

Ramirez had to bite his tongue. "We aren't here on drug-related business at the moment."

"So you say. But what do you think I can do?" he added. "You are missing two of your citizens. If they are in my country, they are here illegally and will be arrested if we find them."

"They were kidnapped and taken to your country against their will," Grier interjected. He leaned forward. "Look, we don't want to provoke a diplomatic upheaval. We just want to find the people and take them home. Surely you could ask questions and see if anyone knows anything about where they are?"

"I'm sure the ex-president of your country would be grateful," Ramirez added with a cold smile. He was reminding the little politician that he himself had ties to the Mexican government, especially with a man who was known for opposing and attacking the drug traffic here.

The mayor cleared his throat. "You have interesting connections, *señor*," he said.

"I have relatives everywhere. In fact, so does he." He indicated Grier.

Grier smiled nonchalantly.

The little man glared at them.

"So," Ramirez continued in his patient, deep voice, "can we count on you to help find our kidnapped citizens?"

The politician was thinking fast. This had the potential to blow up in his face, especially since the leader of the cartel was on his way here right now. These federal law enforcement people could cause him some big trouble if they were found in his office when the head man arrived.

Mendez got to his feet and smiled from ear to ear. "I promise you, I will do everything in my power to find them for you," he said, suddenly cordial.

"That's kind of you," Ramirez said.

"Jorge," he called to his aide, who rushed in the door with an electronic tablet.

"Yes, *señor*," he said, almost comical in his deference to the smaller man.

"These gentlemen are looking for two American citizens whom, they say, have been kidnapped and brought to our country. Will you make some inquiries and see if you can find anyone who has knowledge of this crime?"

Jorge blinked. "Of course." He hesitated. "Who would you like me to call?"

"You might start with the border patrol and work your way down to the policemen in the towns nearest the border crossing," the mayor said shortly.

"Oh. Yes. Of course! I will begin immediately!"

Jorge went back into his small office.

The mayor threw up his hands. "My nephew," he muttered, glaring toward the door the younger man had just exited. "Incompetent, but my sister loves him. I must do what I can to promote peace in my family."

"Understandable," Grier replied. He glanced at Ramirez, who had the same irritated expression on his face that Grier imagined he was wearing. This little twit wasn't going to do one thing to look for Hayes Carson and Minette Raynor.

Ramirez got to his feet. "Well, we thank you for your... cooperation."

The mayor shook hands with them both, still smiling from ear to ear. "You are most welcome. I will have my people call you if we find out anything."

"Thanks." Grier walked out ahead of Ramirez.

They were back at the bucar before he spoke. "He knows where they are," he told Ramirez.

"I figured that out myself. Any ideas?"

Grier sighed. "We're guests here, but nobody's going to offer us lodging for the night, I'll wager." He looked around at the closed doors and windows. "We aren't exactly attracting pleasant attention."

"So I guess we go back home and hope for the best?" Ramirez said heavily. "I don't want to leave them down here. If they were kidnapped because of something they know, they'll be killed."

"No, it's not something they know. It's who they are. Miss Raynor is El Jefe's daughter. El Ladrón will kill her slowly and probably send videos of it to El Jefe," Grier said with pure disgust.

"Yes, but Hayes humiliated Charro Mendez by arresting him and confiscating his gold-plated hardware. He wants revenge just for that. Not that he won't kill Hayes, too. Of course he will."

Grier nodded. "They found four bodies in a ditch here recently," he replied, looking around. "Somebody got in the way of the drug traffickers."

"Hayes Carson is notorious for that," Ramirez said. "In the old days, before I was married and had a child, I think I'd have come down here undetected and looked for them myself."

Grier smiled sadly. "Me, too. But that's a job for younger men now."

Ramirez pursed his lips. "You know, Minette Raynor's father probably has somebody working on this case right now. And he'd have to rescue Hayes as well as Minette, unless he wanted her to hate him forever."

Grier chuckled. "That would be one for the books—a notorious cartel leader trying to save a sheriff who wants him locked up."

"El Jefe is a prince among thieves," Ramirez replied. "And we have nothing on him on our side of the border. Yet."

"Maybe we should pay him a call," Grier said, thinking out loud.

Ramirez smiled. "Maybe we should."

* * *

Pepito was gathering wood, but his mind wasn't on the task. He was thinking of his wife, and his little girls. He'd been forced to help the Americans escape their jailors, but none of the men he worked for would believe that. They'd think Pepito volunteered to let them go, because everybody knew he had a soft heart.

The Americans didn't know where they were. They had no compass, no way to find the border. He knew that if he didn't return, they would most likely wander around until they were recaptured by Pepito's boss.

That would be bad, because they'd already sworn to tell the boss that Pepito helped them get away. They wouldn't lie to save him.

On the other hand, they might die in the desert. It was very cold and the sheriff was still fragile from that bullet wound. They would be very uncomfortable without any source of warmth, and there were wild animals who lived in the desert. Anything could happen.

He picked up another piece of mesquite wood, his eyes on the setting sun. It was very red on the horizon. Red, like blood.

He groaned as he thought of his poor family, who would be at the mercy of the drug lord once they knew their prisoners had escaped.

There was the possibility that he could sneak into the small village where they lived and get them out, before his treachery was discovered. It wasn't so far from here, and he knew the way. The Americans might die anyway. It would not be Pepito's fault. And if they did get recaptured, then perhaps Pepito could hide from the boss, with his family, until he had the chance to get out of the country and start over.

Yes. He could do that.

Coyotes howled menacingly. He shivered. He hated coyotes. He thought of them preying on domestic animals. Did they attack humans? It sounded as if they were very near the camp where he had left the Americans.

But it was not his problem. He had to save his family. He had to!

The mayor of Cotillo was straightening his tie, in anticipation of the arrival of the leader of the biggest cartel in the country, Pedro Mendez, the ones the stupid Americans called by a humiliating title: El Ladrón.

Pedro was coming to see the prisoner that Charro had hidden in a cabin in the desert. It would be a particularly interesting visit. El Jefe's daughter, in his power, and Charro had made it possible by sending his best enforcer, Lido, to kidnap her. The sheriff hadn't been part of the deal, except that he was with Miss Raynor and they couldn't leave him behind to talk.

"Jorge, are they almost here?" Charro called to his aide.

The younger man came to the door. "Yes, sir," he replied. "They are bringing many men with them. It is a convoy of no less than four armored SUVs," he added. "Just in case the American federal agents think to try something. I told Señor Mendez about the visitors. He was not pleased that they had the audacity to come here."

"You should have let me tell them, you fool!" Charro raged. "I am the mayor. I am in charge here, not you!"

"I am very sorry," Jorge said, lowering his eyes. "I did not think."

"You never do." Charro reached out and slapped the younger man viciously on one cheek. "You idiot!"

"Excuse me, is this the mayor's office?" a pleasant deep voice interrupted.

They both turned to the door. There were two men, one tall with long loosened thick black hair down to his waist, the other short and mustached and grinning.

"I am the mayor. Charro Mendez," the smaller man said, regaining his dignity. "Who are you?"

"Carson," the taller man replied. He was olive-skinned and black-eyed, but not of Spanish heritage, and it showed. He had on his belt the most vicious-looking knife Mendez had ever seen.

"And you?" The mayor turned his eyes to the small Hispanic man with the newcomer.

The little man was still grinning. "I worked for El Jefe," he said proudly. "I know all about him, all about his operation. I can tell Pedro Mendez how to bring him down!"

Charro's eyes almost popped. "You work for...!"

"I *did* work for him," the smaller man corrected. "But I am not paid what I am worth. This man—" he indicated the tall man at his side "—had a friend who worked for Pedro Mendez. His friend said that Señor Mendez would pay me handsomely for information about El Jefe, and that he could give me protection. El Jefe will try to kill me, for what I know."

Wheels were turning in Charro's mind. He could get rid of his boss's worst competitor, and here was the means to do it. He grinned.

"Welcome," he told the men. "Jorge, bring coffee! Come, come into my office, and we will speak of these things," he added, motioning them into his office with a smile that reached almost to his ears.

* * *

Ruy Correo was a very good actor. He told Charro all about El Jefe's operation, where his contacts were, what routes he used, even the names of the men who headed the distribution hubs in Mexico and the United States. Of course, every word was a lie, but he was so convincing with the information that Charro was almost beside himself with excitement.

"This is very good news," he told Ruy. "And I promise that you will be protected. In fact, you can speak to Pedro Mendez in just a few minutes. He is on his way here right now. He and I and our enforcer, Lido, will go to the cabin where we are holding El Jefe's daughter and her American friend." He smiled coldly. "They will be tortured and it will be recorded. Pedro is going to send the video to El Jefe, to show him how powerful, and how ruthless, and how cunning we are. He had so many men protecting his daughter." He laughed. "And they all failed. We have her."

Carson was lounging against the wall, watching the byplay. His black eyes were narrowed in thought. "Pedro Mendez is coming here?" he asked, and pretended to be impressed. "This is just a small town...."

"Cotillo is the hub for all the drug trafficking in northern Mexico," Charro said indignantly. "It is the most important town we own. I myself killed my predecessor." He indicated the jeweled, gold-plated handle of the .45 automatic at his belt. He made a face. "The American *federales* confiscated my guns. I had so many, all beautiful, all terribly expensive. They will pay for this. I have one of their own prisoner, in addition to El Jefe's daughter. He will die for his arrogance, for my humiliation!"

"Good for you," Carson remarked. "Mendez is coming here, you say."

"Yes, there is a whole convoy," he chuckled. "Armor-plated vehicles, which no ammunition can pierce. Even bulletproof glass. My boss is very careful of potential attackers."

"Smart." Carson's eyes twinkled. "An assassin would be stupid to try to shoot him, anyway."

"I don't know," Mendez replied. "We know of a former government sniper across the border who might be tempted to try it."

He meant Cash Grier. Carson didn't say a word. But he was laughing inside.

"You can speak to my cousin personally," Mendez promised Ruy. "And you will be well paid for your information."

"I am grateful," Ruy said.

Carson stood up tall from his lounging position. "Well, I need to stretch my legs. Is there a cantina in this town?"

"But of course, and there are women, as well," Mendez said with a sarcastic smile. "It is at the foot of the hill, on the right."

"I think I'll go down and have a shot of tequila. And, maybe, sample the local goods," he insinuated with a raised eyebrow at Mendez, who chuckled. "See you later, Ruy."

"Yes, of course."

Carson walked out, his easy, smooth stride not menacing at all. Yet.

"Where did you find this man?" Mendez asked Ruy, indicating the visitor who had just left.

"He has connections to our world, is all I know," the other man replied. "And he is very dangerous."

"Yes, that weapon he carries is impressive. Not as impressive as mine, however," he laughed, smoothing his hand over the butt of his gun. "Now. Let us drink coffee and talk of pleasant things!"

Outside, Carson moved out of sight and reclaimed a backpack he'd concealed behind a building. There was only one road into Cotillo that was well-kept, and it cut across the barren country like a knife. The convoy would have to enter from it.

Carson walked around the buildings and out onto the roadway. It didn't matter if he was seen. It would make no difference. Ruy would find some excuse to leave the mayor's office and make his way to the border. He'd served his purpose with a diversion that gave Carson information and a chance to even the playing field of the drug lords by putting Pedro Mendez permanently out of business.

He moved off the road and waited. He had a fierce temper and he rarely smiled. But he was patient.

A few minutes later, the convoy came into sight in the distance. Carson had rigged a sort of ghillie suit out of netting and vegetation. It was invented by Scots sportsmen and borrowed by Highland soldiers. They were often seen in movies, and some hunters used them, but they weren't in use in the military much anymore, not with the new computer-generated camouflage uniforms that blended with any landscape. But, then, Carson was ex-military. He had no uniform, but he was a trained sniper as well as a field medic. This time, a sniper kit would do him little good against all El Ladrón's armor plating. But he had a few tricks up his sleeve, learned in missions for Eb Scott's counterterrorism group. Those drug lords' vehicles were very heavily armored, yes. But most people neglected to do the same job on the undercarriage...

The lead vehicle, the one containing Pedro Mendez, was easy to pick out because of its over-the-top gold and jewel fixtures.

Even the rearview mirror was priceless. Pity, Carson thought, to destroy such wealth. But, then, this little monster tortured and killed innocents. That couldn't be allowed. A message had to be sent. A warning.

Carson picked up three hand grenades. He pulled the pin on the first one and almost casually tossed it right in the path of the lead vehicle. He did the same on the next two.

Then he ran like hell....

Inside the mayor's office, the explosions were so loud that they shook the building. "What the hell is that?" Charro exclaimed, shocked. "Come on! Jorge, did you hear that?"

Ruy walked out with them. "What could it be?" he asked with mock horror.

"Look!" Charro gasped as he spotted the wreckage of three armor-plated vehicles. "My cousin...!"

He started running toward the outskirts of town. Jorge followed. Ruy put his hands in his pockets, smiled thoughtfully and melted back into the population of the town, gathering quickly to see what the noise signified.

Charro recognized what was left of his cousin. Nobody in those vehicles was left alive.

"Pedro Mendez is dead," he choked. "My cousin is dead!"

"Who could have done this?" Jorge exclaimed. "Only we knew that he was coming!"

"Only we?" Charro turned quickly. "Where is that man, that Ruy? And Carson...go to the cantina, see if he is there!"

"At once!"

Charro looked at the wreckage as the townspeople gathered in horror around him.

"He is dead!" one of the men whispered. "The leader of the cartel is dead!"

"No," Charro said at once, straightening. He turned to the people. "I am now leader of the cartel."

Nobody argued.

One man bowed. "As you say, *patrón,*" he said quietly. "Congratulations on your new job."

Charro smiled. He felt taller already.

Jorge came back very soon, brooding. "I cannot find either one of them. The bartender said that no American had even been in the cantina."

Charro felt sick. "Those Americans. They did this!"

"I fear they did," Jorge said. "What can we do now?"

Charro's eyes narrowed. "We will kill El Jefe's daughter and send him the video. I will go myself. You will go with me!"

Jorge swallowed, hard. "Couldn't Lido go instead? He is very good at torture."

Charro thought about that for a minute. "All right," he said. "Go and fetch him. And have someone take care of the bodies and arrange the funerals."

"Yes, *patrón.*"

Charro thought of the American female. He had seen photos of her. She was quite lovely. He pursed his lips. He would enjoy her for the cameras, and then slit her throat. El Jefe would pay for his arrogance, for killing Pedro Mendez. Charro would see to it personally.

15

Hayes and Minette had awakened from a brief nap, both shivering with the cold. It was a long time since Pepito had left them. Neither of them expected him to return. They were resigned to the fact that he'd sold them out.

"I wonder what that explosion was all about," Hayes murmured.

"Maybe a gas tank blew up," Minette mused.

"It sounded like a grenade," he said quietly. "In fact, like several grenades."

She glanced up at him. "We'll probably never know," she said heavily. She pulled the blankets closer around them. "Well, in a few hours it will be daylight. Then we can start walking again...."

The sound of footsteps was loud in the darkness. Sudden movement caught Minette's attention. Instinctively she grabbed the rifle and shouldered it. Hayes would hardly have been able to lift it, she knew, with his shoulder in such bad shape.

"*Señores,* do not fire, it is me, Pepito!"

She clutched the rifle, waiting with breathless fear to see if he was alone.

He walked into the camp with an armload of wood.

"I am sorry it took so long," he told her. "I had to go very far to find the sort of wood that would make a smokeless fire. Mesquite trees are sparse around here. The Americans covet the wood for their, how do you say, barbecues. So the trees are sold and now they diminish by the year. It is very sad."

"Thanks, Pepito. For not selling us out," Minette said with honest gratitude.

"I gave you my word," he replied and managed a smile, his white teeth showing in the darkness. "I would never break it."

"So we have wood, thanks to you," Minette replied. "Now all we need is a match!"

"Perhaps I could help you with that," came a deep, slow voice from the darkness just beyond the overhang.

Minette clutched the rifle. She felt Hayes sit up, tensely, beside her. Pepito froze in place. They waited.

As the occupants of the camp held their collective breath, a familiar tall man with long black hair walked softly into the camp. Hayes remembered him from the argument back at Minette's house.

He felt around his jeans pockets. "Well, maybe not. I'm all out of hand grenades." He grinned, his teeth white in the darkness.

"You can't start a fire with a hand grenade," Hayes exclaimed.

"Sure you can. You just have to stand way back while you throw it into a woodpile." He glanced at Pepito. "You could ask your big boss, El Ladrón, how effective it is. I mean, if you could sew him back together again." His face was hard as stone.

"I'm sure Charro Mendez will take his place, now, but they'll most likely be along soon to kill her." He indicated Minette. He glanced at Pepito. "You, too, I'm afraid."

Pepito crossed himself, fell to his knees and began to pray. *"Gracias a Dios, gracias a Dios…"*

"What?" Carson asked, nodding toward the man.

"The big boss had his wife and children hostage," Minette explained. "They were going to torture and kill them if he stepped out of line."

"Oh, no!" Pepito panicked, coming to a sudden realization. "Once it is known that Pedro Mendez is dead, they will kill *mi familia!*" he wept.

Carson motioned and four men came into the camp. One looked very much like Pepito.

"They won't kill your family. Tell him—" he indicated their Hispanic companion "—where they are," he told the prisoner.

"You would save them?" Pepito exclaimed. "I would do anything…!"

"Just talk to him. We're running out of time."

"Yes. Yes. Thank you!"

Carson turned to the two people huddled under the rock. He went down on one knee and pulled out a pack. He noted Hayes's gritted teeth. "Coltrain said you'd be in some pain. I've got something for that."

"If I take anything I won't be able to walk," Hayes replied with a weary smile. "I'll manage."

"I'm a field medic. Don't argue." Carson administered an injection. "Any fever, other symptoms?"

Hayes shook his head. "Can you press a hundred and eighty five pounds?" he asked.

"Guess I could," Carson replied. "Why?"

"Because that's how much I weigh and I'm not going to be able to walk if I'm sedated."

Carson smiled grimly at him. "Not a problem. Miss Raynor, are you all right?" he asked her.

She frowned. "Well, actually, I do think I have a hangnail..."

Carson made a face.

"Watch out for her," Hayes advised. "She's hell on wheels with an AK. She rescued us. All by herself." He grinned from ear to ear.

"Yes, well, about that," she said sheepishly. She produced the AK-47 and handed it to Carson sideways with a wry grin. "I actually don't know if it's loaded or if the safety's on...."

"What the hell...you bluffed?" Hayes exclaimed.

She swallowed. "Well, I couldn't actually take the time to check, if you know what I mean. Pepito might have noticed that I couldn't fire the damned thing."

Hayes burst out laughing and held out an arm. She went under it and clung to him.

"I'm never playing poker with you," he told her, and kissed her.

She grinned up at him. "Good idea."

Carson just shook his head. "In case you wondered, it is loaded and the safety's off."

"Too much information," she told him. "I don't want to know." She shivered. "I hate guns."

"You have to learn to tolerate them, though," Hayes told her. "A sheriff's wife has to conform a little bit."

"You marrying him?" Carson asked her.

"Apparently," she laughed.

He shrugged. "I'm not coming to the wedding."

"Wait until you're invited, to refuse," she replied.

"Not coming anyway."

She laughed. "Okay. But thank you for saving us."

"I thought you already did that," he replied and his dark eyes smiled at her. "Saved yourself and him."

"I just got us out of captivity. It's still a long way to the border. We were lost."

"Not anymore."

"I still can't walk much farther," Hayes had to admit, although it hurt his pride.

"No worries, I told you." He held up a hand and made a circular motion with it. A flare lit up the night. Seconds later, the sound of a huge helicopter was heard as it approached. "See?" he added to Hayes, and laughed.

They arrived back at Minette's house exhausted, to be met with tearful, anxious faces when they walked inside. The children grabbed first Minette, then Hayes, sobbing the whole time. Aunt Sarah managed to get a hug in, wiping her eyes, as well.

Two men sitting in the living room got up and came to meet them. Garon Grier and Rodrigo Ramirez smiled.

"Glad you made it out," Rodrigo told them. "We were just leaving town after a fruitless discussion with the mayor of Cotillo when somebody—" he looked past them at Carson, who was standing just inside the doorway "—apparently tossed a hand grenade right into a convoy of high-level drug lords."

"Slight correction." Carson held up a finger. "It was three hand grenades, not one."

"We have no idea who did it, of course," Ramirez continued with a glare. "If we did, we'd probably have him hanged."

"If you did," Carson replied, unperturbed, "a few of his friends might have something to say to my first cousin's husband."

"Your cousin's husband?" Garon Grier asked.

"Yes. He's the senior senator from South Dakota." Carson smiled blithely.

Grier actually groaned. "He's on the committee that has to approve our budget requests."

"Ours, too," Ramirez said with a grimace.

"So, can we call that a standoff?" Carson inquired.

Grier threw up his hands and turned away.

"We were going to do everything in our power to gain your release," Rodrigo told Minette. "I had to telephone my cousin to get us into Mexico past a border guard."

"Your cousin?" Hayes asked.

He nodded. "He was president of Mexico until the recent election."

Carson glared at him. "Name-dropping. Very uncouth."

Ramirez actually grinned.

"We were on our way out of town, to call in our negotiators to deal with the mayor," Grier added, "when the convoy blew up."

"But the wheels of government turn slowly," Ramirez added.

"Too slowly for some of us," Carson interjected.

"You're lucky not to be on your way to federal prison," Grier said shortly.

Carson made a face at him.

"Come on, guys, I believe in the rule of law as much as you do," Hayes added. "But in this case, Minette would have been long dead before diplomacy did its work. And so would I."

"I have to agree," Ramirez said quietly. "I owe my life to one of your colleagues," he added to Carson, "having suffered a kidnapping myself some years ago."

"Which brings us to the point of our visit," Grier replied. "I believe you have some information about a DEA agent who might be working with the cartel across the border."

Hayes nodded. "I was on my way to meet with the computer tech when they grabbed us. But he had the computer and had just accessed the hard drive...why are you looking at me like that?" he added, frowning.

Ramirez sighed. "We were hoping he'd told you something."

"No. But he was at my office..." Hayes continued.

"We found him about an hour ago," Grier interrupted solemnly. "In a ditch."

"What?" Carson exploded.

"He was tortured and killed," Grier continued. "And the computer was taken, as well."

"I'm sorry. I'm so sorry!" Hayes exclaimed. "God!"

"He was a good man," Carson said through his teeth.

"We'll find who did it. I swear we will," Hayes promised him. "In the meantime," he added, "thanks. For getting us out." He held out his hand. Carson shook it. "If I can ever do anything for you, well, anything legally," he added with a wry smile, "I promise to do my best."

"You can find who did that to Joey," Carson replied. "Not that we won't be looking, as well." He held up his hand when Hayes and the others started to protest. "No hand grenades. I swear."

They nodded.

"At least, not on this side of the border," Carson said under his breath.

* * *

The excitement was over. Hayes was saddened by the death of the young computer whiz, but so happy to have Minette safe and home again. Her father had called, overjoyed at her rescue.

"I was dubious about the man's offer of help," he confessed to Minette on the speakerphone, "but obviously he knew what he was about. I will give him anything he wants, for the rest of his life, for saving you. Also, that man Pepito, he is now working for me. Doing something legal, *niña,* I swear it," he added quickly. "His family lives in this country now, on my rancho. I am teaching Pepito how to work with horses. I think he will be a natural."

"The man will try again, won't he?" Minette asked sadly. "To kidnap me, to kill Hayes..."

"Oh, you mean El Ladrón?" El Jefe was honestly surprised. "They did not tell you?"

"Tell me what?" she asked, exchanging puzzled glances with Hayes.

"El Ladrón was so excited about your capture that he wished to see you tortured," he said grimly. "So he and his lieutenant were in the convoy that was on its way to the mayor's office. Someone, I cannot think who, lobbed a hand grenade into his SUV."

"He's dead?" Minette exclaimed.

"Oh, yes, quite dead, along with the boss who was going to torture you for him. I assure you, we have dealt a savage blow to that drug organization. Which leaves only mine in command of the entire territory," he added with a smug laugh.

"But, I thought the Fuentes gang controlled it," Minette replied.

"Niña," he said softly, "the Fuentes brothers were my first cousins. There is one brother left. We are family." He chuckled.

She caught her breath. "Well!"

"You do understand that if you do anything illegal here, I'll have to arrest you," Hayes told him. "I'll do it sadly. But I'll do it."

"I know that. No worries, I have no intention of breaking the law on American soil. I have my daughter's welfare and reputation to consider!"

"Thanks," Minette said softly. "And thanks for sending that absolutely certifiable lunatic to save us."

"As I understand it, you saved yourself, and the sheriff."

"I helped," she said modestly.

"Pepito has told me everything. Including about the jeweled, what you call it, toilet-roll holder? I have hardly stopped laughing since. My daughter, the Amazon warrior!"

She laughed self-consciously. "I guess we never know what we can do until we're put to the test," she agreed.

"I am most proud of you," he added. "Your mother, God rest her blessed soul, would be very proud, also."

"Thanks."

"Sheriff, your injuries were not complicated by the kidnapping?"

"No, I'm doing very well," Hayes replied. He looked at Minette lovingly. "By the way, I'm marrying your daughter."

"Yes, so I have heard," he chuckled. "This does please me. In return, I will make sure that none of my people break the law in your jurisdiction. You have my word."

"I'll be grateful," Hayes told him with a wry twist to his lips.

"And for the time being, it would be as well if no one knew our relationship for certain, niña. I will always have enemies," he added quietly. "It is a by-product of the desperate times in which we live, and the trade in which I involve myself."

"We'll be vigilant," Hayes promised him.

"That is all I ask."

"Are you sure you want to marry me?" Minette asked later, when they were alone in Hayes's bedroom after the children and Sarah had gone to bed. "I mean, I run a newspaper—and what a scoop I'm going to have on the front page next week!—but my father is a notorious drug lord."

"My brother was a notorious drug user," Hayes reminded her. "We both have things to live with, or live down, whichever it is." He pulled her close. "The important thing is that we have each other."

She smiled slowly. "Yes."

He bent to her mouth. "Have I ever told you," he whispered into her lips, "that I love you quite madly?"

Her heart jumped. "No."

He smiled. "Well, I do."

She linked her arms around his neck. "I love you, too," she said, a little shyly.

His smile grew wider. "I had a feeling," he mused. "Move over here...."

He eased her down on the other side of him. He was wearing pajama bottoms and nothing else. She was in slacks and a T-shirt. But a few minutes later, those articles of clothing were on the floor.

"This is not...a good idea..." she panted, even as she opened her legs so that he could slide between them.

"We're getting married as soon as...we get a license," he groaned, sliding his good hand under her hips to lift her up.

"We've publicly announced...our intentions...oh, God!" he groaned so harshly that she thought he was dying.

About the same time she heard the groan, she felt the hardness of him go right inside her, with an enthusiasm that almost dampened the sudden, sharp pain that made her grind her teeth together.

"I'm sorry," he whispered brokenly, even as he kept moving. "I can't...help it!"

"I know." She didn't have to be told that it had been years for him. He was so hungry that he could barely contain it. She felt his mouth covering hers, his hand going between them quickly to touch her in ways that shocked at first, and then delighted her.

"Try to relax," he whispered. "I'll make it as good for you... as I can."

"It's all right." She moved with him, lifting to the sudden urgency of his body, feeling his hand tease away the pain and replace it with a tension that grew and grew and grew until it exploded in a hail of white heat that enveloped her, consumed her.

She heard the quick, sharp movements of their bodies against the crisp sheets, saw the ceiling come and go over Hayes's shoulder as he drove blindly for satisfaction. She thought there wouldn't be time, that she wouldn't catch up to him before he found his own satisfaction. But her body followed his, arched up to receive it, ground itself against his hips until she felt the heat suddenly burst inside her, just as he groaned hoarsely and shivered, again and again, arching down into her with all the power of his hot body.

She clung to him, her lips on his chest, on his throat, as the furious heat washed over them and left them breathless and damp with sweat.

"Too quick," he whispered apologetically. "I'm sorry...."

"No. I felt it," she whispered back, flushing. "I really felt it."

He lifted his head, still breathing heavily, and looked into her melting dark eyes. "I hurt you."

"Collateral damage," she breathed. "Not unexpected after such a barrage."

"Shock and awe." He grinned.

"Yes."

The smile faded. He held her eyes while he moved, slowly, rotating his hips. She gasped. He did it again, watching for signs of discomfort.

Fascinated with this new adventure, she looked down. He saw her curiosity and lifted his hips, let her watch, as he eased down again, penetrating her very gently.

"So that's what it looks like," she whispered huskily.

He smiled. "And how it feels."

She looked up into his face, saw his eyes go to her breasts, their tips hard as stone, her body rippling as he moved on it.

"I never dreamed it would be so, so intimate," she swallowed.

"I never dreamed it would be so perfect, the first time," he whispered back. "The only thing I didn't like was having to hurt you."

"It only hurt a little." She felt more confident now. She lifted her own hips and moved them and watched his face contort. "And you can make it up to me. Right now. Like...this..."

He shuddered as she moved under him.

"Don't fight it," she whispered huskily. "Don't hold back. Don't hold anything back...go inside me, as hard as you can, as deep as you can...!"

The words burned him, whipped his passion into white-hot

urgency. He pushed down into her and caught her close, riveting her to him while he drove into her, his eyes wild with passion, his face rigid with tension.

"Watch me," he whispered. "Watch. Watch!"

She couldn't have dragged her eyes away to save her life. He shivered and shivered again, and then arched up and cried out as the pleasure brought him almost to unconsciousness.

All the while, she was riding the crest of that heat, feeling it swell inside her, feeling the raging torrent sweeping her closer and closer and closer to the edge of some unimaginable delight, some incredible joy...

It came suddenly, like being dropped from a great height. She gasped and then fell through layers and layers of feeling, until at last she arched up and sobbed endlessly, clinging to him, lifting to him, grinding against him as she tried hopelessly to cling to that silvery pleasure for as long as possible. But it was fleeting and quick and gone.

She wept.

He cradled her against him, smoothing his hand up and down her spine, still joined to her as intimately as he could be.

"It doesn't last," she sobbed.

"No. But the memory of that will last us until we're old and gray, I think," he whispered breathlessly. "Not even in my wildest dreams was I ever that sated."

"I never had wild dreams," she whispered. "I didn't know what it was like, what it could feel like." She kissed his chest. "I guess we can't miss something we've never had."

He kissed her forehead tenderly. "No." He tilted her face up to his eyes. "And now you belong to me. Completely."

"And you belong to me."

He eased away.

"No," she protested weakly.

"The kids will come in to see me first thing in the morning. I really think they don't need to find us like this," he said, tongue-in-cheek.

She looked at him boldly, her eyes lingering on his body. "You're beautiful."

He laughed. "So are you, honey."

She sighed. "We jumped the gun."

"We blew up the gun," he mused.

She hit him gently. "Oh, Hayes, your shoulder!" she exclaimed.

"It will survive," he promised her. "It's a little sore, but it was worth it. A few days' setback, maybe. Nothing more deadly. Honest."

"Okay."

He got up slowly. "Come on. We'll have a nice bath and go to bed."

"A bath? Together?"

"Saves water and soap," he said.

She laughed. "Okay!"

They showered, touching and kissing, and then they dressed. Hayes kissed her good-night and she went back to her room to sleep. She finally managed a few hours before the kids came bouncing into her room and jumped onto the bed.

"Minette, we're hungry!" they exclaimed.

She laughed with pure delight. "I'll come cook breakfast right now!"

"I want oatmeal," Julie said.

"I want eggs!" Shane said.

"You can have both. Get out and let me dress, though."

"Yes, Minette." Julie led the way.

Minette dressed, feeling a new and strange soreness that, she assumed, was from her nocturnal exercise. She cooked breakfast, exchanging soft glances with Hayes.

"I suppose you should all know that Minette and I are getting a marriage license today," Hayes told the others.

"We're getting married to you?" Julie exclaimed. "Oh, Hayes, that is so wonderful!"

She jumped out of her chair and ran to hug him. So did Shane.

"You can live with us and we can watch movies together. And we'll protect you so nobody ever shoots you again!" Julie promised.

"That's right," Shane said solemnly. "And we can watch wrestling together!"

Hayes hugged them, trying to hide the brightness of his eyes until he had it under control. "I'll buy more movies," he promised.

Sarah got up and hugged him, too. "You know how I feel," she laughed. "No need to tell you how proud I am to add you to the family."

"Thanks, Sarah."

"Now all we have to do is line up a minister," Hayes told Minette.

And they did. The wedding was a social event. Everybody showed up, even people who weren't actually invited. The happy couple said their vows at the altar, kissed and were pelted with rice and confetti all the way out of the church and into the beautiful sunlight.

Minette's photographer captured images of her in her couture white wedding gown with its delicate pastel embroidery echoed in the fingertip veil and the bouquet she carried. She tossed it, and watched with dismay as it was caught by a foreign-looking tall man with a mustache who grinned at her. Her father!

She looked at Hayes aghast. He shrugged and grinned.

She ran and hugged her father. "Thanks for the wedding present," she said. "But you shouldn't have!"

"Jaguars are the safest cars on the market. This one is a special order, it has armor," he added with a sly grin. "So I am certain you will be safe when driving it. I like your family, niña," he added gently. "They are precious, the children."

"Yes. Very precious." She reached up and kissed his cheek. "I'm glad you came."

He shrugged. "My daughter was getting married. But I must go now." He indicated a few men in suits on the sidelines.

"Where did they come from?" she exclaimed.

"They are either from government agencies, or they are aliens in disguise," he said gleefully. "Who knows." He lifted his hand and waved at the men in suits. Amazingly they grinned and waved back. He shrugged. "Hey. Without me, they wouldn't have jobs, yes?"

"Yes." She had to concede that. "Stay out of trouble," she told him firmly.

"Of course!" He winked at her, put on his sunglasses, motioned to his bodyguard and exited the fellowship hall. The men in suits followed dutifully behind.

"Is this a wedding or a bust?" she asked Hayes.

"Actually," a deep voice said from behind her, "it's a bit of both."

Cash Grier grinned at her. His beautiful redheaded wife, Tippy, was on his arm, wearing a green creation that made her look like a cover girl. Which, of course, she was.

"I couldn't miss the wedding. I just hate taking her out in public." He indicated his wife with a sigh. "Before the day is over, I'll have to arrest my own officers for lewd behavior. Stop that drooling!" he snarled at one of his patrolmen by the door.

The young officer snapped to attention, looked flustered and left.

"See?" Cash sighed, exasperated.

"I'll wear a bag next time," Tippy promised, and went on tiptoe to kiss his rugged cheek.

He hugged her close. "Never. I love showing you off too much," he chuckled. "Even with the complications." He glared at another officer who was openly staring at Tippy. The man cleared his throat and went back to the punch table.

"He won't have those with me," Minette laughed, pressing close to Hayes. "I'm just ordinary, I am."

"Huh!" Tippy scoffed. "Holding off a drug dealer with an AK-47 and you're just ordinary?"

"Yeah? Well, you stopped an assassin with a cast-iron skillet," Minette shot back.

"Stuff of legends," Cash said smugly.

"Both of them," Hayes agreed, pulling Minette close.

"I totally agree. Toast!"

He picked up a glass of punch and called for attention. "To the sheriff and his lady. Many happy years, many children, much joy!"

"Hear, hear!"

They all drank.

* * *

"What was that part about many, many children?" Minette asked sleepily with pure joy in her voice and in her eyes as they lay in a satisfied tangle in a bed in Panama City, Florida.

"I'm working on it," he mused. "Leave me alone. I'm tired."

"Tired! Pshaw!" she scoffed.

"Pshaw?" He sat up in bed.

She shrugged. "Crackers and milk?"

He laughed and lay back down, pulling her close. "We could have gone overseas, you know," he murmured.

"The places you want to go wouldn't work. Carson seems to be wanted in at least two of them."

He glared. "Why did we have to bring him along on our honeymoon?"

"Well, it's not as if he's in here with us," she pointed out. "The last I saw him, he was glaring at a pretty young blonde who was flirting with him on the beach. He took a margarita to bed with him."

"Some help he'll be if we're surrounded by drug lords after revenge," he murmured.

"He had two of his friends with him. My father sent them along." She shook her head. "It's going to be a very strange marriage, Hayes."

He kissed her nose. "A very happy marriage."

She closed her eyes with a sigh and pressed close. "Merry Christmas."

"That's next week," he pointed out. "We'll be home then."

"I'm celebrating early. Merry Christmas."

He pulled her closer. "Merry Christmas, honey."

She curled up in his arms and went to sleep.

* * *

The next morning, they had breakfast and walked along the beach, watching the tide roll in and out on tiny white foaming waves.

She danced in and out of them, because it was too cold to go wading.

"We have to come here in warm weather and bring the kids," he said, smiling. "They'll love playing in the sand."

"You really don't mind that I've got a ready-made family, do you?"

He shook his head. "They're my kids. I love them."

"They love you, too. So do I," she added softly.

He bent and kissed her. "I love you, too, honey. Forever."

"Forever."

She looked out over the Gulf of Mexico, her eyes bright with love and happiness, looking forward to a future she'd never expected. Her hand tangled in Hayes's and she moved close to him.

"Life is an unexpected journey," she said philosophically.

"With unexpected rewards." He kissed the top of her head. "And that's enough philosophy for one day. Race you to the coffee!"

"You're on!" She gasped and pointed behind him. "Is that a pelican?"

While he was diverted, she burst into a run and made the door just seconds ahead of him. She was still laughing when he reached her.

16

Just before Christmas, four men met in the back room of a restaurant in Jacobsville, Texas. They were all wearing suits, except for the sheriff. All of them had sidearms.

The oldest of the four was taciturn as he looked from one face to the other. "We have a lead on the computer tech who was killed," Garon Grier said quietly.

"Someone connected to the late, great El Ladrón, I'll bet," Hayes Carson replied.

"Actually, no," Rodrigo Ramirez said.

"Someone connected to a low-level but vindictive politician, in congress," Jon Blackhawk interjected. "And rumored to be thinking of running for an even higher federal office in a year or two."

"You can't mean him," Rodrigo exclaimed.

"Yes, I can." Jon was grim. "We know about his connections to the drug trade, we know he uses bribes and threats to get what he wants out of other legislators. Imagine that talent catapulted to the highest levels of government."

"We still have a free press," Hayes commented.

"Reporters have families. So do the CEOs of the corporations that run the news media," Jon said. "Do you really think that people who massacre journalists across the border would hesitate to do it here?"

"I had hoped so," Hayes said. "But I guess that's not realistic."

"So what do we do?" Ramirez asked.

"We wait," Jon said grimly. "We keep our eyes open, we look for connections we can prove. And we hope that we can find that computer that Eb Scott's tech was killed trying to probe."

Lassiter hadn't spoken. He was standing a little apart from the others with his hands in his pockets. "What about the sniper that El Ladrón was sending after you?" he asked Hayes.

"The one who was actually working for my new father-in-law?" Hayes chuckled. "He went back home."

"Pity," Lassiter said. "We might have used him."

"For what, bait?" Ramirez asked.

Jon shook his head. "Some members of the drug cartels are stupid. Very stupid. But the man who's running the territory now, the little mayor of Cotillo, has a brain. He also has one of the most intense intelligence networks we've ever come across. I'm surprised he didn't die in the grenade attack."

"He was entertaining us at the time," Garon Grier interjected, nodding toward Ramirez. "We left just in time to avoid the explosion."

"Yes, well, it turns out that one of our local mercs had some extra hand grenades that he used to practice on the armor-plated vehicles with," Ramirez said with a hint of humor. "He was also visiting the mayor at the time. It's only a trick of luck that Charro Mendez wasn't there to meet the convoy. If he had been..." He let his voice trail off.

"That man, Carson," Hayes said. "He's quite something."

Ramirez lifted an eyebrow. "He has a serious attitude problem."

"Could be, but Minette and I owe him our lives," he pointed out.

"I suppose so." He frowned. "Didn't he feed somebody to a crocodile overseas?"

Grier chuckled. "He takes credit for it, but I have it on good authority that Rourke was the instigator. Carson helped."

"Who did he feed to the crocodile?" Hayes asked.

Grier's face became hard. "A man who tortured a wealthy young journalist who was covering the attack on Barrera. Apparently she and Rourke go way back."

"And who's Rourke?" Jon Blackhawk asked. "The name is familiar, but I can't place it."

"He works for Eb Scott occasionally, but he mostly does jobs for K.C. Kantor. The man is rumored to be his father, but nobody knows the truth."

"Kantor." Grier shook his head. "There's an interesting man. He started out as a merc, bought stock in some company and became a millionaire in a few years. Now he's based in South Africa, and if there's any sort of revolution going on, you can bet he'll be backing the rebels against the corrupt governments."

"An interesting man," Hayes commented.

"How's the therapy coming?" Ramirez asked.

Hayes sighed. "It's going to be a long haul," he said. "The kidnapping did some damage, but eventually I'll regain most of the use of my arm. Sadly it's going to be a longer time before I can shoulder a shotgun. So I guess Zack is going to be on the firing line in any gun situations from now on." He looked depressed.

"Neither of us can go busting down doors with guns blazing, either," Garon pointed out, nodding toward Ramirez. "We have wives and families and we confine ourselves largely to administration now. Fieldwork is best suited to young men."

"I'm young," Ramirez taunted. "I can press a teddy bear!"

Grier burst out laughing. "Yeah. Me, too."

"I wouldn't mind having more kids than Julie and Shane," Hayes said dreamily. "Children are terrific."

"That's right, Minette has two little siblings," Grier noted. "You didn't mind?"

Hayes shook his head. "They sat in bed with me and we watched movies together, and they said they'd protect me from bad men." He still almost got choked up when he recalled that. "They're great. Both of them."

"Well, by the time your own come along, you'll be experienced," Ramirez chuckled.

Hayes grinned. "That I will." The smile faded. "Pity that Charro Mendez didn't go out to meet his cousin when the grenades went up."

Garon frowned. "You think he knew it was coming?"

"Someone said he had visitors, just before the grenades went off," Ramirez recalled.

"Yes," Garon replied. "A tall man with long black hair down to his waist, an informer told us. And reportedly an employee of El Jefe."

Hayes chuckled. "Carson."

"Exactly," Grier said. "He's quite efficient."

"Deadly," Hayes agreed. "And he carries an illegal weapon that he says your brother—" he nodded toward Garon Grier "—gave him a permit to carry."

"My brother was a sniper," Grier pointed out.

"What does that mean?" Hayes asked.

"Just that men who share deadly occupations form friendships."

"Oh, good Lord, Carson was a sniper?" Hayes burst out.

"A very good one, according to my brother. But he's doing jobs for Eb Scott and Cy Parks these days."

"Cy Parks quit the business," Hayes recalled.

Grier leaned forward. "And pigs fly. Just because he doesn't participate in commando raids doesn't mean he doesn't help organize them. He's got about three ex-mercs on his payroll. He has enemies, too."

"If they know about Carson, I don't imagine they'll bother Parks," Ramirez said. "And before you forget, I was one of those mercs before I joined the DEA. I'm still a wanted man in several countries overseas. Though, fortunately, not in this one."

"Truly," Grier agreed.

Jon Blackhawk sighed. "Well, I suppose Charro Mendez just inherited El Ladrón's crown."

"Inherited it, yes. Now let him try to keep it," Ramirez said somberly. "Your wife's father will be on his toes now and looking for a way to put Mendez out of business," he told Hayes. "There's another issue, as well. We still have a high-level mole in my organization. I don't dare talk to anyone except Cobb about that. We can't afford to advertise the fact that we even know he exists. With that computer missing, and the data most likely destroyed, he thinks he's safe."

"That gives you the edge," Hayes told him. "He's much more likely to give himself away if he does think he's safe."

"It's a big agency," Ramirez said heavily. "Very big. And I can't remember the agent who came with me to your drug bust. So that leaves us with nothing."

Hayes was thinking. "Did you stop anywhere on the way down here that day?"

Ramirez thought for a minute. "Not on the way, no." He hesitated. "We did stop at the police station. I wanted to talk to Cash Grier. But he was out."

"Did the agent go inside with you?"

"I believe he did." He shook his head. "Oh, that's a long shot. That's a very long shot."

"Someone in that office might remember seeing you with him, might be able to describe him. Cash's secretary, Carlie, was she working that day?"

"Sorry," Ramirez said with an apologetic smile. "I don't know the names of any of his personnel...."

"Medium height, jeans, T-shirt, short dark wavy hair, big smile," Hayes described her.

"Smart mouth?" Ramirez said with a faint grin.

"That's Carlie."

"She's memorable," Ramirez had to admit. "Yes, she was working."

"From what I've heard, she has a photographic memory," Hayes continued. "If she saw your agent, she'll know what he looked like."

"Finally," Ramirez exclaimed. "A break!"

"Yes, but we can't advertise it," Hayes said. "We don't need another tragic death because the drug traffickers panicked."

"I see your point. Okay," Ramirez told him. "I'll drop by casually and talk to Cash before I do anything."

"I'll go with you," Garon added. "It won't look suspicious, if people think I'm dropping in on my brother."

Ramirez smiled. "Nice angle."

"I can be devious," Garon chuckled. "I used to work on the FBI hostage rescue team a few years back."

"I'm impressed," Ramirez said with a smile.

Lassiter checked his watch. "I have a few calls to make. But if you need any help that I can give, I'm always available."

Hayes's eyes narrowed. "Just who do you work for?" he asked.

Lassiter grinned. "Nobody you know."

"You worked for my wife's father," Hayes pointed out.

"As a cover," Lassiter replied. "El Jefe fed me enough information to hang Mendez out to dry, before your buddy Carson turned him into human sushi," he sighed. "So that assignment's off the table now."

"There's another Mendez," Hayes pointed out. "El Ladrón's cousin, the mayor of Cotillo."

"He doesn't have a footprint on this side of the border, well, not one that we can find," he amended. "Pity. We get a lot of our budget from the Rico statutes."

"We?" Jon asked. "We, who?"

"Sorry. Need to know." Lassiter shook hands all around. "It was an honor to work with you. Maybe we can do it again one day."

"MIT?" Hayes mused.

Lassiter chuckled. "Yes. But can you really see me in a classroom teaching physics?"

"Not hardly," Hayes had to admit.

"My dad was totally outraged that I wasted that expensive education. And he doesn't approve of the work I do—neither does Mom. They think it's too dangerous. But I just smile and do what I please. My dad's a great guy."

"So I've heard."

"I hope you get back on your feet soon," he told Hayes.

"Thanks. Coltrain says I'm making great progress. But for now, I'll just sit at my desk and give orders."

"Nothing wrong with that," Lassiter agreed. "See you guys."

Hayes watched him go with narrow-eyed curiosity. "'I met a man who wasn't there...'" he quoted.

The others burst out laughing.

Across the border, at a deserted cabin, just after Carson got Hayes and Minette out of the country, a man with a gold-plated, jewel-gripped automatic pistol was raging at his enforcer and his aide.

"You let them escape?" Charro Mendez raged at his enforcer Lido.

Lido wasn't a man who feared much, but he knew what Charro did to people who crossed him, and he began to sweat.

"I left Pepito here to guard him. Pepito knew we had his wife and children under surveillance, that we could kill them whenever we wished!"

"Then where is Pepito?" Charro raged again. "And where are my prisoners?!"

"I do not know," Lido said, swallowing hard. "But I will find them..."

Charro pulled out his weapon and shot Lido twice in the chest. He watched the man fall to the ground with disgust.

Jorge started backing up, his hands held out in front of him.

Charro glared at him. "I cannot kill you," he said, irritated. "My sister would never forgive me."

"What about him?" Jorge indicated the dead man on the ground.

"Leave him," Charro said with contempt. "Let the coyotes feast on him." He bent down and retrieved the automatic that was still in Lido's belt, unfired. "He has ruined my plans. El Jefe has his daughter back and he will now want revenge."

"We have much protection," Jorge began.

Charro laughed coldly. "Ah, well, at least we can pay Pepito back for his treachery. Come. We will take care of his family personally. Stop flinching! Be a man for once!"

"But I cannot kill a child," Jorge wailed.

Charro sighed angrily. "Then we must find someone who can. Come."

They arrived back in Cotillo to find a house burning. Charro went down the hill to look, with Jorge beside him. "Is that not Pepito's house?" Jorge exclaimed.

"I think it is." Charro walked over to a crying woman. "What happened here?"

"The house caught on fire, *señor*," she sobbed. "I saw the woman and her children, and even her husband, inside it! They are all dead!"

Charro relaxed. So he had his retribution after all, and he would make sure that everyone in his organization knew the penalty for betraying him. He would say that he set the fire himself, to punish Pepito and his family.

He turned and walked away with Jorge beside him.

The sobbing woman looked after him. She smiled coldly. Out

of her pocket she pulled five hundred-dollar American bills. What a small service for such a price. She would find work across the border, financed by this windfall, and never have to worry about living in fear again. She did wonder where the tall American with the long black hair got so much money, but she didn't ask questions. He set the house on fire and told her exactly what to say to the mayor before he left. He was handsome, that one, and she was single and pretty. But he was all business. He did not flirt, and his eyes said nothing that his lips did not echo. He was cold as ice. Just as well, she thought. She did not need the complication of a romance in her life right now. She was going to be free of the drug wars, and that was something.

Carson made one call from his cell phone to El Jefe.

"It's done," he said. "He bought it."

There was deep laughter. "So now, Pepito and his family are safe with me, and Charro will not try to come over and kill them. I will tell him. He will be very grateful. If I can do anything for you..."

"Thanks, but I don't need anything." He hung up. His black eyes searched the horizon. Somewhere out there was a man who'd killed his friend, the computer tech, Joey. He'd been protective of the boy, who had no family and no ties. It was like losing a brother.

He put away the cell phone. The missing computer had a code that it would transmit when it was activated. That had been Carson's idea, but Joey had implemented it. Back at Eb Scott's impressive compound, a computer was on, waiting for that signal to come. He had no idea if and when some computer tech would try to retrieve the information that Joey had painstakingly recovered. But he imagined they would be curious enough to try to read the hard drive. When they did, Carson was going to follow the hidden signal to the source; and there would be payback.

"What did you find out?" Minette asked her husband when he got home that afternoon.

"Let's see, that Lassiter works for some agency we've never heard of, that Mendez is smarter than he looks and that we may have a way to find out what that DEA agent looks like after all."

"We do? How?" Minette exclaimed.

Hayes started to speak, looked around and smiled. "Just kidding," he said. But his eyes were making a comment—he couldn't be sure that the room wasn't bugged. He was taking no chances. A politician with ties to the drug cartel was going to be very dangerous, and he might need help from Minette's father to avert disaster. There was also the worry that when they found the traitorous drug agent, there would be reprisals from Charro Mendez. But he wasn't going to talk about that in a room that he hadn't had Zack sweep for bugs. He smiled at Minette. "I wish I had a few leads in the murder of the computer technician."

"I wish you did, too. I'm sorry."

He pulled her close, still wincing a little. "I got you something for Christmas," he said. "Something I think you'll like."

"Did you?" She grinned. "I got you something, too."

"What is it?"

"I won't tell."

He kissed her. "Please?"

"I won't tell."

"Pretty please?" He kissed her again.

She looped her arms around his neck and kissed him back. "Never."

He sighed, and just kissed her.

On Christmas morning, the kids tore into their presents as if the world was ending. Sarah was exclaiming over warm socks and a sweater that Minette and the children had given her. Hayes was sighing over four ties that came from the wives of his deputies. They were both still reeling from her father's unexpected gift, a yearling from one of his prize racehorses to, as El Jefe put it, begin her own line of thoroughbreds. She and Hayes had each given him a colt from their palominos, which he honestly seemed to love.

Minette handed Hayes a box, gaily wrapped with many ribbons. "Open that."

He studied her quietly and then the box. It was long and huge. "What is it?"

"Open it and see."

He tore off the wrapping and wrenched off the end of the box with the strength of his good arm. He caught his breath. "A new spinning rod!" he exclaimed.

"Top-of-the-line. I got one for me, too, so we can go fishing next spring," she said, grinning from ear to ear.

"You sweetheart!" He leaned over and kissed her, hungrily. "Thanks!"

"Open ours, Hayes, open ours!" Julie exclaimed.

Shane handed it to him with a grin.

He laughed and undid the wrapping paper and ribbons. Inside were three new cartoon movies. He gathered the kids up close and hugged them.

"You angels," he exclaimed. "I haven't seen these!"

"Neither have we," Shane told him with a chuckle.

"We want to watch them, too," Julie said. She kissed his cheek. "It's very nice that you're our brother now, Hayes," she added. "We love you very much."

"Yes, we do," Shane agreed, grinning.

Hayes was trying not to break down. "I love you guys, too." They hugged him again.

"Open the others!" Minette told the kids.

They laughed and rushed back to the presents that were left.

"Softy," she chided, kissing Hayes warmly. "I love you, too."

"That goes double for me." He kissed her back. He reached over and produced a small box. "This one is for you."

"Oh!"

She opened the wrappings and discovered a jeweler's box. She looked at Hayes curiously. He nodded at the box.

She opened it, and caught her breath. It was the most beautiful hand-carved cameo she'd ever seen in her life. It was graceful and beautiful, a young girl's head. But not just any young girl. It was her head. It looked just like Minette in a portrait her stepmother had commissioned when she was sixteen. But the artist who'd carved it had put her in a high-necked Victorian dress, with her hair in a bun and a soft, secretive smile on her full lips.

"I...I've never...it's so beautiful!" She started crying.

He hugged her close. "My beautiful Minette," he whispered. "I hoped you'd like it. The guy's been working on it since Thanksgiving. He barely got it done in time."

"I've never had anything so pretty in my whole life."

"There is just one thing prettier than the cameo," Hayes whispered.

"There is? What?" she asked, lifting a face wet with tears but smiling.

"You, my darling," he said softly, his deep voice velvety with feeling. "You are the most beautiful creature I've ever seen."

She couldn't find the words. She knew she wasn't beautiful. But Hayes thought she was. And that was all that mattered. She tucked her face into his throat.

"I love you, Hayes," she whispered brokenly.

"I love you. Merry Christmas."

"Merry, merry Christmas," she replied. "And I hope we have a hundred more, together."

He sighed. "So do I."

She reached up and kissed his rugged chin. "And if you'll stop walking into gun battles," she murmured, "we might just have that many!"

His eyes were soft with affection. "Tell you what. I promise to stay out of gunfights from now on. How's that?"

"That's just what I wanted to hear."

He rubbed his nose against hers. "One condition."

"What condition?"

"That you stop provoking drug lords to firebomb the news-paper."

"Awww. Spoilsport."

"If I have to promise, so do you."

She met his eyes and her own smiled back. "Okay. I promise."

He moved back into his chair and pulled her down onto his lap. "Well, I don't know about you," he said loud enough for the others to hear, "but I'd really like to see a cartoon movie!"

Cheers went up from the kids. Aunt Sarah chuckled.

"So would I," Minette agreed. "Suppose I go and pop some popcorn?"

"You stay right there," Sarah said, rising. "I'll make the popcorn. Hayes would pine if you left him."

Hayes grinned from ear to ear. "Yes, I would. Thank you, Sarah."

"I am your friend," Sarah assured him. "Here, kids, let me put the first movie in the player. There we go! Now I'll hurry up and pop that popcorn. Won't be a minute! I'll feed Rex while I'm in the kitchen."

Minette made a face at her aunt. Then she snuggled close to Hayes and closed her eyes.

A minute later, Aunt Sarah was back. She looked resigned. "Hayes, I hate to bother you, but could you ask Andy to get off the stove?"

"The stove?" Hayes blinked.

"I believe he wants his bananas fried."

Hayes burst out laughing. He and Minette filed into the kitchen behind Sarah. Rex was sitting expectantly near the counter, hoping to be fed. Andy was sprawled over the enamel cooktop of the stove where Sarah had been slicing his bananas. He was digging into them as if he hadn't been fed in weeks.

"Pig," Hayes muttered.

Andy gave him a look, snorted salt out of his nose and went right back to eating.

"Don't you pay him any attention, old dear. You can have your bananas anywhere you want them," Minette said, and scratched him behind his ears.

Andy looked up at her and bobbed his head and blazed his eyes, before he went back to eating.

"He used to be my lizard," Hayes sighed.

"He still is. He just likes me best," Minette said gleefully.

"What are you putting on those banana slices?" Hayes asked.

She chuckled. "That's my little secret. Eat up, Andy. Stove tops can be cleaned," she reminded Sarah.

Sarah shook her head. "Ah, well, I can make microwave popcorn. At least he can't get in there!"

"Yet," Minette enunciated.

Sarah threw up her hands and went to feed Rex.

Hayes tugged Minette close to his side, but Andy didn't threaten or even offer to break anything. He looked down at her. "I think he's cured of being jealous."

She shook her head. "He's just being cautious. He doesn't want to lose his kitchen privileges!"

He laughed and bent to kiss her. "If you say so."

She laid her head against his chest. "It's been a long road, hasn't it, Hayes?"

He understood what she was saying. "A very long road. But it's all rainbows at the end of it."

She nodded. "Rainbows."

Andy gave his humans a wry glance, shrugged in his lizardly way and tucked back into his dish of sliced bananas. And if iguanas could have managed expressions, he'd have been smiling from ear to ear.

17

The traffic through the little café in San Antonio, Texas, was slow but steady. Two men sat in a booth with red vinyl seats, sipping cups of black coffee. One was the mayor of a small town over the border in Mexico. The other was a state senator with an interesting background, most of which was unknown to the voting public.

"It will take a lot of money to get me elected," the politician told the drug lord. "You know what's at stake. If I have the power, I can help you."

"Yes, but there is no guarantee that you can win this election," Charro Mendez said, shrugging. "It may be only a dream."

"Or it may not. I have friends in high places, and some in very low places, who can insure that I get the victory." Mike Helm smiled, a cold, practiced, formal smile that he used when campaigning. "A little cash here, a little intimidation there, and I'm in."

"I suppose it helps that the incumbent is too old to lift a cup and eaten up with diseases," Charro said sarcastically. "He may not last until the next election."

"In that case, I'll be a shoo-in," Helm replied. "I have a friend who'll make sure I get appointed to fill out his term."

"You take much for granted," Charro replied.

The politician just laughed. "I know how things work. That's all. I'm no newcomer to politics. I've been in elected offices since I was out of college."

And done very little with them, except to enrich himself. But Charro didn't say so.

"Listen, I'll make sure you don't get hassled at the border with your transports," Helm said earnestly. "All you have to do is make an investment. Hell, one of your pistols would get me elected. They're worth a small fortune!"

Charro lifted his head proudly. "I was born to a family of farmers," he said. "I worked in the fields from dusk until dawn, until my back almost broke. Then one of the Fuentes brothers took pity on me and gave me a job as a runner. I was very good at it. He kept me on, and I advanced higher and higher until now, I take the place of El Ladrón, may he rest in peace."

"Yes, you're good at your trade."

"I have earned the right to these fancy weapons you see," he added coldly. "They are a sign of my wealth and intellect, they tell people that I am wealthy."

"Sure they do."

"I will be a better *patrón* than my predecessor, and I will make more money than he did. I intend to gain more territory. Only El Jefe stands in my way, and I will find means to deal with him before I am through."

"I believe you. About that cash…?"

Charro's eyes narrowed. "I will help you. But remember your promise." He smiled. It was an icy tug of his lips. "Because I do not forgive betrayal."

Helm had heard about Charro's enforcer, Lido. This man sitting across from him had killed the man in cold blood. Rumor was that he had a new enforcer, much worse than Lido.

"So you know about Lido, do you?" he chuckled. "Good. You can see that I am a man of my word. I have a replacement for him." He indicated a tall, blond man with one eye standing at the door. "He is very good. He calls himself Stanton. I do not know if he has other names."

"He looks shady," Helm muttered.

"But of course he does," Charro replied, and laughed. "He is very experienced in his field."

"Which is...?" Helm asked.

Charro smiled. "Assassination."

Helm reached for his coffee cup and sipped the cold liquid. He was going to have to walk a narrow path with these people. But without their financial support, he'd be stuck in the state legislature forever. He wanted more. He was intelligent, and he was ambitious. But what he wanted most was wealth, tons of it. This man could help him. So he had to be pleasant, even as he was repulsed by what Charro was saying. It would be worth it, in the long run.

At the doorway, Stanton Rourke tried not to look smug. He'd had a friend tout him to Charro as an experienced hired killer, and Charro had sent for him. He had a whole world of fake identities that he could assume when he needed to. This was one of them. He needed to know who had killed the little computer tech, Joey, so beloved by the men in Eb Scott's mercenary group. They all wanted revenge, but first they had to find the men responsible, and the computer that contained enough information on the DEA mole to expose him.

Now he was learning other things of value—that Senator Helm there was dickering with his boss for money to run a campaign for the U.S. Senate. What a combination they made, the little mayor and the tall, sleazy politician. What a pity, Rourke thought privately, that he was going to find the means to bring them both down. But first, he wanted to find the people who killed Joey. And this was the only way to do it.

Hayes Carson was sitting in his office when a stranger walked in the door. Hayes was much better. His arm was healing. The cold bothered it, but the therapy was giving him more range of movement by the day. Marriage suited him, as well. Minette was all he could ever want in a woman. He loved her. He loved her family, too. He was happier than he'd ever been in his life.

He cocked his head as the one-eyed man with blond hair approached him. He frowned. "Don't I know you?" he asked.

The blond man chuckled. "I think you might," he said in a crisp South African accent.

"Rourke," Hayes exclaimed.

"That would be me." He sat down in the chair in front of Hayes's desk. "I wanted to give you some interesting news."

"What?"

"State Senator Matt Helm is having conversations with my new boss about financing his federal senate campaign," he said. "Drug lords with a mouthpiece in congress. Think about it."

"Horrible," Hayes said. "But what do you think I could do about it? Jacobsville is far away from Austin."

"I know. But that was just news in passing." He leaned forward, solemn now. "I'm after the people who killed Joey," he said. "I think my new boss was one of them, but I have to be sure. I don't want to take him down in Mexico. I want him tried for murder here, in Jacobs County, where it happened."

Hayes raised both eyebrows. "Your new boss...?"

"Oh, that. I'm working for Charro Mendez."

"The drug lord...?"

"Hold it, hold it." Rourke held up both hands. "I'm under-cover. If I can find a way to bring him down, I'll do it. But my priority is to find Joey's killers."

Hayes took a breath. "How the hell did you get that job?"

"It's a long story. I have friends in odd places. Just wanted you to know what's going on."

"I was sorry about Joey," Hayes said quietly. "He was one of the best computer techs I ever knew."

"He was sort of our mascot," Rourke told him. "We miss him around the camp." His face set in hard lines. "Revenge is a bad motive, but justice is a good one."

"Did you help Carson feed somebody to a crocodile?" Hayes asked suddenly.

Rourke just stared at him, with that one dark eye. He didn't say a word.

"Eloquent," Hayes pronounced, and laughed shortly. "All right, I won't pry."

"Good thing. I'm always discreet." He stood up. "I'll take my leave. I just wanted to let you know that I'm looking for evidence. If I find the culprit, or culprits, will you have them prosecuted?"

"You bet your life I will," Hayes said curtly.

Rourke nodded. "That's all I ask."

"If you can get them to come across the border voluntarily," Hayes added with a sigh. "Extradition is a pain in the...well, in an unmentionable spot."

"I can guarantee they'll turn themselves in," Rourke said. He smiled slowly. "Because the alternative will be so very, very messy."

"Don't you go feeding people to alligators around here," Hayes said, wagging his finger at the man.

"You don't have any alligators around here."

Hayes shrugged. "Well, if we ever *do*...!"

Rourke just laughed.

Hayes went home and told Minette what he'd gotten from Rourke.

"How about Carlie?" she asked. "Have you talked to her?"

"Yes, I have. Cash Grier got an artist he knows to make a drawing of the man she saw. It's in my desk drawer."

"Did it jog your memory?" she asked.

"Sadly, no." He sighed. "You know, I think I may be getting old."

She slid her arms around him and pressed close. "Hayes, you'll never get old."

"Think so?"

She reached up and bit him softly on the earlobe. "The kids are in school, Aunt Sarah's gone to the grocery store. We have about forty-five minutes.... Hayes!"

He backed her into the wall, stripped her from the waist down, dropped his slacks and went into her without a second's hesitation.

She hung there, shocked, delighted, shivering at the instant passion he'd kindled in her.

"I read about this in a book," he whispered as he pushed into her, moving his hips so that she began to moan. "It was the most erotic thing I ever read. So I thought, why not try...it?"

His voice trailed off as the desire blazed to fever pitch. He thrust down into her soft body, his face rigid with need, his body corded like wood as he moved on her.

She arched toward him, unbuttoning her shirt, unhooking her bra, then unfastening the buttons on his shirt with trembling hands. She rubbed her bare breasts against his chest as he built the rhythm until he was buffeting her so hard that the picture on the wall began to shake.

"Hayes," she whimpered. "Oh, Hayes...!"

"Yes, baby, yes," he whispered hoarsely. "Yes. Now!"

He moved so hard, and so fast, that she climaxed instantly and shuddered with the fever of it while he thrust into her again and again until finally his own body corded and convulsed. His groan at her ear was anguished, but she knew that pleasure, not pain, provoked it.

They clung to each other in the aftermath, shivering, damp with sweat, still hungry.

"Not enough," he said through his teeth.

"Not enough," she agreed breathlessly.

She picked up the strewn clothes and walked up the staircase bare to the waist, with Hayes right behind her.

They made it to the bedroom, behind a locked door. He laid her down on the bed and slid over her, his mouth anguished on her hard-tipped breasts as he began to arouse her all over again.

She cried out when he went into her, still burning for him,

still hungry and insatiable. She looked at his face the whole time, her eyes open, so that he could see the pleasure he was giving her with the quick, hard thrusts of his hips.

"It's never...enough," she whispered, shaking.

"No. And it doesn't...last...oh, God," he groaned and began to shake, too.

"Yes," she whispered, pushing up, helping him. "Yes, yes!"

He cried out, his lean body arching, his face contorted and red as he shuddered and shuddered with fulfillment.

She went with him all the way, her body so attuned to his that each thrust brought her higher and higher and higher, until the tension burst and she convulsed under him.

They lay together, shuddering, in a tangle of damp flesh.

"I can't ever get enough of you, Mrs. Carson," he whispered hoarsely. He kissed her tenderly, his lips gently probing hers. "And I want so badly to make you pregnant..."

She laughed breathlessly and kissed him back. "We have all the time in the world. When it happens, it happens."

"Well," he said, lifting himself to look down at her with proud, hungry eyes, "if what we did downstairs didn't accomplish it, this might."

She lifted her eyebrows. "You can't do it three times in a row."

He eased down on her. "Would you care to bet on that?" he chuckled, and when he went into her, she realized that, yes, he could do it three times in a row. But she was much too involved to say so.

A few weeks later, she started throwing up while at the office. She went straight to the sheriff's office after she stopped by Dr. Lou Coltrain's office for a pregnancy test.

Hayes was filling out a form. He looked up as she entered

the room. "Well, hello, gorgeous," he said with a grin. "Are we going out to lunch together?"

She went around the desk, turned his swivel chair and sat down in his lap. "We can't go to lunch. I'm sick."

"Sick?"

"What do they call it?" she asked with mock memory loss. "Oh, yes. Morning sickness. That's it."

"Morning...sickness..." His expression was impossible to describe. He was torn between delight and pride and wonder. "We're pregnant," he whispered.

She grinned. "Yes. I had a test. It's positive. We're pregnant."

He kissed her with aching tenderness. "We'll have three children. What a magical year it's going to be!"

She sighed and snuggled close. "Yes," she agreed.

He smiled and pulled her closer. After all they'd been through, this was like the rainbow after the storm, the kiss after the cut. He told her so.

She looked up at him with soft, tender eyes. "It's been a long, hard road to get here."

He nodded. "But, then, it's not the destination, baby. It's the journey."

She grinned. "Some journey!"

"Some journey. Suppose we go by Barbara's Café and get you some pickles and strawberry ice cream for lunch?" he teased.

She made a face at him. "What a horrible combination."

"What would you like, then?"

"A thick chocolate milk shake and an order of French fries," she decided.

"Bad girl. You need protein for our baby." He patted her stomach gently.

"Milk shakes have milk. There's your protein." She laughed. "But I'll settle for a nice cold crisp salad."

"In that case, I'll take you to lunch."

"Nice of you!"

He got up and framed her face in his big hands. "Nothing's too good for my best girl," he whispered, and kissed her. "But no fries."

She sighed. "Okay. No fries."

He took her hand and led her out the door. His mind was full of dreams, of the coming child, of a shared future.

She was feeling much the same. It was going to be the biggest adventure of her life, having a child born of her own body.

"I have ulterior motives," Hayes said when they got to the crowded café.

"You do?" Minette asked. "What are they?"

"Wait and see."

He opened the door, walked into the full dining room, grinned and said, "Make way for my pregnant lady!"

And everybody laughed and cheered.

Hayes looked down into Minette's amused face and grinned again. "I just saved us the trouble of sending out birth announcements."

She burst out laughing. And then she kissed him. And their friends and neighbors looked on with real affection, and gave them a standing ovation.

* * * * *